The
ORFFYREUS
WHEEL

by David Niall Wilson

Then it happened. One of the men on horseback, suddenly disgusted with the wait, and the day, slapped his mount hard with a crop, driving it to a sudden gallop and heading back down the road. The sound of leather on the horse's flank cracked through the air like thunder, and despite Frederic's tight grip on the reins, their horses shied. The young driver fought them. He called out to the frightened animals, but it was too late. They bucked and the carriage slid sideways, up and over the rise at the top of the road and onto the slope.

Johann called out frantically, trying to climb back out of the carriage and help, but a sudden lurch drove him back inside, and he was forced to take a seat, bracing Barbara with his body to keep from pummeling her as he was tossed about. Rosina clung to the bench across from them, eyes wide. She gave a sudden terrified scream, and the horses shied again.

They were moving, sliding down the embankment toward the rough, muddy waves. Frederic cracked his whip and shook the reins, but the horses were off balance, and by the time they regained their wits enough to pull, they couldn't get firm footing on the road. The weight of the carriage slid down, gained speed, and the horses, straining and slipping, were dragged after it.

The animals lunged, valiantly tugging at the harness, but the weight, and the slope of the hill was too much for them. With a shuddering moan, the carriage slid sideways on its wheels, miraculously avoiding a snapped axle, and plunged into the water. The current caught the wood solidly and pulled, and as those seated above watched in horror, the carriage, horses and all, was swept from the bank and into the center of the river, whirling around as the terrified animals paddled and fought to free themselves.

They spun so that the horses faced downstream, and then, as the waters of the river swept around a bend, they were simply gone. Only the echo of Johann's and Frederic's hoarse shouts, and the screaming of the women, remained to echo in the cool, damp air.

For Trish, who I love with all my heart,
Katie, who I believe could invent Bessler's Wheel
Bill, who would find a way to fix it if it broke
Zach, who would figure out how to connect it to the world...
Zane, who would help me lift it into place and be there if it fell
And Stephanie - who would help us share it with the world.

Acknowledgments

There are a lot of people who helped to make this book possible. It was originally conceived for an agent who did not want me to write it. Thanks to Nanowrimo, and a new agent, Robert Fleck of the Fleck Literary Agency, I ignored that other agent. I'd like to thank the folks at the original Amazon Shorts program at Amazon.com – this book, serialized – was a bestseller in that program. For research and background, John Collins, and for the original inspiration so long, long ago, Johann Bessler.

One day, maybe free energy will be a possibility. For now, even having an idea that could create it is dangerous…

Author's Note:

I became aware of Johann Bessler and his wheel several years ago when an agent I no longer work with suggested that I find something historical, some mystery like that involved in Dan Brown's popular novel *The DaVinci Code*, to base a thriller on. I presented her with several options – this one included – all of which she shot down.

I couldn't let it go. I met a man in the UK who had written a book about Orffyreus, and Perpetual motion, *PERPETUAL MOTION: An Ancient Mystery Solved?* His name was John Collins, and we became correspondents. I read his book, which is fascinating, and it is that book that much of my fictionalized account of Bessler's life is derived from.

I've taken considerable license with history and science in my account. I wanted a great story, and I wanted to present it in such a way that the unfair treatment this brilliant man received so many years agois presented as not so different from what he might expect today. Perpetual motion could free us or condemn us as easily as our forays into nuclear power have done.

I hope that one day we'll know the full truth of The Orffyreus Wheel, if it exists, or that someone else will discover what Bessler found so long ago. If possible, I hope this book will spur interest in the subject and tempt new minds to be bent to the task.

You can still get Mr. Collins' book - and you can find more information at such places as:

http://www.besslerswheel.com

Or John's site:
http://www.free-energy.co.uk/

David Niall Wilson

ONE

Rain whipped against the heavy glass panes of the windows, counter-pointing the rhythm of the crackling wood in the fire. Edgar leaned back into the deep leather of his chair. He was not a young man, and he had come to what he termed a "proper appreciation" of finer things. The desk before him was dark, polished mahogany, and in its center sat a half empty bottle of whiskey. There were two tumblers, but only his own was full. In an ashtray to one side his pipe rested, still smoldering, but nearly forgotten.

Lightning flashed and he glanced out the window. A car turned in at the end of a winding drive, slicing the darkness with the brilliant beams of its headlights. Reflexively, Edgar reached out and grabbed his whiskey, taking a long sip. He continued to watch the window, but the lightning left him blind. As it faded, he caught a glimpse of himself, reflected in the glass. Graying at the temples, deep brown eyes – aging well. The whiskey was also well aged. It was Scotch, single malt, but he barely tasted it. As he replaced the glass on the desk, his hand shook.

He glanced at the tray on his desk and the large folder it held. He knew the visitor was the man known to him only as Black. Edgar had been waiting for this visit for nearly an hour, watching the rain beat against the windows and thinking.

He'd almost taken the folder lying on his desk and its carefully assembled contents and left.

It was tempting to know, to understand what it was that was so valuable about that single sheet of onionskin paper. Edgar shook his head, as though to clear away such thoughts.

Understanding was not his business. He was a seeker.

Somewhere below, a car door slammed. Edgar waited, considered another sip of his whiskey, and then decided against it. He turned his chair slowly, rose, and left the office. The hall beyond was dark, but dim bulbs glowed behind smoked shades on the stairs, and he was used to the lack of illumination. Edgar descended slowly through the deep chimes of the doorbell; the sound masked his footsteps.

He opened the door and stood back. Black was a tall man, and as usual he was draped in a full-length overcoat and a dark, wide-brimmed hat. Rain ran in small rivulets down the expensive cloth of the coat, and for just a moment, Edgar watched those glittering trails. It postponed the moment when he'd have to meet his visitor's eyes. He had never liked a man less.

Edgar was not a coward, his work precluded it, but this man standing and dripping water onto the rug in his foyer disturbed him. There was something about the coat, and the hat, the way the man's features always seemed obscured, even when you stared directly into his eyes that wound like cold sweat through Edgar's pores.

"Come in, Black," he said, reaching to take the man's coat. The hat followed, and, once Edgar had hung them and turned back, he chanced a direct glance into the other's eyes. They were slate gray and devoid of emotion. It was dark in the foyer, and Black's hair curled down over his forehead. It would have been rakish on most men, but in this instance sinister was a better word.

He carried a small leather satchel that he did not relinquish with his hat and coat.

"Follow me," Edgar said, turning and starting slowly back up the stairs.

His visitor remained silent, but fell in behind without hesitation, making no sound as he walked. Edgar barely contained his desire to turn and make sure there was anyone there at all.

The two entered the office and Edgar went straight to his desk. Once he was beyond the heavy polished wood surface, the whiskey bottle in his hand, his unease lifted slightly. This was his place. He had met a lot men and women this way, he in his large, leather chair, and they seated across from him in slightly less comfort – slightly lower to the ground; the familiarity of it gave him strength.

He poured two fingers of the amber liquor into each tumbler, stoppered the bottle and offered the second tumbler to his guest. It was accepted in silence. Finally, after tasting the whiskey and nodding appreciatively, the man spoke.

"You have it, then." It was a statement.

Edgar, his whiskey gripped tightly in one hand, seated himself once more in the leather chair behind his desk. It was his turn to nod in silence. Then, after a moment's pause, he was the first to break it.

"It was not easy. I have been to three countries in this search. I have bribed, threatened, and called in favors. I have been to every fiber-optically connected data source available."

He fell silent and glanced at the computer console in the corner. The monitor was dark, but several lights blinked in a random sequence.

"I am not interested in your methods, Mr. Kline," the man replied. Then he took another sip of the whiskey. "If we did not believe you had the capability to supply what we needed, I would be seated in another office, in another city."

Edgar knew it was true. The man owed him no explanation, nor did he truly want one. It was the situation that grated on his nerves. The melodrama. Late-night solitary meetings, names that were so obviously false that he'd not even bothered running routine background checks. And then there was the object of the search. He caught himself before he could glance at the folder on the far corner of his desk. He glanced, instead, at the satchel his visitor carried.

"You have the money?"

Without answering, Black stepped forward. He placed the case on the desktop and undid the clasp with a sparsity of motion that was eerie in its precision. He moved like a machine.

Edgar watched as Black spread the satchel open and lifted free stacks of tightly bound bills. Hundreds. Edgar's mind calculated as Black's hands deftly stacked the bills. It was all there; $100,000 for the search, and another $50,000 for his silence. For the questions he would never ask that would itch at the back of his mind for the rest of his life. Bought, and paid for, his father would have said. Edgar stared at the money a moment longer, then smiled thinly and finished his drink.

He reached to a small wooden tray on the corner of his desk and pulled out a wide manila folder. In that instant, he thought he saw the first flicker of animation dance across Black's face, but it was gone in the space of a single breath. Edgar slid the folder across the desk.

Black opened it and stared at the contents in rapt concentration. His brow was furrowed, and Edgar watched in silence, wanting to pour himself another drink, but unwilling to break the tension of the moment.

Edgar knew what the other man saw, but was left with all the burning questions. What was it? Why did it matter? Why would anyone pay such an exorbitant amount of money to possess it, and to ensure no one was aware that they did?

"Is all in order?" Edgar asked at last. He stood slowly, chancing a glance over the folder to where Black's finger traced down the document inside. He was able to make out the single word at the top – ORFFYREUS. The rest was a meaningless jumble of symbols and phrases. Black closed the folder with a snap and tucked it under his arm.

"I believe so," he said curtly. "Where is the original located? This is a very good likeness, perfect to our needs, but . . . "

"I do not know," Edgar answered with a shrug. "I purchased the secret, just as you are purchasing it, and I'll tell you this; the man who sold it feared for his life. I do not think he would have told me the location of the grave if his life were forfeit in the bargain."

"You have done well," Black said after a short hesitation, "amazingly well, and more quickly than we had dared hope. You may be certain that if we require such a service again, you will be the one we call."

"I appreciate that," Edgar replied, making a conscious effort not to grab the money and start stuffing it in a drawer, or to go for the loaded Beretta in his desk. "I don't suppose," He added, "that I will ever know whom you refer to by 'we'".

"The Americans have a saying," Black smiled coldly. "Such things are on a 'need-to-know' basis. I'm afraid you have no such need."

Edgar chuckled nervously, and this time he did reach for the whiskey.

"One for the road?" he asked, proffering the bottle to his guest.

"I don't think so," Black replied. "It is not a good night for driving under the best of circumstances. I would hate to be involved in an – incident."

Edgar nodded, and refilled his own glass. "I won't be venturing out, myself," he said, raising his glass to toast the storm beyond the windows. "I know when I'm overmatched."

"That is a very commendable trait," Black said softly. "Very commendable. I would guess it could be well-applied to most of life."

Edgar glanced at the man, but saw no hint of imminent danger in the ice-chips Black called eyes.

"Safe trip, then," Edgar said. He took a sip of the whiskey, placed the tumbler back on the desk, and stepped around toward the door. He waved his hand, gesturing that Black should precede him down the stairs. He doubted the man was likely to push him, but you never knew. A man with no more life in his eyes than Mr. Black, whoever he really was, might be capable of just about any treason.

They descended the stairs in silence, and Black grabbed his hat and coat before Edgar could offer. In a dark whirl, Black returned himself to shadows. Not even the glint of those eyes penetrated the gloom.

Edgar opened the door, just as another flash of lightning split the sky. It was much closer, and the crash of thunder made him wince. In that second he saw Black's face very clearly. The man watched him in the manner of a snake, waiting to strike, and Edgar took a half step back before he caught himself.

Black turned in that instant and started down the stairs to his car. The rain obscured Edgar's vision, reducing the other to a dim shadow, then to nothing. The car door slammed, and Edgar turned away, closing and locking the door carefully.

Though he was alone, the short climb back to his office drew another shiver up Edgar's spine. He couldn't shake the sensation that though departed; Black was watching him and waiting for something.

He returned to his seat and his whiskey. He glanced briefly at the money, stacked so neatly and precisely on the mahogany surface, but he gave it little thought. There would be time to deal with it in the morning, shuffling the cash through various accounts and business acquaintances until it dissolved into his other assets without a trace.

He wished he had something new to investigate. He's spent a long time on this one, too many hours and too little sleep, and he found that he couldn't shake the image of that single sheet of paper and the boldly scripted word - ORFFYREUS. Symbols danced before his eyes. He growled and reached for his pipe. It didn't matter. Nothing mattered but the stacks of lovely green bills on his desk, and the continued departure of the twin red taillights winding out toward the end of his drive.

Black drove slowly. He had hesitated only long enough to secure the folder in a black leather briefcase on the seat beside him, then to lock it. He took special care not to let any of the water dripping from the brim of his hat contact the paper. It had taken too long to acquire it.

Now, as he turned from the driveway and onto the quiet road beyond, he chanced a glance in his rear-view mirror, a last sight of Kline's home. He saw that the light was still on in the office, overlooking the drive, and he imagined the man sitting there, watching out the window and drinking.

Black reached under the front seat of his car and pulled out a slim, plastic control. In the center was a single button, gray in the dim interior of the old Cadillac. Black depressed the button, slipped the control back under his seat, and drove on.

Moments later, as he turned off a side street three blocks away and hit the entrance ramp to the freeway, the sky lit with another flash. Not lightning. This time there was flame, and the thunder that followed was a deafening crash. Black floored it and merged with traffic as Edgar Kline's home exploded, raining dust, debris, and hundred dollar bills on an unsuspecting city.

Not looking back, Black pressed play on the CD player in his dash. Mozart filled his thoughts, and at last, he smiled.

"Good evening, Mr. Kline," he whispered. "It was a pleasure."

TWO

The lawn stretched for what seemed a mile beyond the huge draped window. Elly gazed out over the huge expanse to avoid staring at her surroundings. If the grounds beyond the window were extravagant, the office in which she stood was an embarrassment of wealth. The floors were gleaming hardwood; the shelves were lined with row after row of books with raised, ribbed leather spines. Though they were obviously old, they seemed untouched, and the glistened as if they'd been polished along with the furniture. Nothing was out of place.

In her knee-length skirt and plain blouse, Elly felt out of place, and the sensation irked her. She knew it shouldn't matter, but it did. She wished she were wearing a floor length gown, heels, and had her hair coiffed like a queen. She also wished she knew why she was standing; looking out a window at a lawn she'd never seen before, waiting for a lawyer she'd heard of only in the news.

Elly Kassel was a simple woman. She lived alone, had no children or lovers, no family that she was in contact with. She made a comfortable living as a clerk in the offices of one of London's lesser-known solicitors, and she kept to herself. When the large, officious envelope arrived at her home, she'd thought it a mistake. She'd been ready to call out and bring the mail carrier back to her door, when her eyes slid past the glossy seal on the envelope and her gaze locked onto her own name. She'd never seen it printed in such a fashion, and the sight of it had shocked her to silence.

Ratliffe and Brownridge, Solicitors.

She'd heard the names. She'd read them in the papers. She'd even handled briefs and paperwork for clients who were associated with them. She'd never expected to see one of them in person, let alone speak to them, and yet here she was. She had their letter, folded carefully and tucked into her handbag. She'd shown it to her few friends, Connie at work and old Marge who lived in the apartment across from her own. They'd been no help at all, oohing and ahing over the letterhead and not really taking in the scope of the letter's contents.

"Ms. Kassel,

It is our duty to inform you of the passing of your grandmother, Eleanor Lillian Kassel. Our firm has been employed in the execution of Ms. Kassel's last will and testament, and you have been named as sole beneficiary. We would be pleased to speak with you at your convenience.

Sincerely,

Dorian Brownridge."

The letter was short, but it had opened floodgates of questions and memories. Elly knew little or nothing of her family. She'd never met her grandmother, and she had no idea what to expect when she phoned the solicitor's office. The secretary had taken her name, put her on hold, and then returned in a hushed flurry of words that left Elly breathless. If it was no trouble, the woman said, Elly was to come in that very day. Important papers were to be signed, and there was an inheritance involved. No, she could divulge nothing over the phone. No, she knew nothing of the deceased. No, it was not a mistake.

The door behind Elly opened and she started, whirling as if caught stealing something. She blushed, and the man who entered, short, balding, perhaps in his late forties, or early fifties, smiled.

"I did not mean to startle you Ms. Kassel. May I call you Elizabeth?"

"Elly," she blurted, wishing in the instant she could retract it and stick with the more elegant Elizabeth.

"Elly," the man said, still smiling. "Very pretty." He adjusted his glasses, and then stepped closer, extending his hand. "I am Dorian Brownridge. I'm sorry to have kept you waiting. We have a rather tricky case pending – I was forced to oversee the final preparations."

"Oh," Elly said. "It's no trouble. I was just admiring your view. It's – lovely."

Brownridge glanced out the window, his pleasure at her compliment obvious.

"The first office I considered was nearer to the front of the building," he explained. "The view was of the drive, and the road beyond. I'm fonder of nature, so I moved back here. I have never regretted the choice."

Elly didn't know what to say, so she smiled and waited. Her hands were clasped behind her back, and she blushed again when she realized she was bouncing nervously on the balls of her feet. At 5'2" tall and only a hair more than a hundred pounds, she knew she probably looked like a schoolgirl waiting for a sweet.

Brownridge didn't seem to notice her discomfiture. He moved behind his desk and shuffled some papers. He tossed aside the first two folders that came to his hand, then glanced down at the third, and smiled again.

"Here we are," he said. "I knew I had it here somewhere. Sometimes I believe that I'll end up before a justice one day, the wrong file in my hand, defending some poor man's life with the details of a paternity suit."

Elly smiled in spite of her nervousness. He was a very pleasant man, and if it had not been for the thick file in his hand, and the tips of papers leaking out around its edges, she might have enjoyed his company. As it was, it was impossible.

Brownridge must have noted her nervousness, because he fell silent for a moment, adjusted his glasses absently, and peered down at the folder in his hand.

"If you'll be seated, Elly, I'll bring you up to date on what we know of your grandmother, and of the estate. Don't let the file fool you; it's a very short and straightforward bequest. Your grandmother was a client for a very long time; all of our dealings with her are listed in this file."

Elly nodded. She was familiar with such files from her own work, though she found herself curious about what sort of dealings a member of her family would have with such a firm as this, and what it could mean to her.

"Your letter said I was the sole beneficiary?" she blurted. Again, she regretted her impertinence. It must have sounded as if she was greedy, and that was not the case. Elly was very happy with her life, just as it was. It was this interruption that was the problem.

Brownridge glanced up from the file, caught her flush of embarrassment, and again, he smiled.

"No need to be embarrassed," he said with a chuckle. "I'm sure this business is quite out of the ordinary for you. Yes, you are sole beneficiary. There were other relatives, but it seems your grandmother, Eleanor, was somewhat of a recluse, and none of them wanted anything to do with her. I wonder," he mused, glancing back at the file, "if they would have felt the same had they known the full extent of her holdings."

Elly's heart pounded. "Holdings?"

Brownridge chuckled again. "Oh yes. As I said, we have been dealing with Eleanor for many years. She gave one the impression of being somewhat of an odd duck. She never went in for expensive clothing, or extravagant possessions. At least," he smiled, "when visiting here in London. I gather that most of your family considered her a crazy old lady, and I suspect that is the impression she intended to give."

Elly's confusion must have shown, because Brownridge set aside the folder and watched her carefully.

"This must be a bit difficult for you to take in," he said. "Eleanor spoke of you often, but I know she never spoke to you, and that was something she and I argued over regularly. She didn't want to spoil this particular surprise, and there were a good number of reasons for her to keep her life private. You'll learn most of those reasons before you are done, I suspect, but it isn't my place to speculate. Shall we get on with it?"

Elly bit her lip, but she nodded. Brownridge shuffled the papers again, extracted a single sheet, and scanned it quickly before glancing up at her once again.

"Your inheritance may seem a bit odd to you," Brownridge explained. He slipped an old, yellowed envelope from the file in his hand and slid it across the desk to her. Next, he opened a second, smaller envelope and handed her an ornate key.

"But what," she started, staring at the key in consternation, "what is it to?"

Brownridge rose and beckoned for her to follow him. In the outer office, his secretary, a middle-aged, gray-haired woman, clattered away at a computer keyboard. Brownridge led her to one corner, where a wooden case the size of a steamer trunk rested on the soft carpet. It was banded in iron, and padlocked. Elly glanced down at the key, then caught Brownridge's eye. He nodded.

"But what is it?" she asked.

The old solicitor adjusted his glasses once again, the smiled at her. "I only wish I knew," he said. "It has been kept in one of the vaults at our bank for decades. The key, and that envelope you are holding, were kept under equally secure circumstances in a bank in America. Your grandmother was a careful woman."

"But why?" Elly blurted. "Why me? Why can't you just tell me what it is?"

"I don't know what it is," Brownridge answered with a shrug. "It has never been opened in my presence. All that your grandmother told us of it was that it was a secret better locked away than in the wrong hands."

Elly stared down at the key in her hand, and then glanced at the envelope. She moved as if to open it, and Brownridge stepped closer to her, quickly, placing one pudgy hand on her own.

"Not yet," he said softly. "There is more to the inheritance, and if you open that too soon, you could forfeit it all."

She glanced at the key, then at the trunk. Brownridge shook his head.

"Let's go back into my office for a bit," he said, placing one hand on her shoulder and guiding her gently. "There's a bit more to tell, and I'm a little pressed for time."

Elly hurried into the office and took her seat, chastising herself for dawdling when Mr. Brownridge had already explained how tight his schedule was. Her head was spinning, and the key in her hand seemed to burn into her flesh as she held it, begging to be inserted into the chest in the next room and reveal its secret.

"There are a few more things," Brownridge continued, taking his own seat and grabbing the file in a no-nonsense manner. "There is the manner of this ticket," he slid another small pouch of papers across to Elly, who scooped it up quickly, not bothering to look at it as she listened. "It is an airline ticket, one way, to America," he explained. "Your grandmother arranged for people to pick you up at the airport in New York City. Your flight leaves in two days."

"But my job," Elly blurted. "I have to work. I can't just take off with only two days notice . . . they'd let me go for certain."

Brownridge looked up at her over the rim of his glasses, his eyes twinkling. "I don't believe you will find that to be a problem. I am not at liberty to discuss details, beyond the ticket, the chest, and the envelope, but let me say this. Your grandmother was well off, Elly. Very well off. Now the same can be said of you. Take the ticket, and take the trip. You will never regret it."

"But . . ." the rest of her retort died on her lips.

Mr. Brownridge rose and placed his hands on his desk, watching her. It was obvious he considered the meeting to be ended, but it took her a second to catch up with him. Her hands were still shaking, but she held tightly to the key, and the envelope.

"The trunk," she said. Her words trailed off.

Brownridge was moving again, his hand comfortingly on her shoulder. "Don't you worry about a thing," he said. "We will make sure the case is on the plane when you arrive. A car will arrive to drive you to the airport. It has all been pre-arranged."

Elly didn't try another 'but' because she sensed how it would end. Brownridge escorted her through the opulent outer-office and into the hall beyond. At that point, a young man with thick glasses and a friendly smile appeared as if by magic to escort her to the front of the building.

Elly mumbled something as she stumbled through the front doors and found herself standing, alone, on the top step of a very long stair of gleaming white stone. She didn't know which way to turn. Her car was below, and she would have to go home, but....

Then she remembered the envelope, still clutched tightly in her hand. She held it up in the sunlight where she could read the front of it. It bore only a single word – or name – she couldn't be certain. It said ORFFYREUS.

THREE

Elly's flight left her nearly breathless with excitement. She had flown before, but never such a long flight, and certainly never First Class. The deep, cushioned seats and eager flight attendants lent an eerie quality to the journey. Elly was a simple woman. She had a small home, simple clothing, and simple tastes. Everything she owned she'd worked and saved for. She knew where every item came from, how much it had cost, and why it had been purchased.

The treatment she'd received from the airline was alien and nerve-wracking. Above her in the luggage rack she had a small overnight bag. She'd packed enough in her one other suitcase for about a week, though every time she'd called Mr. Brownridge to worry over it, he'd chuckled and assured her that it would be no problem, she could purchase what she needed when she arrived. She didn't like the sensation of being swept along without a say in what happened around her, and she would have felt a lot more comfortable if she'd been in the rear of the jet, stuffed in between two other passengers who didn't wear clothing that appeared to be painted on, or flash diamonds that glittered across the cabin when they waved their hands.

It was a relief when the seat belt light flashed off. Elly rose and grabbed her bag. She smiled weakly at the flight attendant in passing, and was walking so quickly by the time she hit the end of the departure ramp that she nearly tripped as she entered the airport.

Her relief was short lived. JFK International was a haze of rushing people, loud voices, intercom messages, and turmoil. Elly stood, feeling very lost, and very alone, her overnight bag clutched tightly in both hands. Then she turned, and she saw the man with the sign. It was a plain white sign with the words Elizabeth Kassel written in sharp, black letters across the front. The man was dressed in a dark uniform, and he did not smile. Elly stepped closer to him, raised her arm tentatively, and he caught her gaze.

Stepping closer, the man held out a hand. "I'm Jonathan," he said. "I've been sent to escort you. Please follow me."

Without another word, he turned and started off down the concourse to her right, winding his way quickly through the teeming crowds. Elly stumbled along in his wake, trying keep up, and nearly crashing into several other travelers as something in one store or another caught her eye. More than once, Jonathan turned to observe her progress impatiently, but each time, as Elly neared him and started to speak, he turned again and hurried off.

As they reached the turnstiles leading to the baggage area, Elly heard a commotion behind them. There was shouting, and the sound of something large crashing. She stopped to listen, but at that moment, Jonathan grabbed her by her arm and dragged her toward the doors.

"But," she said, struggling against his pull, "my baggage."

"It has been taken care of," Jonathan assured her. "I don't mean to seem impatient, but we are nearly late."

"For what," she asked, growing suddenly irritated. "If I'm the one who is inheriting things, shouldn't they be waiting for me?"

He stared at her for a moment, as if sifting her words through some complex filter in his mind for the right answer. "It is just that we have been waiting a very long time to meet you," he said at last. "I have strict instructions to meet you and bring you along with all haste. I'm sorry if I seemed short." He hesitated only a second for his words to sink in. "Shall we go?" he asked.

Elly caught him glancing back the way they'd come, but the tumult had died out, and only the normal sounds of crowds and electronically enhanced voices could be heard. Elly pursed her lips, and then nodded, allowing Jonathan to take her arm again and lead her toward the front of the building.

People hustled all about them, carts of luggage, overnight bags, golf clubs - even a large sky kennel with a napping Doberman rolled past. There were several counters for information of various sorts, hotels, rental cars, a confusion of color and sound. Jonathan wound through it all to the doors and escorted her out to the walk beyond. They crossed one lane, then another. Moments later, he was opening the back door of a sleek, black limousine. Elly slid inside.

There was a window between the rear of the limo and the driver. Elly saw the back of Jonathan's head, but she couldn't speak with him. Or at least, it didn't seem as if she could. There was no indication of an intercom, though she thought there probably was one. She glanced around the opulent interior of the car, taking in the bar, a small television and stereo setup with a DVD player and a small selection of movies.

There was a card on the seat beside her with her name on the front. Elly picked it up and read the contents quickly.

"Enjoy the drive. There are refreshments if you should want them, soft drinks, wine, beer, spirits, and please feel free to use the stereo, or enjoy a movie. It will take a little while to get out of the city. Please relax, and I will explain all I know about what is going on when you arrive."

The card was signed Max. Elly knew no one named Max, nor had Mr. Brownridge mentioned anyone by that name. She had a number she was to have called, and the name Cynthia Lyons as a contact, if she was not met at the airport.

Elly sat back. She eyed the DVD player for a moment, but the silence, after the flight and the craziness of the airport, was too pleasant. She turned and flipped on the stereo. The station that it was tuned to was playing modern rock, and she began pressing the preset buttons quickly. She settled on a light jazz station, turned the volume down low, and leaned back in her seat. It wasn't long before the smooth, comfortable roll of the limo and the equally smooth rippling notes of the music caused her to drift, and then doze.

When the limo finally pulled to a stop, Elly was startled to wakefulness, not by any sudden motion, but by the sudden lack of it. It was still light out, and she glanced quickly out the window. The city was gone. She had a quick moment of vertigo as her mind caught up with reality.

They were parked just outside the doors of a garage that was easily large enough to house a dozen vehicles. Jonathan opened her door for her without a word, and then closed it behind her. He didn't offer to take her overnight bag, for which she was grateful. There was something about the way the man acted that bothered her. Something not quite right. She'd met plenty of servants and footmen in her time, though she'd never been on the receiving end of their attentions. None of them had such an attitude. She supposed she was being paranoid, but she was happy to have her possessions close by her side. She wished she had her luggage, as well.

She turned and stared up at the huge old building beside the garage. It resembled nothing so much as a European castle, complete with ramparts and stone columns. It would have been imposing in any urban setting, but here, in the middle of nowhere, as far as she could tell, it was brooding and ominous.

Jonathan turned and strode off toward a side entrance to the building, and Elly called out after him.

"What about my other bag?"

He slowed, turned, and replied almost impatiently. "As I said, it is being taken care of, Ms. Kassel. Please, follow me. All of your questions will soon be answered."

Then he mounted the steps, and, just as she had in the airport, Elly was forced to hurry after him to avoid being left behind. She gritted her teeth and promised herself that, as soon as she found someone in charge and ascertained her place in this madness, she would find a moment to put Jonathan back on the right track. Then, laughing to herself, she hurried up the stone steps and into the building.

Listen to yourself, she thought. You already sound as if you're rich.

Then she was inside. If the outer expanse of the building had been impressive, the interior was awe-inspiring. There was a foyer large enough to be a ballroom in most large homes. A huge, winding stairway spiraled up into the shadows, lit dimly here and there by wall sconces and topped by a huge crystal chandelier.

Jonathan ignored the stairs, however. He stepped through a shadowed arch, and when Elly followed him, she found they were in a small hallway, hiding the modern convenience of lifts from the decadently opulent old-world décor of the foyer and main hall. It was only moments before a dim light flashed on and the door of the first lift slid open quietly. Jonathan stepped in and, seeing no other choice, Elly followed.

She wanted to ask him where they were, what the building was, who owned it, and a million other things, but she kept her silence. He probably would not have told her, in any case, and as things progressed she was less and less certain she wanted to know the answers. This was not at all the sort of greeting she'd expected, after speaking with Mr. Brownridge. The solicitor had always been so upbeat and pleasant. Had he been leading her on, just trying to get her on the plane and across the ocean by any means possible? She couldn't shake the sensation that something was just – wrong.

The lift shot up with dizzying speed, though there was absolutely no sound of the machinery behind it. Elly wished she'd taken the time to count the number of stories the building boasted from the windows outside. Though it took only seconds to reach their destination, the weightless sensation brought on by the lift lingered as she stepped from the car and into the thickly carpeted hall beyond.

The corridor was lined with heavy doors to the right and left. At the far end, toward the rear of the building, was a larger, double set of doors, and it was toward this entrance that Jonathan now led her. The hallway was lit only by the dying afternoon sunlight filtering in through high windows. The ceiling, though they were on what must have been the top floor of the massive structure, was at least 12 feet from the floor, and the windows opened at about the ten-foot level. There were more of the sconce like lamps along the walls, but none had yet been lit.

Ornate furniture lined parts of the wall, sitting chairs, a Victorian style settee, and several very old mahogany tables.

The walls were hung with portraits in gilt oak and gesso frames, polished and gleaming in the dim light. Elly couldn't make out many features of the paintings, hung as they were in shadow, but from what she saw they seemed a gloomy lot – pale of face, dark haired and frowning.

It was a long hall, and with Jonathan's self-imposed silence, images of prisoners walking their final mile, and witches being escorted before Bishops of the Inquisition came to mind. The more nervous he made her, the angrier Elly grew. Whoever was beyond that door was going to hear about it. All of it. Her grandmother had died, and while she'd never been close to the woman, Elly expected more respect from those handling the woman's affairs – her own affairs now. By the time she stepped through the large double doors into the office beyond, her eyes blazed, and she gripped the overnight bag so tightly her knuckles were white.

As she passed him, she glanced at Jonathan's face. Just for a second, she thought she saw a smirk on those cold lips. It sent a quick shiver running icily through her anger, but it didn't even begin to overcome it.

The office was well lit, but with low, table-level lamps, two in the corners and one on the large oak desk near the rear center of the room. Behind the desk was a window, overlooking the rear of the building. In a high-backed leather chair facing that window, a man sat. Elly saw a pale reflection of his features in the window, and she recoiled in shock. In that reflection, he might easily have been one of the men portrayed by the portraits in the hall. Pale, colorless eyes gazed back at her from that mirrored impression, then the chair spun slowly, and the man rose.

"Elizabeth," he said, not a question, but a smoothly rehearsed statement. "I have waited a long time to meet you."

He turned the chair, rose, and stepped from behind the desk gracefully. The man was tall, a few inches past six feet, and very dark. His hair feathered back over his ears with streaks of gray that might have been distinguished if he'd been less handsome. Dashing was the word that slipped into the forefront of Elly's mind, though it didn't linger there. The next word that came to mind was oily.

"My name is Maxwell Black. May I offer you a drink?"

Elly stared at the hand he held out to her, but she didn't take it immediately. She clutched her bag tightly and stood shaking with repressed frustration and anger.

"You may not," she said, surprising herself. "You may tell me who you are, beyond your name, and you may tell me exactly what is going on, where we are, and why. I have lost my grandmother, who I hardly knew, and I have flown a very long way with no more than an envelope, some mysterious comments, and vague promises of inheritance to keep me sane. Now this."

Elly flung her arms wide, nearly losing her grip on the bag in the process. She indicated the office, the building, everything, in fact, associated with them.

"All of this. I am not a plaything, Mr. Black, nor am I a child. So, what you can do for me, if you please, is to explain what I'm doing here, what my inheritance entails, and why everyone is acting like I'm the heroine in a very bad spy novel."

Black blinked, nearly taking a step back. He was clearly amused by her outburst, but there was something cold in the humor that did not put her at ease. He poured himself the drink she'd refused, whiskey neat in a crystal tumbler.

"I can understand your frustration," he said, starting over. "I really wish you would reconsider the drink, as it is a very long story. I don't know everything, of course, but I know enough to set you at ease on a number of issues, including your inheritance.

"I apologize for our rather unorthodox greeting, and for Jonathan, who I know can be surly on occasion. Extraordinary times, as they say." He sipped from his drink and watched her closely, as if to gauge the affect of his words.

Elly's expression softened slightly, but she made no move toward a chair, or a drink. She stood in silence, waiting for him to continue. Before he could do so, however, a red light flashed on his desk. He slammed down his drink, and at the same moment, there was a crash from the hall outside the door. Loud voices broke the silence, cursing and crying out. There was the muffled thump of a gun being fired.

Elly backed toward the bookshelves lining the wall, hand to her mouth in dismay.

"The envelope," Black said tersely. "Do you have the envelope?"

Elly glanced down at her overnight bag, still clutched tightly in her hand, then back at Black. She didn't answer.

"Give it to me," he demanded. He was moving now, not to the doorway to see what the sounds from beyond the door might be, but directly at Elly, his hand outstretched. She felt the anger surge up inside her again. She backed toward the door.

"Give it to me you stupid girl," he growled, lunging at her.

Elly struck without thought. She swung the heavy overnight bag to the side, then back, cracking it into the side of Black's head. He had no time to dodge. The man's momentum carried him past Elly and face first into the bookshelf, where he struck hard.

Elly leaped past him and grabbed the door. Black was already shaking his head groggily and trying to rise. She had only seconds to act and no time at all to think. With a quick twist of the knob she opened the door and stepped into the hallway beyond, slamming the door behind her.

She ran in the direction of the lift she and Jonathan had used to ascend. There were sounds of a struggle nearby, but she couldn't pinpoint them. Breathing hard, running as fast as she could with her bag in one hand, Elly entered the small hall where the lifts opened and pounded on the button. There was a soft whir, and the light above the door came on.

She waited, her mind reeling and her breath coming in ragged gasps. A door opened, and she heard a curse. Black, it had to be him. She pounded on the button again, but the lift remained silent and still. Footsteps sounded in the hall and she pressed frantically on the button. She heard Black breathing, and she pressed herself against the lift doors, tears brimming in the corners of her eyes.

"Elizabeth," Black called softly. "You have been a very bad girl. Come out now, and give me that bag and we can talk about it."

Elly didn't know what he wanted, or why he was so anxious

to get her bag, but she knew she had no intention of handing it over to him. She drew back her arm, gripping the bag's strap tightly, ready to swing it around again if he came into sight. The lift door slid silently open, and she slipped inside, just as quietly. Elly pressed the CLOSE button and waited what seemed an eternity. The doors began to close.

Black cursed, and she heard him lunge into the small alcove. She thought he was going to reach the doors and prevent their closing, but at the last second, he tripped and crashed into the wall. The doors closed with a solid SNICK!

Elly pressed the number one and fell back against the wall. She was far from safe. If Black took the stairs, how quickly could he reach the ground floor? Could he beat her there, at a dead run, or would the winding length of stairs give her the chance to get outside? If she did, then what?

No time to think about that either. The lift sank swiftly through the dark interior of its shaft, and before she could fully gather her thoughts, the number one lit, and she was moving again. She dashed through the door, ready to swing her bag again, if necessary, but Black wasn't there. She looked around wildly. Above her, she heard pounding footsteps on the stairs, circling. Descending.

The door to the front of the building and the concrete stairs beyond was to her left. She ran to it and yanked it open. As she slipped into the late afternoon light, someone grabbed her firmly, but not painfully, by the arm. She swung, leveling the overnight bag in a tight swing. It never connected. The bag was caught, easily, and the grip on her arm tightened slightly.

"Elly," a voice said, close by her ear. "Elly, you have to listen to me."

She stopped struggling, gathering her thoughts. As she stood, she glanced around the periphery of her vision for a means of escape. Then she stiffened.

Elly.

The voice had said Elly, not Elizabeth. She hadn't corrected any of them, not Jonathan, who'd barely spoken to her, or Mr. Black. Who was this?

"We have to move," the voice continued, calm, but filled

with tense urgency. "The others can hold off Black and his man for a few minutes, but unless we want serious trouble, we have to get out of here. There will be more of them soon. They won't be happy."

"Who are you?" Elly demanded, spinning. She took in the man beside her at a glance. He was tall, over six feet, with dark hair and dark eyes. He looked to be in his thirties, maybe late twenties, well muscled and smiling, though the smile was tense.

"My name is Benjamin," he replied. "I tried to meet you at your flight, as planned, but it seems Mr. Black had other ideas."

Elly stared at him. None of it made any sense.

A sudden cry from behind her intensified her confusion. She heard voices from the other side of the door. It might be Black, or Jonathan; it might be Benjamin's companions, whoever they were. She had to make a decision, and she knew it had better be the right one. The man released her arm, and that was all it took.

"Where do we go?" she asked.

"Follow me," he said. He launched down the steps at a run, and she stumbled along behind him, her overnight bag banging off her leg painfully. She was not used to this kind of physical exertion, and she was getting tired.

The door slammed open behind them, and, as she reached the bottom step, Elly turned.

Framed in the doorway, Black glared at her. Blood dripped down his forehead where he'd struck the shelves, and his neat, rich clothing was in a shambles. His eyes blazed, and he lunged after her, but at that moment, two more bodies hurtled through the doorway. One was Jonathan, and the other was a blonde man Elly had never seen. The two grappled, a gun held between them, and as they careened through the doorway, the crashed into the unsuspecting Black's back.

With mingled cries of surprise and rage, the three toppled and fell, crashing and rolling down the steps. The gun went off with a loud crack, and a bit of stone chipped off the nearest column on the huge porch.

Benjamin turned back to the struggling men.

"Get to the car, there," he pointed at a sleek, dark Volvo

pulled up to the curb. Its engine was running, and there was someone – a woman – behind the wheel. Benjamin rushed back the way they'd come without another glance, and, with no other option open to her, Elly did as she was told. She reached the sedan, yanked open the rear door, and slid into the soft leather seat. It was cool inside, and dark. Elly turned to look back the way she'd come.

"Hold the door," the driver said urgently. It was indeed a woman, long flowing red hair covered her shoulders, and her hands were gloved in black leather. Elly couldn't see her face, but she caught a bright flash of the woman's eyes in the rear-view mirror.

"After that fall, Eddie will be hurt. As soon as they're in, we've got to move."

"But," Elly started to speak, but the woman shook her head.

"Not yet," she said. "Wait until we're on our way out of here."

Elly turned back to stare out the door. Benjamin was pulling the blonde man free of the tangle on the ground. Eddie. The woman had said the man's name was Eddie. Eddie was limping heavily, and as he managed to lurch free, Jonathan tried to regain his feet. He had the gun in his hand, and he swung it toward Benjamin, but he was far too slow. The big man had already launched a kick that connected hard with Jonathan's hand and sent the pistol flying to the side. Black still lay where he'd fallen, and, as Benjamin and Eddie made for the Volvo as quickly as possible, Jonathan turned to his boss, just for a second, before stumbling after his gun.

The woman in the front seat leaned over and opened the passenger side door. Benjamin thrust Eddie roughly into the back seat with Elly, who cowered into the far corner as the man's body fell heavily onto the leather seat. Benjamin closed the door behind him. Then he leaped into the front, and before he had hit the seat, they were rolling.

Gravel spat from beneath the Volvo's tires, and they skidded down the first few yards of the long, curving drive at an angle before the car righted itself at a deft tug of the wheel and shot away into the growing twilight.

FOUR

Elly leaned as far into the corner as she could and pressed against the smooth leather seat and the cool vinyl rear door. Eddie, the man in the seat beside her, slumped in her direction and threatened to lay his head on her shoulder if she allowed it. He was in pain, and she wished she could help, but had no idea how she could do so. She also had no real idea why she should.

The Volvo cruised smoothly through the darkness, and for several miles, no one spoke. The woman concentrated on her driving; Benjamin turned in his seat and did what he could to examine the injured Eddie. When he was satisfied he'd done all that he could, he turned to face forward once more and spoke.

"He'll be fine. He's taken quite a smack to the head, but the cut is superficial. We'll clean it up, give him some aspirin, and he'll be back to himself in no time."

Elly nodded, even though no one was watching her, then felt foolish and sat up straighter. She assumed he'd been talking to her, but he might have been speaking to the driver. Suddenly the silence was too much.

"Who are you people?" she asked.

The question was so inadequate that she bit her tongue in frustration, but she had no idea what else to ask, or how to word it. She didn't want to cause a repeat of the sudden evil transformation she'd witnessed in Maxwell Black, but neither did she want to be dragged along without a say in what happened.

Benjamin turned again, met her gaze, and she was astonished to see that he appeared contrite.

"I am terribly sorry, Elly," he said. "My name is Benjamin

Wright. This is Cynthia Lyons, and the man threatening to lay his head on your shoulder is Edward Carter. We call him Eddie, and I'm certain he will hope you do the same.

"We were set to meet you at the airport, but, as you have no doubt observed, we were detained. I take all blame for this; I should have expected it. It comes from my being too trusting, I suppose, or naïve. I did not think that even Maxwell Black would stoop to kidnapping you straight from the airport."

"But..." Elly started to speak, but Benjamin held up a hand to restrain her.

"Give me a moment, Elly, and then I'll do my best to answer any questions you still have."

Elly sat back, released the breath she hadn't realized she was holding, and stared at him, her lips pursed.

"I was your grandmother's Personal Assistant," he told her, lowering his voice. "I am very sorry for your loss, though I realize that the two of you were not close. This all must seem very surreal to you, and I apologize for that, as well. It has been necessary to keep things as quiet as possible. I'm sure you will realize the truth in this, once you've heard our whole story.

"I'll tell you this immediately, so that you can rest a bit easier. Maxwell Black is an evil man. He works for an organization that would very much like to steal the secrets your grandmother possessed and bend them to his own purpose. We have gone to great lengths to make certain this can never happen, and tonight, we came very close to failure.

"You have every right not to trust us, and I would be surprised, indeed, if you did, but I want to assure you that we are acting in your best interests, and on the instructions of your grandmother. From this moment on, consider me at your service, as I was at hers."

Elly didn't speak for a moment. She tried to sort it all out in her mind, but everything jumbled together, and she still had to lean away from Eddie, who showed no signs of becoming more animated any time soon.

"Where are we going?" she asked.

"We are going to your estate," Benjamin replied. "You have a home here, a part of your inheritance, and the servants and staff are waiting to greet you. I'm sure, in fact, that they are nearly frantic by now with worry."

Elly blinked. "Estate?"

Benjamin smiled with genuine warmth in his voice as he replied.

"Oh yes. Your grandmother was a very well to do woman, Elly. I keep forgetting that you know nothing of her work, or of your inheritance.

"We still have a bit of a drive ahead," Benjamin said softly. "Why don't you rest? We'll have time to speak once we're safely inside, and perhaps, once you see how things stand, you will more easily understand what I have to tell you. We have a lot to talk about, and even more to accomplish."

Elly didn't reply. She turned away from Benjamin's frank, open stare, and gazed out the window at the passing signs. The car was headed back toward New York City. At least she would be closer to the airport if she decided to turn and run back to her old home and her old life. At least, in the city, she would feel as if she could run.

Benjamin fell silent, and the only sounds were the hum of the tires on the pavement and the slightly harsh, heavy breathing of Eddie, who Benjamin had pulled to the right and settled against the far side of the car, giving Elly more breathing room.

She would dearly have loved to take Benjamin's advice and rest, but there was so much bouncing around in her mind that she was afraid to close her eyes. What if she awakened in another bad situation? What if they only smiled to put her off her guard, as the oily Maxwell Black had tried to do?

Of course, Black had not gotten himself injured trying to rescue her, as the man breathing fitfully and moaning softly beside her had done. He had also tried to hurt her, and thus far, none of her new companions seemed inclined to be anything but solicitous, if a little short under the extreme circumstances.

Elly glanced over her shoulder more than once, scanning the expanse of road stretching out behind them for lights. Soon they were on a busier road, surrounded by gleaming headlights and the dark silhouettes of other vehicles.

"No one followed," Cynthia told her in a soft voice. "I've been watching closely. They know where we are going; there is no need to chase us."

"But," Elly exclaimed in sudden alarm, "If they know where..."

Cynthia's laughter stopped her, and she frowned.

"I'm sorry," Cynthia said, still chuckling. "They know where we're going, and that is why they tried to take you from the airport. They can't follow, and you will be perfectly safe from them once we arrive."

Elly fell silent again. None of what she was hearing made any sense, and the more she heard, the more she despaired that it ever would. Better to sit back and wait patiently, see where this strange troupe would lead her, and deal with the situation when it arose. In any case, barring throwing open her door and launching herself out into the fast-moving traffic, there was little else she could do.

The city swept up on her in degrees. On the way out of New York, Elly had been tired, and the deeply shaded windows of the limousine had made any effort at tracing her route away from the airport impossible. On the way back in, with the lights gleaming and the sky aglow like a man-made borealis, it was a very different experience.

Highways wound in and over other highways. They drove into a long, dark tunnel that was bisected every few yards by lights, and then slipped out the other side. The farther they wound into the city's heart, the more imposing it all became. Elly watched, mesmerized, as skyscrapers stretched from the sidewalks to the sky, taller and taller, glass and mirror-bright metals, concrete and dark stone.

Finally, they turned slowly into what she thought was an alley. Elly saw almost immediately that this was a deception. They had driven onto a ramp that led down beneath a large, glossy white building that stretched so far to either side that it seemed to cover the entire city block. Elly nearly spoke then, to ask where they were, but she knew it didn't matter. She would find out soon enough, and any explanation they could give her in the following moments would only add to the confusion.

Wherever it was, they were far away from Black, and Jonathan, and that was a good start.

They pulled into a parking spot near a bright light, and Elly saw that the car they rode in was only one of a long string of identical vehicles, lined up and stretching into the shadows. She opened her door quickly and climbed out, waiting as Benjamin pulled Eddie carefully out the far side and, supporting him on one shoulder, turned toward the light. Cynthia moved ahead of them, already talking on a cell phone, or a two-way radio. Elly followed the three of them, watching in amazement as doors ahead slid open and a group of people streamed out.

Eddie was eased from Benjamin's shoulder and moments later four young men in lab coats lifted the injured man and placed him on a gurney. They strapped him on carefully. Moments later, as Elly and the others stepped in through silently sliding doors that closed behind them with a soft click, Eddie and the gurney disappeared down a hall and into a side-passage.

"We'll bring your things to you," Benjamin told her, taking her gently by one arm and directing her in a different direction. They entered an lift and a few moments later entered a different hall, less-brightly lit and covered in a deep, lush carpet. Benjamin and Cynthia strode quickly down that hall, Elly hurrying at their heels, and at last they came to a halt in front of a dark, lustrous wooden door. There was a brass plate on the door, and Elly saw with surprise that it bore her name.

Benjamin reached out, turned the knob, and held the door open for her. Elly stepped inside and, when Benjamin flipped on the lights, she gasped. She stood on the threshold of the most amazing office she'd ever seen. The desk was semi-circular, off center from the door to allow anyone entering the room to catch sight of the far wall – a single glass window without seam or blemish. Elly could make out stars, and the moon, though they were dimmer than they would have been from the patio of her flat in London. The lights of the city glowed so brightly, even at such a late hour, that they obscured the heavens.

Elly wished she'd paid attention in the lift. How many floors had they come up? The ride had been so quick and so smooth, that she'd not thought to count. Or had there even been lights for the floors? She couldn't remember.

"This is..." She hesitated, and Benjamin laughed softly.

"I know," he said. "It's overwhelming. Your grandmother spent a lot of hours staring out that window. It points east, you know. Toward London."

Elly glanced at him, then back at the window. His words had put a dizzying perspective on the view. She was so far from anything she'd called home.

Benjamin strode across the room to another door and Elly turned to see. He held that door open, as well, and beckoned to her.

"There's plenty of time to go through the papers and books later," he said. "Through here are your quarters. Her quarters. They are just as she left them – it was a stipulation in her will."

Elly stepped through the door. This time she managed not to gasp, but just barely. The rooms were elegantly furnished, dark mahogany and thick carpet, leather seats gathered around a coffee table and faced off with one of the largest high-definition televisions she'd ever seen. There was a bar along one wall with a beautiful copper espresso server and crystal stemware glittering from hanging racks.

Elly turned in slow circles. The place was imposing, but not in the same way the office had been. She felt a presence – her grandmother? – in the décor, in the tilting, disorganized books on the shelves, and the sparse artwork hanging from the walls. There were more doorways leading off from this main chamber.

"That's the hallway that leads to the bedroom," Benjamin pointed to her right. "Over there, to the left of the bar, is the entrance to the kitchen. It's only a small one – most of the cooking and eating is done in a central location. Lily," he hesitated, then corrected himself with a rueful grin, "your grandmother, was a very people-oriented person. She spent her quiet time here, but she liked to be out with the others, sharing meals, learning about their lives."

The man grew silent for a moment, and Elly turned to him. Before she could speak, he continued.

"She was an amazing woman, Elly. Your grandmother was

well-loved here, and you'll find that she has touched all of our lives in one way or another."

Elly nodded, and then turned back to the room. There was a knock at the outer door, and a young man stepped inside. He pulled a cart on which Elly's luggage sat. All of it, the trunk, which she hadn't seen since she boarded her flight in Heathrow, and the bags she'd carried.

Without a word, the young man placed the bags by the door and wheeled the trunk into a corner where it would be out of the way.

"Thank you, Tom," Benjamin said with a smile. He turned back to Elly. "I'll leave you alone for a while now and let you settle in. Everything you see here is yours. Everything you don't see but might need is yours for the asking. Your phone has several numbers programmed in for inter-office calls. I'm number 2, Cynthia is number 3 and if you dial the 0 you'll get the kitchen. If you need an outside line, dial 9 first."

"Thank you," Elly said softly. She was already walking toward the hallway and the bedroom beyond when the door clicked shut behind her, and she was alone in her grandmother's home.

The hall was a short one. As she entered it, there was a bathroom to her right, long and sleek, all white and black and chrome. It might have been too cold and modern, but with the teal towels and shower curtain infusing it with cool color, and an out-of-control spider plant in a hanging basket above the sink, it relaxed her. The tub was wide, deep, and jetted on all sides.

Elly turned away and stepped into the bedroom. She found the light switch to the right of the doorway and flipped it on. Another surprise – the room was absolutely different from every other in the huge apartment. The bed was old and wood framed. Octagonal posts jutted up at each corner, topped by hand-carved pineapples from which brightly colored swatches of fabric were strung. There was a patchwork quilt, a pair of fluffed, down-filled pillows, and a nightstand with a single lamp on it.

In the corner, almost invisible from the doorway, and to Elly's right, was a television stand. The remote sat on the nightstand beside a box of tissues, and a short pile of books. Elly crossed the room, sat on the bed, and turned on the lamp. She ran her hand lightly over the quilt. It was old, soft, and warm. There was a window across from the bed. She knew it must be thick safety glass, but the interior wall had been designed with a wooden frame, and a sill. She stared out over the glowing lights of the city toward the horizon.

Elly stood, returned to the main room, and grabbed her bags. She carried them quickly to the bedroom and closed the door behind her. It was a silly precaution, she knew, but it made her feel better. If they wanted in, they would come in. It was just that the smaller, closed-in room felt more secure. More like home.

Elly slipped opened her bag, pulled out a nightshirt, and quickly undressed. Whatever this place had to offer her, it could wait until she had at least tired to sleep. Her mind whirled with the events of the evening. Too many questions, too few answers, and now – all of this.

She flipped back the covers, slid between, and lay back on the pillows. Glancing to the nightstand, she noticed the books again. Without thinking, she reached out and grabbed the top book off the stack. It was a journal. She opened it briefly, took in the smooth, even letters and the carefully filled pages. Then she closed it. Tears slid from the corners of her eyes and down her cheeks. Her hands trembled.

There would be time, she knew. Her grandmother lay between the covers of that journal, and she knew she'd go through every word of it, searching for answers to her questions. Just then, she was weary to the point of exhaustion, and suddenly very aware of the amazing, powerful woman who had left everything earned and learned in a long, active life, to Elly.

She reached out to set the journal aside, and stopped. The second book in the pile was old. It was bound in brown leather, faded, like an old wallet, as if it might have been carried in someone's pocket and rubbed smooth. The title was tooled into the leather and darkened with age. Elly ran her finger over the letters, tracing them slowly.

It read, simply, "Orffyreus."

Elly switched off the light, fighting the urge to open the book and read. The letters had etched themselves into her vision, and even with the light switched off, they strobed through her thoughts and confused the beginnings of her dreams. Despite her nervous energy, Elly was asleep in moments.

FIVE

In her dream, Elly fled down a corridor. She glanced over her shoulder, but there was no one in sight. She heard deep, rasping breath and pounding footsteps, but somehow she stayed ahead and just out of sight of her pursuer. She saw the blinking light of an lift ahead. The lift car rose from three floors below. It was too slow. She knew she would reach that door while the lift car was at least a full floor beneath her, and the footsteps drew nearer. She turned a final time, but there was no one.

The lift slipped between floors, and she heard a sound, like a soft chime. The doors opened and she gasped, lurching inside. Someone was already there. She caught sight of polished shoes and dark, creased pants. She raised her gaze but...

The alarm continued its mellow, soothing intrusion. Elly sat up groggily and fumbled with the unfamiliar mechanism until the clock was silent. The pillows were incredibly soft, and it took her several shakes of her head to clear the cobwebs of sleep from her thoughts. The events of the night before came back in a rush, and she pulled the warm quilt around her tightly. The room wasn't huge, but it was large, and just then, alone and closed in on the top floor of a building she'd never seen before, overlooking a city that might as well have been a landscape on the planet Mars for all her familiarity with it, the space seemed huge and empty.

She glanced at the clock. It said ten o'clock. She stretched and slid her legs off the side of the bed. Standing, she noticed the open window and the bright sunlit sky beyond, and she backed away from it. Then she laughed softly. Anyone this many stories up and staring in her window was welcome to the view. She glanced out over the city. It was different by day. She could see for quite a distance, but mist, or clouds obscured the very tops of the buildings surrounding her. Most of them were lower than her window, though there were others that stretched up and beyond. She stood and watched several birds wheel through the clouds, then turned and found her suitcase.

In the bathroom, Elly gazed longingly at the tub, but it was going to have to wait. She needed food, and she needed answers, and she could get neither by lying around in the tub, no matter how inviting. She showered quickly, made herself as presentable as she could on short notice, and went to the front door. She half expected this to be the moment when she discovered herself to be a prisoner, but the handle turned easily, and she stepped out into the corridor. There were no open doors except that of the lift at the far end. Elly closed the door behind her and walked to the lift.

Once inside, she inspected the buttons. To her relief, the labels on the controls weren't limited to simple floor numbers. She pressed the button that read dining hall and watched the doors whoosh shut before her. Moments later the gentle tugging sensation in her stomach told her the lift was dropping fast. Everything was metallic and smooth. Even the mechanism that ran the lift was eerily silent.

The doors slid open, and Elly stepped into a corridor she'd never seen before. The scent of fresh coffee reached her first, followed by a variety of other equally tantalizing aromas. She walked down the corridor, glancing into doorways as she passed. There was a lounge with snack machines, a small room that reminded her of the boardrooms used by lawyers on television. Finally, near the far end of the hallway, she found a cafeteria. It was large and open, tables lined the walls and were scattered across a tiled floor. There were a number of people, some in suits, others in different colored lab coats, eating, drinking and laughing at the tables. When Elly stepped in, everything grew quiet for a moment.

Determined not to make a scene, she quickly made her way among the tables to the counter and the coffee. By the time she slid a blue tray down the line toward food, a Styrofoam cup of coffee steaming in front of her, the general noise had returned, and she felt the weight of their combined gaze lift from her shoulders. She chose a pre-packaged egg and cheese sandwich and a small Danish, as well as a cup of orange juice to join her coffee on the tray. There was tea, and she stared at it longingly, but she recognized none of the brands, and didn't want to take a chance.

There was no checkout at the far end, and Elly was standing there, a bit perplexed, when she heard a friendly voice call out from behind her.

"Good morning."

Elly turned to face Cynthia Lyons, who had just picked up a tray of her own.

"Good morning," Elly replied noncommittally.

"Give me a second to grab some coffee and a muffin," Cynthia said brightly, "and we can sit together. I'm sure you have questions."

Elly didn't answer. She stared at the young woman. In the better light of the morning she saw that her driver for last night's escapades was approximately her own age. The long red hair Elly had noticed was braided and hung over one of Cynthia's shoulders. Her eyes were hazel and her smile bright. Also missing was the tight leather. Today, Cynthia wore blue jeans and a teal smock that accented her eyes.

Cynthia grabbed a steaming cup of coffee and a bran muffin. Once they were balanced safely on her tray she turned and nodded toward a table near the front entrance to the dining hall, against the wall. "It's a little bit quieter over there," she said, "and if anyone important that you should know, or know about, walks in, I can point him or her out to you."

Elly nodded. "Thanks," she said softly. She wasn't ready to trust anyone just yet, but Cynthia seemed genuinely friendly, and it was good to not be alone. The building was immense, and the more time Elly spent watching people hustle back and forth, carts pushed past the windows, and listening to the laughter and shouted greetings of people she didn't know, but who theoretically worked for her, the more surreal and overwhelming it became.

They sat at a small table, Elly with her back to the door.

Cynthia attacked her muffin immediately, washed the first bite down with some coffee, and glanced up at Elly, smiling.

"I can't imagine what you think of us after last night," the girl began. "I don't know what to say except that it was almost as strange for us as it was for you. Eddy is doing fine – we can go and see him later, if you want. Benjamin has scheduled the entire afternoon for you, but until then I told him I'd show you around a little and try to make you a little more comfortable with the situation."

Elly sipped her orange juice. "But…" she said at last, turning and waving a hand to encompass the dining hall, the corridor beyond, and the building as a whole. "What is this? Who are you people, and why on earth would my grandmother want me to come here? Who is that man, Maxwell Black? Why did he kidnap me, and how did you know?"

Cynthia laughed, and it was rich, honest laughter. Elly felt a little better hearing it, though she pursed her lips at having caused such an outburst.

"I'm sorry," Cynthia said, still grinning. "I know I said I'd answer questions – I just kind of thought they might come one at a time."

Elly looked at her, blinked, and then laughed herself. "Sorry," Elly said. "I guess I don't even know where to start asking."

"Well," Cynthia replied, "this 'place' is The Orffyreus Corporation, that's a good place to start, I think."

Elly started. "Orffyreus? That word - or is it a name? - keeps popping up. It's on the envelope my grandmother left to me, and it seemed to mean something to Maxwell Black."

"It did," Cynthia said, her expression suddenly grim. "Your grandmother put together the solution to a secret that has evaded science for hundreds of years. Maxwell Black is aware of this, and he would go to any length to pry that secret loose from us. He must be getting desperate if he's resorted to kidnapping, though. He should have known that you wouldn't have what he needed before you'd even spoken to us."

"He wanted the envelope," Elly said. "He tried to take it, just when Eddie crashed through the door and snatched me out of there."

Cynthia nodded. "I'm not sure how he knew about the envelope," she replied, "but it wouldn't have done him any good without the trunk, which he didn't even try to take. Whoever supplied him his information didn't tell him everything, and that's good. It doesn't mean that we don't have a spy, but it does mean the spy isn't very good."

Elly frowned again. "But why would there be spies? What are they spying on?"

Cynthia's smile was a little wan when she replied, "Orffyreus. They want the secret of Orffyreus, and if we let them get it, then everything that we have worked for, everything your grandmother spent a lifetime achieving, will have been so much wasted time. Put very simply, Orffyreus is about energy, very cheap, efficient energy."

Elly glanced around, then finished her orange juice and unwrapped her sandwich. "I still don't see what it has to do with me," she said softly. "I don't feel like I own anything, or like I'm in charge of anything. I'm confused, and a long way from home."

"Well," Cynthia replied, "you'd better get used to the owning part, anyway. This is all yours, and there's more. When you're done eating, I'll show you your office."

"I've seen it," Elly replied. "It's right outside my apartment."

Cynthia smiled. "That's your personal office – like a retreat. You have a corporate office as well, more business-like, and right next door to Benjamin."

Elly groaned.

"Two offices? Do you know how I lived in London? Do you people have any idea what I'm actually going through here? My entire flat would fit in the office I saw last night. I have never slept in a bed remotely as comfortable as a single pillow on the bed I was in last night. There is one short story to my home. No lift. No kitchen and dining hall. I didn't even have room to own a cat."

She turned and glanced into the hallway beyond the dining room once more. "Now all of this."

Cynthia reached out and laid a hand gently on Elly's arm.

"We'll help you in any way we can," she said. "We wanted to bring you in quietly yesterday, get you settled and discuss things over dinner. Maxwell Black prevented that, and you've been exposed to a lot of things that you should not have been. Not yet."

A great clanging noise interrupted Cynthia's short speech, and both women turned to watch as a rolling cart was pushed past the window and down the hall toward the lifts. The cart was heavily loaded. Three young men and a tall, stately black woman in a bright peach smock rolled the cart. They didn't look up as they passed the window. Elly caught a glimpse of a wiring harness peeking out from beneath the tarpaulin that shrouded whatever was on the cart, and she frowned.

More secrets.

Cynthia seemed to snatch Elly's thought from the air. "We have to maintain some secrecy between departments," she explained. "What we are doing here is very important. We trust our employees – they're screened for every potential threat we can conceive, but there's always something forgotten. Yesterday's fiasco was a good example of that.

"No one group knows the entire plan. Information can be leaked, but only in small doses, and only over time. Time is what we are fighting here. If we can manage to put the final pieces in place, make use of what your grandmother left you, then we will be able to reveal the secret to the world, and it will be too late for the Maxwell Blacks of society to either exploit our work, or stop it. Until then…"

Cynthia stared off after the retreating hulk on the cart.

Elly swallowed the last of her sandwich and took a sip of the coffee. Before she could say anything more, a young man hurried in the door. His hair stuck out in all directions at once, and his eyes were dark and intense. He was small and slender, and he wore thick, rimless glasses that slid down his nose every couple of seconds, only to have him push them nervously back up. He had a sheaf of papers in his hand, and gave the impression of being late for several things at once.

"What is it, Charlie?" Cynthia asked. She didn't seem ruffled by the young man's nervous state.

"Paperwork," he muttered. Then he glanced up, saw them both watching him, and broke into a wide grin. "I'm sorry," he said, extending a hand to Elly, who took it before she could give the action any thought. "I'm Charlie Lynch. I'm in charge of building security. Benjamin wanted me to get with you this morning and get your identification badge processed. He thought you might want to get out into the city later, and you'll need it to get back in. Of course, since you're here, you know we can get you back in without it, but it simplifies things a great deal."

The words spilled out in such a rush that Elly's mind seemed to process them at a speed a word or two behind that in which they were spoken. When he released her hand, she held it up and laughed. "Slow down, please. Identification badge?"

"Sure," Charlie said. He grabbed a long cord that dangled around his neck and held up a shiny plastic card with a photograph and other information printed on the surface. The bottom of the card was a magnetic strip.

"We use these to get in and out of the main lobby, and also for access to the various labs and facilities within the building. This strip," he pointed at the bar code, "is programmed to allow you into whatever areas you require access to, and to deny you access to others. Yours will, of course, be granted full access. You might have wondered about the lack of a lock on your apartment door?"

When Elly didn't reply, he went on. "The lift you rode down on is the only access to that floor. All of the rooms there are for your private use. There is also a stairway exit for emergencies. Mr. Wright is the only other person with access to your floor, and after certain hours even his is revoked. Without you pressing the proper code sequence in your quarters, no one can get in – or out – of your private area. I'll come up and explain the security panel to you, and show you how to choose your private codes this evening. Last night we had everything opened up so you could get in and out without trying to learn all of this too quickly."

"Everything is happening too quickly," Elly replied with a shake of her head.

"If you could just sign this," Charlie said, "I can get on with processing your badge. We have all of the pertinent information.

If you were a new employee we'd do a background check and a fingerprint scan before we processed the paperwork, but obviously this is different."

Elly took the pen he'd held out to her. She couldn't see any harm in it. If she wanted to get in and out of the building, it seemed she was going to need this badge. She signed her name in a quick squiggle on the paperwork, and Charlie scooped up pen and paper and spun on his heel, headed for the door.

"I'll have this done and delivered to you before you leave Benjamin's office," he called over his shoulder. Then he was gone.

Elly sat back, a little breathless, and turned to catch Cynthia's amused gaze.

"Charlie is a little – enthusiastic," Cynthia explained. "He's a nice enough guy, and very good at what he does, but sometimes he gets caught up in it all and tends to forget the rest of the world is out here. We excuse his little quirks, because – as I said – he's very good at what he does. Nothing in the Orffyreus complex moves without one of his cameras or microphones picking it up and one of his computers recording it. I wouldn't be surprised if that program he's so proud of could distinguish who was sleeping in what room by the rhythm of their snoring."

Elly downed the last of her coffee, and Cynthia stood up. They carried their trash to a receptacle and headed for the door. "There's a lot to see," Cynthia told her, "but most of it we'll save until after you and Benjamin have talked. It won't make much sense without the background to put it all in context."

"Let's just start with the office then," Elly said. "I don't want to see another confusing thing, but I think I can handle a computer and a desk."

Cynthia nodded, and led her off toward the lifts. Elly noticed as they stood waiting that the lift she'd exited was off to the side, a single door width. The others were larger and very busy. She could trace the cars as they moved up, and down the buildings center. She tried counting the floors again, but she didn't get past thirty before they reached the end of the hall.

Cynthia stepped into the lift, and Elly joined her. They shared the space with a gray-haired man who was lost in some figures on a clipboard. He glanced up, smiled distractedly, and then went back to work. The lift dropped rapidly, but this time Elly was able to make out the numbers. Forty-two floors. She tried to imagine that in her head, tried to stack forty-two long hallways and hundreds, maybe thousands of rooms one on top of the other, all filled with people talking, walking, working – on what? Her head throbbed, and she concentrated on watching the numbers light up, one after the other. They stopped on three, and the door opened. The man with the clipboard looked up again, saw the number, looked mildly irritated, and went back to his numbers. Cynthia stepped out into yet another hall, and Elly followed.

This area was less elegant and more utilitarian. The doors were of plain, blonde wood, each with a small brass plaque indicating the occupant and his title. They passed one marked with Cynthia's name, and Elly read the words "Executive Assistant," beneath the name. She filed the information away. At the end of the hall were two slightly larger doors. They opened into the corners at an angle. One read Dr. Benjamin Wright, CEO – the other drew Elly up short for a moment. Elizabeth Kassel, President. The plaque was larger than the others lining the hall.

Cynthia slipped past her and opened the door, holding it so Elly could step inside. The room was large, but not overpowering. A solid, serviceable mahogany desk stood near the center and beyond that were tall windows with the blinds pulled. Soft fluorescent light lit the room, and the walls were lined with bookshelves and filing cabinets.

There was no clutter. This space had apparently not been left exactly as her grandmother had kept it, and that was fine with Elly. She was ready to step into something she could adapt to herself for a change. There was a slender computer terminal on the desktop and a large, thin LCD monitor. Elly stepped around the desk and sank into the soft, comfortable leather of the chair. The screen on the computer blinked at her, solid blue with a design of some sort of wheel in the center.

"You can log in if you want," Cynthia told her. "I can step you through setting up e-mail. There will be a brief indoctrination, probably tomorrow, with one of the tech guys to show you the rest of what's available."

Elly nodded.

Cynthia pulled another chair around to sit beside her. "We should have just about enough time before Benjamin is ready to see you," she said.

Elly leaned forward, placed her hands on the keyboard, and stared at a portrait of her grandmother on the wall across from her before they began. The face that stared back at her from the canvas was older, aged by years and lined by smiles. Still, she had the eerie sensation that she was staring back at herself.

SIX

It was around noon when Elly finally glanced up from the computer screen. Benjamin Wright stood in the doorway, dressed in a light gray suit and smiling widely.

"I see you've made yourself at home," he said, nodding at the computer.

Elly glanced back at the over-sized screen and wondered if things like this would ever feel like "home."

When she didn't reply, he nodded. "It isn't going to be an easy transition. If you'll step over to my office, I'll see what I can do to open a few of the locked doors for you. Orffyreus is a truly remarkable project – I'm looking forward to sharing it with you. Your grandmother intended to finish the final stages before she brought you here, but ... well, we do what we can do, don't we?"

Elly stood and stepped around the desk. She already knew from a couple of extended moments of daydreaming that the screen would lock if the keyboard remained inactive more than five minutes at a stretch. More security.

As she followed Benjamin through the door and into the hall, hurried footsteps pounded to their right, and both turned. It was Charlie. He wasn't running, exactly, but he was walking so quickly and with such intensity, that he looked like a large, gangly insect scuttling across the carpet. He waved a white card in the air, and Elly knew it must be her promised ID.

Charlie skidded to a halt beside them and Benjamin chuckled. "Calm down, son," Benjamin said. "We weren't going anywhere."

"I finished your card," Charlie said, ignoring Benjamin.

He was gripping it very tightly, and Elly had to smile at his intensity.

"It's been programmed to give you access to any door in the building," he said hurriedly. "There are four colors we use for security. Green is open to all employees, Blue is restricted to permanent employees, no visitors or temporary staff. Yellow requires a clearance – I can give you the criteria for that any time you're available, and then there are the red areas."

The words had come out in such a rush that Elly simply stared. Benjamin stepped forward, placed a hand on Charlie's shoulder and took the card gently from the younger man's fingers.

"I'll explain the color code and security, Charlie. Thank you for expediting this. I appreciate it, and I know Elly does as well. But let's not hit her with too much all at once."

Charlie smiled sheepishly. "I just got carried away, I guess. We were all pretty worried yesterday." He blushed and turned away.

"Thank you," Elly said.

Charlie turned and smiled at her. Then he hurried off toward the lifts.

"Charlie takes his work very seriously," Elly commented.

"It's a serious job," Benjamin replied. "We're fortunate to have him with us. Your grandmother found Charlie in a halfway home about twelve years ago. A number of the staff came to us in that way. Lily used to watch for children with special abilities, children who were having trouble fitting in because they were bored, or had some special aptitude. Charlie is a genius with computers, but his real love is intrigue. If he could live out a James Bond spy novel, he'd be in heaven. He's a perfect fit in security." Elly noticed that it was the second time Benjamin had called her grandmother Lily, though he was obviously trying to avoid the familiarity. She wondered if there had been something more between the two than employer and assistant, but decided to file away all personal questions until she had some idea where she was, and why.

She glanced down at the ID card in her hand. It was attached to a metal clip and she hooked it to her blouse. She felt better with the badge, not standing out in the crowd of others, all sporting the same small plastic cards.

"Come on in," Benjamin said, holding wide the door to his own office.

Elly entered and looked around. The desk that centered this room was semi-circular and made of some dark wood she couldn't identify immediately. On the walls surrounding her, she saw maps, diagrams, framed blueprints and a series of white boards with scribbled notations across them. There were small groups of chairs gathered around a couple of the charts, and bookshelves lined the walls, stretching up high enough that a rolling stepladder had been added to the room's décor in order to reach the uppermost shelves.

"As you can see," Benjamin chuckled, "I like to keep myself busy. We are growing near to the culmination of a lifetime of work – my lifetime, in any case. It's an exciting time, but hectic. Please," he gestured at a padded leather chair beside his desk, "sit down."

Elly curled into the chair and Benjamin Wright seated himself behind the imposing façade of his desk. He looked a little tired right at that moment, but imposing. Elly glanced around the room again. She couldn't imagine being aware of and involved in so many things at once.

"Just what is the work you do here," Elly asked at last. "I've heard over and over what wonderful things my grandmother was about, and how you have all spent your lives and your energy helping to make her dreams reality. What were the dreams? What is the reality? And what, to cut to the chase, is Orffyreus?"

Benjamin grinned. He grabbed a large sketchpad on his desktop, flipped to a blank page, and began to draw rapidly. Elly watched in amazement and confusion as he drew a large, nearly perfect circle and began ringing it with the letters of the alphabet. He worked quickly, and his sure hands rendered the image in a matter of moments. When he was done, he circled the letters B E S L R and then, at the bottom of the sheet, he wrote the name Bessler. Next he drew straight lines across the diameter of the circle, bisecting the letters directly across from those he'd circled. O R F Y E was the result. He then wrote the word – name? — Orffyre beneath Bessler and turned to her.

"Does the name Johann Bessler mean anything to you?" he asked.

Elly shook her head.

"I didn't think it would, but I figured I'd better ask. Johann Bessler was an inventor. He lived in Europe in the 1700s. At some point in his life, he took on the name Orffyreus – the Orffyre being the diametrically opposed letters from this circle with the addition of the US on the end, an affectation of Romanism. It is one of Bessler's inventions that brought you these thousands of miles to an inheritance you never dreamed of."

"What did he invent?" Elly asked, fascinated.

"The Orffyreus Wheel," Benjamin replied, sitting back and watching her for a moment, steepling his fingers. "A perpetual motion device. The impossible. Johann Bessler invented a wheel that could be set into motion by a soft touch of the hand, and would run, very literally, until its parts wore out. That was his claim."

"And you believe this?" Elly asked.

"I didn't," Benjamin admitted. "Your grandmother did, however, and she could be very persuasive. The result of her belief you see all around you."

The reality of what he was saying seeped into Elly's mind slowly. World politics and the ecology weren't things she'd given a lot of thought to.

"So," she said at last, fearing she'd sound even more ignorant than she felt at that moment, "this man, Orffyreus, invented a wheel that would keep spinning without fuel or power?"

"Exactly," Benjamin replied, nodding. "But the invention is much more than a simple wheel. The implications are staggering, though I know they don't leap out at you. Think about your flat back in London," he said. "Think about the money you pay, month in and month out, for electricity. There are a number of ways that electricity can be generated. Some cities use water power to generate it, others use different sorts of fuel, and in slightly older times, they used the wind. What if that electricity required nothing to create it? What if, once the mechanisms were in place, the power just kept coming forever and you never had to worry about fuel? What if great machines could run pumps and lifts, generators and anything that requires a steady generation of force, but nothing was required to keep them in motion?"

"It would be cheaper," Elly said thoughtfully.

"Yes," Benjamin agreed. "Cheaper, and more efficient, and the cost would only go down over time. These are just the initial benefits of such an invention as Bessler's wheel. Given time and enough thought, and there could be engines running without gasoline or diesel. Things that were once too costly could fall within the realm of possibility. That is what this is all about, a world of possibilities."

"But," Elly cut in, "If this man – Bessler – invented his wheel in the 1700s, why don't we already have all of those things?"

"That is a very good question," Benjamin replied. "The simple answer is that, for all the progress in the world, things haven't changed very much. When Johann Bessler invented his wheel he had a couple of expectations in mind. He thought he'd make a pile of money and be well off for the rest of his life, and he thought people would congratulate him and tell him how wonderful his invention was. Neither of these things happened.

"Johann was a shrewd businessman. He knew that if he let too many people in on the secret of his wheel too easily, they would just recreate it and he'd be left on his own. He guarded the secret jealously. He had a price in mind for the secret, a very great price, particularly in those days, and he kept to his guns. To my knowledge, and according to the papers that have passed down through the ages, only one other living man was privy to the secret of the wheel, a nobleman who became Bessler's patron in later years. The rest of the world spent their time in small-minded attacks on the man, and in attempts to discredit him and his invention as preposterous. The attacks were very successful, and the secret of the wheel died, for all intent and purpose, the day that Bessler himself died."

"Except that it didn't," Elly said softly. "If the secret was lost, then I wouldn't be here, and you would be working on something else."

Again, Benjamin nodded.   "Your grandmother spent a great deal of time, effort, and money in research," he said. "She traveled to Germany, and to Poland, to London and several other countries. She visited the places where Bessler made and presented his wheel. She read the correspondence that has survived between the "great minds" of the day, most of which was aimed at debunking the wheel's existence. She read Bessler's journal – the one that was discovered at his death. It was a prodigious task, and one that no one had thought to attempt before her, though several have come into the race since. You've already met Mr. Black."

Elly frowned. "So, Maxwell Black knows about what you are doing here?"

"Not all of it," Benjamin admitted. "He knows enough to be a hindrance, and he believes that he may know more. His own network is very active, and I believe he may not be far from discovering some secrets on his own. It won't matter. We are nearly ready to go public with your grandmother's work. We have to prove our case beyond any shadow of a doubt, and, as Orffyreus himself knew, we must be careful how, and where, we reveal the secret."

"Surely they can't ignore all of this?" Elly waved an arm vaguely toward the hallway, and the floors and labs beyond.

"Not ignore, exactly," Benjamin said. "But if you think of the people who would gain the most, and those who would stand to lose the most, by the presentation of such a device, you can begin to grasp the scope of what will come next. The oil companies will fight us, and I mean that very literally. The government will try to swallow us. There are plenty of less-savory applications for the wheel, and we have worked long and hard, patenting small portions of the technology here and there and spreading it out so that the various parts would be nearly impossible to piece back together legally. We've even patented a few processes and devices that do nothing at all, just to confuse the trail."

Elly had a sudden vision of great battle machines, or huge ships, prowling the ocean without the limitation of fossil fuel. Her face clouded.

"What does this have to do with me?" Elly asked. "I mean, other than that I inherited from my grandmother, why all the secrecy? What's in that trunk, and the envelope?"

"A lot of what your grandmother discovered is wrapped up in that trunk," Benjamin replied. "I wanted to keep it here, under lock and key, until the time came to send for you, but she was a wise woman. Lily felt it was important to keep the information in more than one place, and she gathered together the things she discovered on her journeys through Europe into that trunk. The envelope contains some instructions, some diagrams, and the one, single scrap of paper that brought it all back together."

"What is it?" Elly asked, glancing at the door, and thinking about the envelope resting on the counter in her apartment.

"Orffyreus left very little to chance," Benjamin replied. "He left lengthy accounts of his life, journals and diagrams, books of notes – pieces. One of the things in your trunk is the remnant of his original wheel. It's missing pieces, and I suspect Bessler himself destroyed them. He encoded the secret, and there was only one paper in the entire world that could help one to decipher the code. You might think that's an exaggeration. Codes have been simplified over the years, and with computers, almost anything can be broken, but this case is different. Bessler was a mathematician, and he lived in the days when Calculus was being invented. Add to that the fact that he was a genius, and you can imagine the complexity he could bring to something like a code."

"And that code is in my envelope?" she asked.

Benjamin nodded.

Elly shuddered. "Black had that paper so close to his hand he could have brushed his fingers over it. If I'd only known..."

"If you'd known, your grandmother didn't believe you'd come at all," Benjamin replied, smiling. "Having met you, I tend to agree. All of this is hard enough to believe when you are sitting in the middle of it – imagine trying to convince yourself of it after a phone call, or a letter. Besides, the fact that you didn't know what it was was intended as a further security precaution. You could not give away information you didn't have, and it would become clear to anyone quite quickly that you didn't know who Bessler was, let alone how to recreate his wheel. It helped us to keep you safe, and it helped us to keep the code safe."

Elly shook her head. She couldn't seen any reason the papers, and the wheel itself, for that matter, would be safer with her. It was true, though, that they had both been locked in the safe at Ratliff and Brownridge, and that she'd known nothing about it.

"What will you do with them now?" she asked.

"I have some suggestions," Benjamin smiled, "but that decision is up to you. They are your inheritance, after all. Your grandmother was a woman of straightforward thought and decisions. She determined a long time ago that she would pass this on to you. She watched you, you know, even when you didn't realize she was there. She took care of little things when she could, without being too obvious."

Elly flushed. "I thought she'd forgotten all about me," she said softly. "I wish she would have visited, or written me letters..."

"Too dangerous," Benjamin replied quickly. "She didn't want you in danger from people like Black until things had already broken wide open. At that point, there would be no danger from those trying to prevent us from discovering the secrets of the wheel, or creating it. The danger then would have been in the political realm, and she believed once we reached that point you'd be safe enough here."

"You said you had suggestions?" she said at last.

"I was going to suggest that you open the trunk," Benjamin said. The notes your grandmother took, and the journals and articles she collected, are all in there. The original wheel, or what's left of it, is there as well. I thought we might rebuild it, if you have no objection. I think it would look good on your desk, and I, for one, would love to see the actual wheel that Johann Bessler attempted to amaze the world, be the very one that brings his discovery, at long last, into reality."

Elly stared at him for a moment. Less than ten minutes before she hadn't even known of this wheel. Now, here this man was, a man who she barely knew, suggesting she rebuild what was possibly the most important and amazing invention of the ages and keep it for a novelty.

"Read the journals," Benjamin said, catching the dismay in her expression. "Learn more, and by all means, learn it the way that Lily intended for you to learn it. We can speak of the wheel itself again later."

Elly nodded. She rose slowly, turning and taking in the drawings on the walls.

"How big was his wheel?" she asked finally. "If it will fit on a desk, how can it do all of the things you say it can do?"

"That was just the first wheel," Benjamin replied with a smile. "Bessler made several more, one large enough to lift a seventy pound weigh repeatedly that ran for eight weeks in a sealed, locked room – a test that was witnessed by some very important people. This evidence, and all of the rest, was refuted, ignored, and ridiculed until Bessler smashed his wheel into bits with a hammer."

Elly walked over to one of the diagrams on the wall. It was a blow up of a very old drawing. It pictured a large wheel with pendulum weights on either side. She reached up and ran her hand across the paper.

"That was the last wheel," Benjamin told her. "That was the one that should have shown the world."

Elly nodded, and then turned to face him.

"I'm going to go open that trunk," she said. "I'll see what I find inside, and I'll see if I can find anything from my grandmother that would tell me what she expected of me. I want to know why I was chosen. I want to know why she couldn't spend time with me sooner – most of all, I want to understand what it is that she was doing all of these years, and how it came to be…" She waved her arms again, "this."

Benjamin nodded.

"If you feel up to it, we usually have dinner together, just the top staff. That would include Cynthia, Eddie, when he recovers, Charlie, and a couple of others that you haven't met. If you decide to join us, just give me a ring and I'll send someone to show you the way."

Elly nodded. She turned and stepped back into the hall. She hesitated at the door to her own office, but decided she'd seen enough for one day. She walked slowly down the corridor; found the lift that gave her direct access to the floor where her apartments were located, and leaned against the rear wall as the door slid smoothly shut behind her.

The trunk was locked, but the key the lawyers had given her fit and turned smoothly. Elly tilted up the lid and leaned it back, gazing inside. There was a tray in the top that was lined with notebooks, journals, diagrams and books. She leafed through them, and on the right side was a packet of notebooks bound in a yellow silk ribbon. Beneath this ribbon was an envelope with her name on it. Her heartbeat sped, and she lifted the notebooks and the card from the box and carried them to a table by the window. She unwound the ribbon, pulled free the card, and began to read.

"Dear Elizabeth,

Since you are reading this, I'm either in the next room, hoping anxiously that we will connect, or beyond that connection and hoping that you will understand, and that you will carry on the work that I have started. I know that Benjamin and the others will treat you with the same love and respect they have shown to me, and I wish that the times and circumstances could have been different. I would have loved to be part of your life sooner; I couldn't risk putting you in danger.

I'm attaching this card to my journals. I've written them in a story form – it seemed easiest, as if I were speaking to you directly. I hope my small ability with words will be adequate to such a momentous task. Johann Bessler was a genius – a man gifted well beyond his means, and his time. When you have shared his story with me, take out the wheel. Compare it to my notes. See if you can see what I have seen – the key that was missing. Remember, no matter what happens, that I have loved you, and that I have done the best that I could for you, in the best way that I knew how.

Love, your grandmother – Lily."

Elly set the card aside, tears welling in the corners of her eyes and trailing hot and wet down her cheeks. She stared off through the window. The sun had passed overhead and was on its way back down the far side of the city. All she could see, gazing east toward England, and home, was the shimmering heat rising from the city, the silver fog and the darker smog, all touched by the golden orange glow of encroaching evening. When the tears had dried, cool on her cheeks, she reached for the first of the notebooks.

Her grandmother's handwriting was beautiful, like Calligraphy, evenly spaced, slanted right and filled with loops and swirls. Elly traced a few of the letters, and smiled. So like her own. She rose, stepped to the bar along the wall, and found that there was a small rack filled with unopened bottles of wine. She chose a red without really glancing at the label, located a corkscrew and a glass, and headed back to the table by the window.

With an empty ache inside for the loss of a grandmother she hardly knew, Elly began to read.

PART TWO: ORFFYREUS

"Whither ye rays of gravity may be stopped by reflecting or refracting them, if so a perpetual motion may be made one of these two ways..."

Sir Isaac Newton

SEVEN

Johann Bessler lay back on his simple cot. His eyes burned with tears of frustration. Moonlight leaked in through the curtained windows of his workshop and drew long shadows from the base of each piece of furniture, making stalking bears and dragons of the shadows of trees as they moved in the grip of the breeze beyond his window.

On a scaffold near the center of the shop, a large cylinder hung suspended on an axle. Dust motes floated about the still form and glittered like tiny fairies in the moonlight. Bessler avoided the sight of it. It should be moving. It should be rolling and rolling and never stopping.

He tried to rest, but his mind was a furious swirl of calculations and formulae. Though his eyes were closed, he couldn't escape visions of gears and armatures, clocks and the great organ he'd been constructing under the tutelage of his cousin. He couldn't rid himself of the still, stationary wheel, mocking him in the darkness.

As he lay there, he poured himself back bitterly over the months and years of struggle, the schooling, the study, making clocks, making organs, preaching and teaching, and the medicine. All of the bits and pieces he'd worked so hard to form himself from were of little use to him now, when what he wanted so very badly was to get the bits and pieces of something else in the proper order. He knew it could be done. He knew he should have done it already, but the wheel did not turn. No matter what he tried, no matter whom he consulted -- mechanics, clock-makers, engineers, mathematicians, even a Rabbi. None of it was enough. He was not enough.

Eventually exhaustion claimed him, and he drifted into a deeper darkness.

In his dream, he walked through his cousin's workshop near the great organ. He thought it odd that his feet seemed not to touch the ground, but ignored this, drawn by a glow near the center of the magnificent instrument's inner workings. He passed around the corner and found that the rear of the organ was open. Inside there was a glow so bright that he could not make out any of the machinery. He tried to examine the mechanics and wondered briefly if there was a fire causing the brilliance.

Drifting closer, Johann reached out, gripped the sides of the rear panel, and steadied himself as he leaned in closer. There was no heat, so it did not seem to be a fire. Perplexed, he leaned further still, until the ends of his hair and the tip of his beard were bathed in the silver glow.

He cried out as those hairs pulled taut. Something inside had reached out to grip him and draw him in. He held tightly to the sides of the organ and tried to call out, but it was as if he floated in molasses, and when the words were finally formed, so slowly they blurred to odd sounds and made no sense, he heard nothing.

For a frozen moment he clung on the brink, and then, with a tug of impossible strength, whatever had grasped him drew him in and down, through the light and into the organ, though he felt no painful crash of flesh on gears, or wood, but only a sizzling bright tingle that rippled down his body... and then a bright SNAP of energy.

Johann tumbled forward and fell, his heart slamming in his chest and his throat constricted by his continued effort to scream. He couldn't breathe. Air rushed past him far too quickly and everything ahead and below was a glowing, silver mist.

Then he sat up and clutched his chest. He was bathed in sweat and had to bite hard on his lip to keep from crying out. He looked around the shop wildly, unable to calm his heart. Such a dream -- and what could it mean? Should he go and check on the organ? Was it a sign?

Then, in that moment of utter confusion lost in a whirl of disconnected thoughts, it came to him. Johann sat up in the bed, flung his legs over the side and gripped the sheets. The sudden intensity of the revelation overwhelmed him, bits and pieces of so many days and years fitting themselves together smoothly and...

He stared over at the cylindrical wheel, and broke into a broad grin. He knew. Just as he had been certain a few hours earlier that he would never bring the wheel to life, it had come to him. A revelation. A vision. Whatever. He understood completely what he needed to do to make that wheel spin, and to keep it spinning, and he didn't know whether to finally let loose with the scream he'd been holding back, leap up and dance a jig, or rush into the streets and spread the word that he was a genius.

So he did none of these things. His lethargy was forgotten, and the world around him came into sharp focus. There was no hurry to finish this now. What he would build would not be another prototype with wings of hope fueling its debut performance, but the finished product. The real thing. He could not have explained how he knew this, but he did.

Hooves pounded on the street beyond his window. He rose and stepped closer to see who it might be. There was a carriage outside, and the young driver hopped down and hurried up the short steps, a rolled bit of paper clutched tightly in one hand.

Johann opened his door just as the boy was about to knock.

"Yes?" Bessler asked, "Can I help you?"

"Pardon me sir," the boy said, bowing slightly, "but are you Johann Bessler, who is said to be able to cure those who are ill?"

Johann nodded and took the paper.

"I was sent to bring you to my Lord, sir. His wife is very sick, and there's another lady nearby who is also feeling poorly."

Bessler read the symptoms, nodded, and turned away from the boy without a word. He bustled around his workshop, grabbed his bag and flung things into it in a haphazard manner. The boy watched, mystified, as Johann grabbed first one bottle, then another and packed away philters and jars of ointment, lenses and metal instruments.

"Give me just a moment to clean myself up, and to change," Johann said at last. "We will go at once." But they did not. Once Johann had made himself presentable, he locked his workshop carefully and placed his meager baggage on the coach. He then directed the boy to a small chapel outside the town, and there he had the driver wait as he entered. He knelt before the altar in the empty building, the high windows bright with the morning sun, and a breeze blowing through from the still open front doors, and he gave thanks to his God. In those moments he considered many things, but chief among them was faith. Faith had driven him and dragged him, aided him in moments of loneliness and goaded him to anger with his own inabilities. Faith had given him the answer. His faith. It was nearly half an hour before he returned to the carriage and drove off into the afternoon sunlight.

Johann did not return immediately to his workshop and build his wheel. Instead, he visited the rich patrons, and he cured their women. These jobs brought him small local fame, and he was able to treat and cure a number of others, gathering a small amount of capital and traveling into the mountains. Now that he had the secret firmly entrenched in his brain, he wanted to think about its uses.

There were mines in the Erz Mountains, and water mills nearby. He learned what he could of the mechanics behind both, and thought of ways his wheel might serve. Water pumps for the mines with an independent source of propulsion would mean that depths might be accessible that had previously been beyond the means of the miners. With an energy source that could pump the shafts dry and keep them that way efficiently, safety would be improved throughout the operation. All the while, as he traveled, Johann treated the sick and wounded, building a reputation as a man of medicine.

One morning, as he inspected the mechanism of a large water mill, he heard the now-familiar clip-clop of approaching hooves. He was growing used to the immediacy of medicine, and hurried to meet the driver without hesitation.

"You must come," the man cried, out of breath.

"What it is?" Johann asked.

"It is my lord's daughter," the man said, "Dr. Schumann's daughter. She is very ill, sir, and the doctor asked if you will come to see to her."

Johann stood still for a long moment, watching the boy's face. Dr. Christian Schumann was a respected medical man himself, and an eminent citizen. If he sought help beyond his own means, then the situation must be desperate.

"I'll come at once," he said, knowing that he was putting his reputation on the line. He was being asked to succeed where a trained medical doctor had failed. It was an important challenge that could make, or break his reputation. Johann squared his shoulders and swung quickly up beside the driver. He was traveling light that day, and had luckily decided to bring his medical bag along, so they would not be delayed in retrieving it.

"What has happened?" he asked, as the young man drove the horses down the rutted road and up toward Schumann's imposing manor. "What is wrong with the girl? And who are you?"

"My name is Frederic, sir," the young man responded. "I work for the head groomsman, and drive sometimes. Young miss Schumann has taken to her bed. She's been there a long time. I hear them say she's bad, twists and turns like a demon has hold of her. I saw, just for a moment, and the cries..."

Frederic broke off, his voice choked with emotion, and Johann turned to watch the road before them in grim silence.

"Can you help her sir?" Frederick asked when the silence had grown too much for him to stand.

"We'll see," Bessler replied. "I believe that I can. Drive, man, drive like the devil was on your tail. Every precious moment we waste on this road is one moment less likely I'll be able to help your mistress."

Frederic slapped the reins across the backs of the horses and they leaped forward, careening up the narrow mountain road toward Schumann's home. Johann clutched his bag and stared resolutely ahead, running over possible causes for the symptoms Frederic had reported in his mind. He would need to work quickly, but if he were right! It was obvious the girl was experiencing seizures, but what type? What cure? Johann leaned back and closed his eyes. He let the memory of the blinding radiance fill his thoughts, and visions of a turning wheel.

When Johann entered the girl's bedroom, he was greeted by Schumann himself, looking very haggard and worried, flanked by three women. The girl was bound in place by leather straps. She bit hard on yet another bit of leather, and her eyes flashed. They registered nothing when Johann stepped closer, laying his hand across her brow.

"There is no fever," Dr. Schumann said tersely. "Unless she has gone mad, I can find nothing wrong."

Johann said nothing. He stepped around the bed and reached for the girl's wrist. He timed her pulse against his pocket-watch. While it was somewhat quicker than normal, this could be attributed to the incredible energy the girl was expending. She writhed against the sheets and pressed up and away from the bed as if it burned her. Despite her condition, Johann could not help noticing she was beautiful. When she arched again, he noticed something else.

"She is with child?" It wasn't a question, but Johann was only cursorily acquainted with Dr. Schumann and wanted to be as delicate as possible.

The Dr. nodded impatiently. "I am not an imbecile, Bessler," the man snapped. "I have examined her, and I can find nothing wrong. If I were not at my wits end, I would not have sent for you. I understand that, though you lack proper university training in medicine, you have brought about some miraculous cures. It is a chance I take, you see."

Bessler nodded. He watched the girl and tugged idly at the tip of his beard. Something bothered him, but he couldn't place it. He had seen a person in this state before, or a state very similar, but something blocked it from his thoughts. He glanced up at the three women, arranged in a semi-circle on the far side of the bed. There was a tall woman who resembled the girl on the bed very strongly, and another who might have been her twin.

Schumann caught Johann's glance and said, "My wife, Helena, and her sister, Anna. The other woman is... She is not important. My daughter is important, can you help?"

Johann wasn't listening. He had caught the gaze of the third woman. She was stooped, older than the sisters, and her eyes glinted like dark jewels. She glared at him, and Johann felt the pressure of some emotion – hatred, he thought - rolling off the woman in waves. She didn't speak, but she kept one arm bent at an odd angle behind her back, hiding something from the others in the room.

Johann began to pace. He could not think with that woman staring at him, and he was embarrassed that she should have such an effect. What was he missing? What had he forgotten? Several times Schumann looked ready to speak, but bit it back. The man's daughter was sick, possibly dying – even his professional pride was not worth that. As Johann turned yet again to pace beside the bed, he happened to glance down. At the edge of the wooden frame, protruding from beneath the linens, he saw a greenish crust of bread.

He almost leaned to pick it up. He squatted part way down, placed his hand on the surface of the bed as if that had been his intention all along, and surreptitiously kicked the crust out of sight. Then he turned to Schumann and said.

"I can help her. I will need full cooperation, and if you grant me that, I believe I can have results within a few hours, but we must act quickly if she is not to lose the child."

"What do you need?" Schumann asked quickly. "Anything at all. I have medicine, equipment – it is at your disposal."

"I need nothing that I did not bring with me but a pan of cool water, a towel, and to be left alone with her."

Schumann frowned, but Johann met his gaze. He knew he must keep his eyes averted from that old woman's at all cost, or it would be lost. If she suspected what he knew, she would poison his words, or set the mother and aunt against him.

"Why in God's name must you be alone with her?" Schumann demanded. "I'm a doctor, man, I can help."

"Not with this," Johann insisted. "The procedure is a very delicate one, and I will be happy to share it with you when your daughter is healed, but there is no time remaining for discussion."

As if to emphasize this, the girl began to shake uncontrollably. The frame of the bed rattled, and she bit savagely into the leather restraining her teeth. She spun her gaze to her father, to her mother and the old woman, to Bessler, nothing but animal rage showed in her expression.

"Christian," Helena Schumann cried. "I can't leave her now. Not like this! This man…"

Dr. Schumann stepped around the bed and took his wife by the arm, not roughly, but firmly. "Come along, Helena," he said, keeping his tone even and controlled. "If this man can save our daughter's life, I say we must leave him to it. I have done what I can, and I have failed. I know you want to be with her, but if you would like to be with her for years rather than moments, then perhaps it is time we listened to someone else."

He turned back to Johann. "You have one hour, and I will return for an explanation."

Bessler nodded. "You alone, then, Dr. Schumann, and you will not be disappointed. May I get the water?"

Schumann nodded and stood stolid and unwavering as the three women hesitantly preceded him from the room. The old woman was last to leave, and she turned in the doorway. Johann finally met her glare. He leaned down then, pulled free the chunk of moldy bread crust from the linens, and held it up where she could see.

The woman started back into the room, and Johann stood fast. She hissed with rage, and only the intervention of the girl's aunt, who gripped the older woman by the upper arm and dragged her toward the door, prevented a confrontation. Johann's heart slammed in his chest and he looked at his hand. He'd gripped the bit of bread so tightly that it crumbled between his fingers.

Moving quickly, he carried what remained of it to the nightstand. He put it aside and opened his bag, which sat beside him on an old, ornate chair. He drew out his mortar and pestle and a small vial. He also extracted an old, worn journal, which he thumbed through quickly.

He found what he sought, grunted his satisfaction, and dropped the bread into the tiny bowl. He added a small amount of alcohol and began to grind the bread steadily, working it into a fine paste. Johann worked quickly. He wanted to be certain of what he said before Dr. Schumann returned. If that woman, or either of the other two, returned with Schumann, he knew he'd have to keep them away from the girl at all costs.

He glanced at her and found it very difficult to draw his gaze back to the work at hand. She heaved on the bed and pressed up into sweat-soaked sheets that were snarled about her like great linen snakes. The leather bit cruelly into her wrists and her ankles, and her belly was so full with the child that it rolled ponderously from side to side as she fought with flagging strength against the constraints.

He wished that he could release her, but that would come later. She was a danger to herself now, and even more of a danger to her unborn child. There was a tap at the door, and a woman he'd not seen before, a servant, slipped timidly into the room. The girl had a fresh towel in her hand, and a large basin of fresh water.

"Bring it here," Johann called to her sharply, "quickly."

The girl hurried past him and placed the bowl on the nightstand, then turned to gaze at her young mistress in the bed for a long moment before slipping back out the door in silence. Johann had been afraid she'd been sent by the old woman, and had been prepared to restrain her if she attempted to slip anything to the girl on the bed, but nothing suspicious took place, and he set aside his instruments.

Johann dipped the towel into the fresh water and began to very carefully bathe the girl's face. He cleared away the sweat and drew the stray locks of matted hair from her eyes. She fought him at first, eyes wide. She ground her teeth into the leather strap, and he spoke to her softly, not really paying attention to what he said, just running the words together in a steady drone of sound. Her struggles weakened slowly, and after about half an hour, her eyes closed, and her breathing eased. Johann continued to bathe her face and her neck, working the cool water in under the leather bonds at wrist and ankle when she ceased her frantic gyrations.

When Schumann entered he found that his daughter was breathing raggedly, but resting. He stepped past Johann to the bed, reached out and brushed his fingers over the girl's cheek, then looked up. His expression was a mix of incredulity, and gratitude. "What did you do?" he asked at last. "What did I miss? God. My own daughter and I could do nothing."

"You did everything you might be expected to do," Johann assured him, "and probably more. Your daughter is not suffering from a disease."

Schumann's gaze grew troubled. "What do you mean?" he asked. "What you saw when you arrived here, Herr Bessler, was not a 'well' girl."

"No," Johann agreed, "but neither was it the suffering of a sick girl. She has been poisoned."

"What?" Schumann stepped back from the bed, his eyes flaring with sudden anger. "She has been here, in my own house, all this time. She has been in the care of her mother since this began."

Johann turned to the nightstand and grabbed the pestle. He held it out to Schumann, who took it, glancing down at it in irritated fascination. "What is it?" the doctor asked.

"It is what remains of a piece of bread crust I found beneath the bed," Johann replied. "It is moldy, and I believe that you will find, if you examine that specimen, that it is infected with the Ergot fungus."

Dr. Schumann stared at the paste in consternation. "What in the world does a piece of moldy bread have to do with my daughter," he asked at last. "She has been fed this mold," Johann replied promptly, "over a period of time. It causes convulsions, delusion – it is used in some religious ceremonies. It has also been found to be the cause behind certain instances of demonic possession."

"How do you know that?" The tone of Schumann's voice had dropped very low, as if he suddenly feared to be overheard. "In all my years at university, I have heard nothing like it."

"My own studies," Johann replied, "come from the roads and the mountains. I have seen this personally, and a priest, who had discovered a plot to have a local woman put to death, shared the secret with me."

"It is that woman," Schumann whispered, "the one you saw with my wife and her sister. The sister has brought her into my home, and I feared it might come to trouble, though I suspected nothing like this."

"Where is the father?" Johann asked, gazing back at the young woman.

"My Barbara is unwed," the doctor replied, his features setting themselves in grim lines. "There was a young man... but that is of no consequence. We must do what we can."

Johann nodded. The girl moaned again, but not in the wild, uncontrolled fashion in which she'd cried out at Johann's arrival. The two men stepped closer to the bed.

"She is in labor," Johann said, brushing the damp strands of hair from the girl's eyes. "It is a bad time. There has been too much strain already, and she is tired."

Schumann moved up beside him and stared down at his daughter. His expression was unreadable, and Johann wondered which woman he was really thinking of as he stared at his youngest daughter. The girl? Her mother? The aunt, who he obviously did not care for, and who had brought the old witch into their home and their lives, or perhaps the old woman? There had to be some resolution; that was certain.

"She may do this again," Johann said softly. "Whatever the old woman's motive, her goal has not been reached. Your daughter is not safe with her – possibly not with her mother."

Schumann turned on him then, eyes blazing, but the fire died before the words could reach the man's lips.

"I know," he whispered at last. "I know. If one of them knows what has happened here, then all of them do. They smile sweetly when I am in the room, but I've come upon them many times, whispering where they think none will hear and muttering about secrets and hunting for hidden treasures, falling silent the moment they know I'm in the room. I did not think they would go this far."

"They may mean to sacrifice the child," Johann said. He tried to keep the emotion from his voice, and the concern that he was overstepping some unknown boundary. "They may mean to sacrifice them both."

Schumann's hands rested on the edge of the bed, very still. He stiffened, but his face did not flush with anger. It paled, and his mouth set, if possible, into even grimmer lines. He turned to Johann then.

"You must help me," he said quickly. "There will be very little time. We must do what we can for the child, but as soon as my Barbara is able to travel, take her. Take her far from here. Take her where she will be safe.'

Johann's eyes widened in shock.

"But I..."

"I know of you, Herr Bessler," Dr. Schumann said, resuming his attentions to his daughter's comfort. The man had calmed visibly and was breathing more steadily. His expression had melted to a mask of resolve. "I know of your life, your travels and your experiments. A Perpetuum Mobile, isn't it?"

Not knowing how else to respond, Johann moved to the far side of the girl's bed and helped the doctor to position the girl, whose breathing grew heavier and rougher with each passing moment. At last, he nodded. "I am very close," he added, as though in defense.

"It is impossible," Schumann proclaimed, dismissing the subject. "I believe your experiments will go nowhere; they are an empty pursuit." He raised his gaze to meet Johann's. "I will give you money to pursue it, however, because I believe that you yourself will come to something. Marry her, Bessler. Take my daughter to wife, without a word to any other soul, and take her from this place. Love her and care for her as I no longer can without the weight of scandal dropping onto all our shoulders."

Johann stepped back from the bed. His mouth dropped open. On his lips, defenses of his work lay stillborn and fell away. In the back of his mind, the knowledge that had come to him in the dream burned as brightly as ever. He turned to the bed and watched the girl's tortured face. Her moment of birth was very near, and Johann's heart went out to her. Even in that moment, she was beautiful. He thought of the old woman, her glare, and the depth of hatred he'd sensed there, the evil glee with which she had watched the girl's suffering. He remembered her eyes as he'd held out the moldy bread to her, showing her what he knew.

Johann stepped closer to the bed again, placed a hand gently on the girl's arm where it was still strapped to the bed, and he nodded. "If she will have me, I will do it." He said. "I will not take her away against her will, but I believe that once she has heard what has happened here…"

The girl screamed. It wasn't a wild, crazy scream, as she'd unleashed before. This scream was pain, and her body shuddered with the labor. Both men cried out and set to work. The girl who'd brought the pan of fresh water appeared in the doorway, startled, and Schumann called to her to bring hot water and more towels.

She hesitated in the doorway. "Mrs. Schumann…" the girl began. The Dr. cut her off.

"No! Don't allow anyone else into this room. No one. Now send for the things I've told you to and be quick. My daughter is giving birth."

The girl darted into the hall, and the sound of pounding footsteps followed. Then, moments later, voices rose. Johann spun to the door, and he saw the helpless serving girl being brushed aside as Helena Schumann and her sister burst through the door. Behind them, bobbing and weaving on her short, stumpy legs, the old woman tried to peer over or around them. Johann caught only a brief glimpse of the rage in her eyes, but it was enough.

"No!" he cried.

Schumann spun. His hands dripped blood, and his eyes blazed. In that moment, Johann thought the man had taken on the aspect of an angel, or a saint. He took a step toward the doorway, lowered an arm to point, not at his wife, but through her, pinioning the old hag with his gaze and his fury.

"Get out," he said. His voice was not loud, but it carried. The force behind the words was irrefutable. Helena Schumann stopped in the doorway, her hand coming to her throat. Her sister fell back a step. The old woman tried to squirm around her then and find a way into the room and to the girl.

"Get out," Schumann repeated. "When I am done here, if that woman is in my house, I will have her taken into custody and burned."

"Christian," his wife pleaded, risking half a step into the room. "She's my daughter."

"Not any longer," the Dr. spat at her. "Not after this. Go. I will come to you when it is finished."

Johann felt the girl's body convulse beneath his touch once again, and turned away from the macabre scene at the door. Barbara's labor pains were very close together now, and she was far too pale. Her breath was uneven and ragged. She clenched her eyes together so tightly her skin stretched taut over the bone of her skull, and for the first time since he'd entered the room, Johann was glad for the leather strap between her teeth.

What followed was a surreal blur. The servant girl ushered a young man in who carried a basin of steaming water. The girl held armloads of clean towels. Dr. Schumann spun and grabbed two of these, dipping them into the water and turning to his daughter in concentration.

"The child has not dropped properly," he said, his voice savage with grief and anger. "I must straighten her."

Johann nodded. He had delivered babies before, but nothing had prepared him for this. He was suddenly very glad for the older man's training, and for his skill. In only a few short moments he had fallen from expert to apprentice, and in those same moments had gone from a concerned physician to a worried lover. Barbara's features imprinted themselves on his mind and heart with each spasm of pain and emotion. He held her, eased her in any way he could, assisted the doctor in positioning her and all the while there was blood. Far too much blood, blood such as he'd never seen.

The women did not remove themselves from the doorway. They stood and stared, two in awe and fear, one in dark fascination, but they did not leave, and there was no time for Dr. Schumann to insist on it. The man's forehead glistened with sweat, and his hands and arms, as well as the towels he kept dipping into the hot, red-stained water, dripped with blood. Johann held the girl as still as possible and whispered to her to help them – to push the child free. He glared at the women in the door, ready to step between them and the bed if they were bold enough to enter.

They did not. The child slipped free with a soft, wet sound that drove into Johann like a sharp blade. He turned from the doorway in time to see the doctor clip the cord. Johann reached for a clean towel without thought. He stepped closer and the doctor placed the small bundle in his arms. Johann stepped away and began to clean the child, brushing the gore and its own filth away. It was a girl, and she had a dark thatch of hair in the center of her head.

Johann worked quickly and efficiently, but his heart had chilled the moment he caught site of the child's pallor, and his trepidation grew with each stroke of the towel. The infant's skin had a bluish tinge, and the tiny body shivered, each breath so tortured he could feel it rattling through him to his own lungs. Then she was still.

Johann did what he could. He tried to revive the child, but it was no good. He cleaned her, and laid her, at last, in a small bundle of towels. Dr. Schumann was just turning from his daughter. He was a ghastly sight. His hair stuck out at odd angles, and was crusted with blood from where he'd reached up to brush it from his eyes. Sweat had half blinded the man, and as he staggered from the bed, Johann nearly took a step back. He managed, with great effort, to hold his ground.

The Doctor stared at him, but Johann could only shake his head. "She never had a chance – the child," he said.

Dr. Schumann stared at Johann for a long time. He stood, dripping blood and sweating, half-crazed with the frenzied effort. Then he nodded, and he beckoned Johann to step closer. Johann did so, with a final glance at the tiny, still form in the towels. He stood beside the bed as Dr. Schumann began, methodically, to clean away the linens.

"Help me lift her," he said. We need to get these sheets off of here, get new ones.

Johann nodded. He breathed a sigh of relief and a short prayer of thanks when he saw that the girl still breathed. The motion of her breast was shallow, and weak, but steady. She had lost a lot of blood, more blood than Johann had ever seen in his life. The heavier loss would be the child, but there was time for dealing with such things later – when she'd had food and gained strength. When he'd gotten her out of there.

Everything shifted for Johann in that moment. His world expanded to encompass things beyond that room, and that poor, tortured face on the pillow became more than Dr. Christian Schumann's daughter. She became part of the vision, against a backdrop of a huge, spinning wheel. He heard Dr. Schumann speaking, but he couldn't make out the words at first. Then the Dr. clasped his shoulders and shook him roughly, and Johann's mind cleared.

"Where is she, Bessler? The child, where is the body of the child?"

Johann spun, confused. The bundle of towels lay where he'd left it. Tiny spots of blood and fluid still dotted it, soaked into the clean white material, but the child was gone. He turned to the door, nearly toppling onto the bed in his haste, but there was no one in sight. Mrs. Schumann and the old hag were gone. The aunt stood in the doorway, regarding the scene with haughty contempt. She said nothing.

"There," Johann managed to say. "I left the body there, wrapped in those towels. She died in my arms, I..."

The growl that erupted from Schumann's throat was beyond rage. He launched himself through the doorway, knocking servants from his path and careening into the aunt as he left the room. Everything he touched was smeared with blood, and the aunt screamed in horror and terror as she bounced off the far wall, barely avoiding an oil lamp.

Johann ignored them. He turned to the bed, and, with calm, sure hands, he unfastened the leather from the girl's mouth. Next he loosened her arms, and her legs. She was groggy, barely aware that someone was near. Johann turned and, seeing the girl Schumann had brushed aside moments before, he called out to her.

"You must help. I will lift her. Put fresh sheets on the bed, and then bring red wine, clean cloths, and more water. Have this cleared away, and quickly."

The girl nodded, and as Johann slid his arms under Barbara's thighs and shoulders and lifted her from the bed, the girl quickly slid the clean sheets she'd already brought into the room onto the mattress. She worked quickly, and when one side had been made properly, Johann laid the girl on top and let the maid complete her work on the near side of the bed. Meanwhile, he packed his own things and found a blanket in the drawers of one a nearby cabinet. He wrapped it carefully about the girl's shoulders and tucked her in.

When another servant arrived moments later with two glasses and a bottle of rich burgundy, Johann took one glass and filled it half way.

"You must drink this," he told the girl, who watched him through hooded eyes, barely aware of her surroundings. "You have lost blood, and strength. Drink this, and then sleep."

She was too weak to sit up on her own, so Johann slipped his arm behind her shoulders once more, propped her up, and held the glass for her as she sipped. At first she didn't want it, and tried to turn her head away, but he insisted gently, and she drank. He made her finish the half glass, and told her he'd wake her in an hour for a second.

Then, like a guard at the gate of some ancient castle, he placed himself at the end of her bed with the second wine glass full in his shaking hand, waiting for Dr. Schumann to return, and watched for the hag.

EIGHT

When Dr. Schumann returned he looked haggard and worn. Blood had caked on his clothing and stained his hands, face and hair. His eyes were open wider than was normal, but his jaw was set, and he moved with purpose.

"I have lost them," he said simply.

Johann could only stare. "The baby?"

Schumann shook his head and frowned.

"I do not know. The baby is gone. They are gone. We must be quick. One of the maids has gone missing, as well, and I fear she has headed into town. I don't know how long we have before they send sheriffs."

Johann held his hands out to his sides. "But, what can we..."

"Hurry, man," Schumann said gruffly. "We must get you on your way. You will take her with you." His voice broke, and he stopped, putting out a hand to steady himself against the bed, "my daughter will need someone to help care for her."

"She should not be moved!" Johann protested. "Surely you know that..."

Dr. Schumann spun. His eyes flashed with crazed light, and this, combined with the stiff, bloodstained hair and the gore smeared over his arms, and his clothing, set Johann back a step.

"Don't you understand, Bessler?" Dr. Schumann said, fighting to keep from screaming the words, "My granddaughter is dead. My daughter is dying. My wife and her crazy sister have stolen the body and taken it off, God only knows where, with that old witch. When word reaches the village, they will come. There will be cries of murder, witchcraft...you have to go."

Bessler's mind spun. It was crazy, but as Schumann's words sank in, their truth became evident. There were many explanations for what had just taken place, but all of them involved murder. Either the wife or sister would be found guilty, the daughter herself, or even Schumann. The Dr. was mayor of the town, as well as physician. His enemies would be swift to pounce on a thing like this, and would worry it until he was locked away, or disgraced.

"If you go quickly," Schumann urged, "they may miss you on the road. If my daughter is not here, they cannot say she has given birth. They know only that she was ill. If the baby is missing, who will know the truth? There will be rumors. There will be accusations; but, without proof?"

Bessler nodded. With the decision made, he was galvanized into action. He hurried to the girl's bed and shook her gently.

"I will have a carriage made ready," Schumann said, turning away. "I must clean myself. I will send Frederic around to help, and to drive you safely away. There is a servant's entrance in back."

Johann nodded, barely aware that Schumann was speaking to him. He was focused on the girl. She must be carried, that was certain. She had lost too much blood, and expended far too much energy in fighting the leather bonds. If she tried to stand, she would fall. If she managed to walk the exertion would do her in.

Johann packed his instruments quickly. The girl, still woozy and barely coherent, followed him with her eyes.

"We must hurry," he told her softly. "We must go away."

"But..." her voice was soft, like the whisper of wind through dried leaves, as though her lungs had no pressure with which to expel sufficient air. "Where is my father? I..."

"Shush," Johann admonished her. "I will answer any question you like as soon as we have gone. When Frederic returns, we will carry you to the carriage."

She looked alarmed, and he placed his hand gently on her arm.

"I know that this must be frightening," he glanced nervously over his shoulder at the doorway. It was empty. "It is very dangerous for you here. A great deal has happened, and you were...away."

She blinked. Her thoughts were still jumbled, but she was struggling to piece his words and her own memories together into something that made sense.

"Who are you?" she asked. Her voice was very small and childlike.

"My name is Johann," Bessler answered.

Frederic burst into the room, took in the scene at the bedside, slowed his pace and nearly tumbled to the floor in his excitement.

"My Lord has sent me," he said, breathless.

Johann nodded. "I know. Quickly, we will have to carry her, and there is very little time."

Frederic stopped and stared for a moment. It was obvious that the notion of such familiarity with the daughter of his employer was a difficult thing for him to grasp.

"Hurry man," Johann barked, frowning. "If they send sheriffs before we get out of sight, all might be lost. If you want to be of service to your mistress, you must help me now."

Frederic nodded resolutely and stepped up beside Johann, who wrapped the sheet carefully around Barbara's too-thin form. The two of them slid their arms beneath her, wrapping her in the covering carefully, and lifted.

"You'll have to show me the way," Johann said quickly. "Dr. Schumann said that there was a servant's entrance."

Frederic nodded. "To the left," he said.

The two slipped into the hall. Barbara would have been only a small burden to either of them – between them she was light as a feather. They handled her very gently, but Johann saw that she was frightened and on the edge of hysteria.

"It will be alright, Princess," he whispered to her. "Everything is going to be fine. You must trust me."

She didn't speak, but wordlessly circled his neck with her arms and clung to him. Johann's eyes fogged with sudden emotion and he had to fight to maintain his balance. Frederic pretended not to notice.

The hallway was empty. They made it to the servant's

entrance without incident and carefully lifted Barbara down the stone steps. The same carriage that had come for Bessler at the mine waited outside, and in moments they had settled the girl on one of the seats.

Johann climbed in beside her and knelt on the floor. He used his body to prevent her from being jostled. Frederic stared in at them for just a moment, shook his head, and turned away. Moments later Johann heard the driver call out the horses, and the carriage took off, moving swiftly away from the rear of Dr. Schumann's home.

There was a cry from the house, and after a moment the carriage shuddered to a stop. Johann, fearing that they'd been spotted, stuck his head out the door of the carriage, staring about wildly.

"What is it?" he cried. "Why have we stopped?"

A quick glance back at the large home answered his question. Dr. Christian Schumann, his hair flying wildly about his face, ran after the carriage. He staggered once and almost fell, and in his left hand he carried a heavy pouch.

It took a few moments for Schumann to reach the carriage. Bessler turned back to Barbara, who stared at him in fright, and patted her arm.

"I will be back in just a moment," he said. "I must speak with your father."

Then, before she could reply, he rose and stepped down from the carriage. Schumann had crossed the final stretch and stood, sweating, panting, and frantic just outside.

"Thank you, Bessler," he panted. "I will always be in your debt. Is she?"

"She's awake," Johann said softly. "She's resting, frightened, and probably half-believes she is delusional and still dreaming."

"You will care for her?" Schumann asked. The older man scanned Johann's face. "She is the best of me, you know."

Johann reached out, clasped Schumann's hand, and met the man's gaze. "I will care for her, and, if she comes to love me, I will make her a good husband. In any case, I will get her safely away from here."

Schumann nodded absently. He took half a step toward

the carriage, as if he intended to climb up and speak with his daughter, then shook his head and turned back.

"There is no time," he said. "Tell her that I love her, Bessler. Tell her what has happened here, that she must stay away from her mother, and her aunt, at all costs."

Johann nodded again. Dr. Schumann held out the pouch he'd carried from the house, and Johann took it, glancing at it curiously.

"This should be enough to get the two of you on the road soon, and to get you started on your work."

"I thought you didn't believe in my work," Bessler smiled.

Schumann almost laughed, but couldn't quite bring it off. "I do not believe in your work. I believe that the sooner you set off down a road, the right road, or the wrong, the sooner you reach the end and know where you will go next."

"Because a thing has never been done," Johann said, "does not mean that it never will be."

Schumann would have said more, but at that moment a wild shrieking rose from the house at his back. His wife and her sister stood at the top step of the servant's entrance, staring down the road at them.

"Go," Schumann said, turning without another word. He started resolutely back up the trail, and Johann leaped back into the carriage, tossing the pouch onto the seat opposite where Barbara lay, wide eyed and staring.

"Drive," Johann cried out to Frederic. "As if the devil were on your trail, drive!"

The carriage leaped ahead, and Johann leaned close, shielding Barbara's body from as much of the rough, bouncing ride as possible. The cries from the house faded, and then disappeared, and the only sound that remained was the steady clop of the horses' hooves on the packed dirt road, and the occasional creak of wooden wheels.

Johann had only two rooms. He lived simply, and all he required was space for his equipment, and to sleep. His food and other needs were looked after by the old woman he rented from. Bringing Barbara into the sparse chambers and laying her gently across his bed, he curses his own frugality.

The girl allowed herself to be carried and situated on the bed without protest. Her eyes never left Johann as he hurried Frederic on his way and then bustled about the room, moving things here and there absently as if their order might enlarge the space and make it more appealing to her.

There had been little conversation between the two of them, and now that they were alone, Johann was at a loss as to where he might start. Finally, squaring his shoulders, he drew a straight backed chair from the corner, after divesting it of piles of notes and books.

"Would you like tea?" he asked.

Barbara nodded. Then she added, "if you'll have some with me, and tell me why I'm here, and who you are. I know your name – you are Johann Bessler. I know my father sent me away, but the last thing I remember is feeling sick. My mother brought an old woman, but…"

"I will tell you what I can," he replied, rising. "First I will brew the tea."

He moved to the fireplace, tossed a log onto the coals and poked at them with a metal rod until they sparked back to life. The making of tea was a ritual he'd picked up on the road. He carried several varieties and mixes with him in a leather pouch. Some were intended to cause relaxation, or to stimulate the mind; others merely fascinated him by their taste. For this occasion, he chose a mild blend of dark leaves sprinkled with a hint of mint.

As he worked, pouring water from a stone jar in the corner and situating the pot on a hook over the now mellow flame in the fireplace, he felt the weight of her attention. She studied him, and this knowledge made him nervous. He nearly spilled the water over the sides of the teapot, and only a miracle kept his trembling hand from missing the hook and sending the entire mess into the center of the fire.

Johann had little experience with women. He'd cured a great number in his travels. He'd spoken with them, learned from them, laughed with them, but always in the course of everyday affairs.

When the water began to boil he sprinkled in the tea leaves and turned back to the bed. The scent of black tea and spearmint filled the small room slowly, and for the first time since he and Frederic had carried her from her sickbed, Barbara Schumann smiled at him.

Johann returned the smile. He lifted her gently and fluffed the pillow beneath her shoulders, helping her into a sitting position on the bed. Her hair, he noticed, was a very pleasant honey-gold, and now that the glaze of the poison was slipping from her eyes, they flashed brilliant blue.

"Tell me," she said softly.

And he did. Johann found that, in the weaving of the story, filling in what details he knew and accepting others that she was able to provide, kept him from staring at her and removed a bit of his awkwardness. By the time the tea had been strained and poured, and they were on their second cup each, he felt almost comfortable in her presence.

"Where will we go?" she asked at last.

The question struck Johann squarely. He had realized they would have to be on the road, and soon, but he'd given little thought to which road, or where he wanted it to lead. He hadn't yet told her of his great work, or of the vision he'd experienced. He would have to do so, because that vision and all it implied would weigh heavily in his decision of where he traveled next.

"We will travel to the town of Gesa," he said at last. "I have family there, a cousin, and we can stay with them. I have work to do and it will be good to be back in a place where I am known."

"But..." Barbara pursed her lips, and then continued, "What is this work? What is it that you do? Are you not a doctor?"

"I am," he asserted. "That and many other things. I might astound you, I think, if I attempted to tell you the extent of the skills I have picked up in my travels. I can build an organ that plays the most wondrous music, or a pocket watch that will keep perfect time. I can build a home, or design a cathedral, but there is one task that I have been born to, and that is what I must pursue with all the knowledge and skill I possess."

Barbara remained silent, but expectant. Johann could see

that she grew weary, and he smiled at her. "It will take me a long time to explain it thoroughly," he said. "I am going to create the world's first Perpetuum Mobile – a wheel that will spin, once set into motion, until its parts wear out, or it is stopped."

"But..." she said at last, "that is impossible."

"So I have been told," Johann laughed softly. "So others believe. We shall see. For now, you must rest. Tomorrow I will begin plans for our journey to Gesa. Your father has given me to care for you, and it won't due for me to tire you instead."

"I heard more than you think," she said softly. "I heard what my father said to you while I lay sick in bed, and I heard what he said outside the carriage."

Johann stiffened, rushing back through his memories wildly and trying to put them in exact order. What had she heard? What would she think?

"I don't know about this machine you intend to build," she said. "I do know that you have saved my life. I know that my father trusts you and respects you. I know that he offered me to you as your wife; and I heard your response."

Johann's already crashing heartbeat thundered. A rushing sound in his ears very suddenly cut off her voice and he shook his head slightly, alarmed, afraid she would speak and he wouldn't hear.

"I would be honored to have you as husband," she said.

Barbara lowered her eyes then, and blushed. Her hands were in her lap.

"I am not pure."

Johann was at her side in seconds, his arm around her back, drawing her head gently to his shoulder.

"I do not care what has happened in your past," he said softly. "I do not care, for that matter, what has happened in my own. My mind is filled with the future, which will now belong to the two of us. I will begin plans for the trip to Gesa tomorrow. You should be strong enough to travel by week's end."

Barbara nodded, the gesture brushing her chin over his shoulder and coating his skin in goose bumps. The scent of her hair dizzied him, and in a moment he slid her back onto the pillows and pulled his blanket up to her chin.

"Where will you sleep?" she asked him, as if just noticing that there was only the one, small cot.

Johann smiled at her.

"I will stay up, for now, and gaze at the stars. If I should tire, I will be as comfortable on the floor as I would in the cot. I have spent long years on the road; another night of roughing it will cause me little discomfort. Tomorrow we will move to the Inn, and soon after that we will make a home of our own."

Barbara nodded, but the gesture sapped the last of her strength, and her chin dropped to her chest. Johann reached down and straightened the blanket again. Then, very softly, he brushed his fingers through her hair.

"Very soon," he whispered.

NINE

It was a quick matter to pack his belongings for the journey. Johann kept very little beyond his notes, his tools and equipment, and his books. There was almost nothing else in his possession he could not replace, and much of what he had was left behind in his hurry to get on the road and away from the area of the Schumann home.

Barbara had even less trouble packing. Before Johann could go out to arrange a carriage to take them to the Inn he'd chosen, which lay just beyond the limits of the city, he heard the clop of horse's hooves in the street outside. He was prepared for the worst. It was possible the Sheriffs had seen him after all. They might want to question him, or Barbara. If they'd questioned the mother, the aunt, or the old witch there was no telling what lies might have been told.

Johann glanced out through his window. It was Schumann's carriage, and Frederic hopped down from the driver's seat to hold open the door. Johann stepped outside.

The young maid who'd brought him the water and fresh sheets climbed carefully down from the carriage. She spotted Johann, and dropped her eyes quickly.

"Good morning, My Lord," she said with a short curtsey.

Johann gaped, at a loss for words, and Frederic stepped in to fill the void of silence.

"My Lord, I have been directed to bring this girl, Rosina, to care for Miss Barbara. My master is afraid she will be questioned by the sheriffs, or that some mischief will come to her at the hands of the other women."

Johann noticed that, again, Frederic blushed when he

referred to the ladies of his household. He was uncomfortable saying anything remotely negative about those he served.

"Dr. Schumann told he would send the girl," Johann replied, nodding to her and smiling. "I didn't know when to expect her, or if the Dr. had changed his mind."

He turned to the maid. "It's good that you have come. I was about to seek a carriage to take us to the Inn. We will be departing by week's end, but for now I want to be free of this place and it's...complications."

Frederic nodded. "I would be honored to carry you and the young lady to the Inn, My Lord. I can't say I'm in a hurry to get back."

Johann caught a slight quaver in the young man's voice. "What has happened?" he asked. Has any harm come to the Dr. Schumann, or his wife? Have they found..."

"They have found nothing," the girl, Rosina, said. She stepped forward and held Johann's gaze a little longer than he would have expected. She studied him, found what she was looking for, and at last looked away.

"They have questioned the girl's mother. Herr Schumann, as mayor, is of course a member of the court. He is directing the investigation."

Johann stared, incredulous.

"But..."

"He had me arrested," the girl said.

Johann fell silent. He knew that he should have expected this, but it still seemed surreal. How could Schumann lead the very investigation he'd told Johann to flee?

"He would have left me in prison, I believe," Rosina said, "had I not begged to be allowed to serve the young lady. He is afraid I'll tell them about what happened – that they could find a way to make me. I wouldn't."

Her voice grew fierce, and Johann stepped forward, laying his hand gently on her shoulder.

"I know you wouldn't" he said. "You helped me when I most needed help, and if you had wanted to cause trouble, you had ample chance while we were all in that room. It is good that you have come."

Johann turned to Frederic.

"If you'll help me to load our luggage, we can get on the road. I have no wish to see this girl, or any of the rest of us, arrested or detained. It's better if we put miles between ourselves and all that has happened."

Frederic nodded. The two men hauled out Johann's equipment, strapped the various crates and boxes to the top and rear of the carriage, followed by the few suitcases and belongings that held the remainder of Johann's possessions. As they worked, Johann thought furiously, and as the last of their belongings were strapped onto the carriage, he made his decision.

"We will not stop at the Inn," he said with finality. "If they are carrying on the investigation, then it can't be long before they are directed this way. We will press on to my cousin's home in Gesa. Can you take us that far, Frederic?"

"I was directed to bring Rosina to you," the driver said doubtfully. "Gesa is a long drive."

"We will send word to Herr Schumann," Johann said. "I'm certain that he would agree this is necessary. The question is simply, who can we trust with the message? If it is received by anyone else at the house, or intercepted by the Sheriffs, we may still be detained before we are safe."

Frederic hesitated for only a moment, and then nodded.

"Leave it to me. I know who to send, and I believe you are right. I would never go against the orders of Herr Schumann, but in this case there is no time to consult him. I know that he wants you safely away, and I will take you. I can deal with the consequences on my return."

Johann nodded. He stepped into the cottage and explained his decision to Barbara and Rosina.

"You are right, we must get away," Barbara said. She was still weak, but her tone was resolute. "My father will not allow this to affect the town; if he finds us he will be forced to act. He will delay in any way that he can without drawing attention to himself, but we must be gone when he arrives."

"You are strong enough for the journey?" Rosina asked, laying her hands on her mistress' shoulders.

"I'll be fine," Barbara said.

They made a last circuit of the small home, gathered the few belongings that had nearly gone forgotten, and then they climbed into the carriage. Frederic held the door for them, securing it when his three passengers were seated as comfortably as possible.

Barbara sat beside Johann. She leaned her head on his shoulder and took his hand. At first he sat very rigid, his face flushed and uncertain what to do with his hands.

As the carriage clattered off down the road and his old life fell away behind him, as it had done so many times in the past, he began to relax. He gripped Barbara's fingers gently and laid his head atop her soft curls. Rosina, seated across from them, glanced away and out the window, but not before the corners of her mouth curled up into a knowing smile.

As the afternoon sun set beyond the horizon, Frederic directed the horses past the inn and onto the open road, keeping close to the center and making as good a time as possible. There were no clouds, and after a short period of twilight the moon ascended, lighting the way with her silver luminescence.

Frederic drove on through the night. They paused at another Inn early the next morning for tea, and to freshen up. While Johann and the two ladies ate a small breakfast, Frederic directed the stable hands to care for the horses, and then curled into his seat to sleep.

As they rested, dark clouds rolled in. Lightning flickered in the distance. There was no rain, at first, but the sky darkened, and the wind picked up. When Johann woke Frederic with a gentle shake, it was as dark as night, though it was still afternoon. The two watched the weather with concern.

"What do you think?" Johann asked, scowling at the clouds. "We could put up in the inn, if they have rooms, and make a run for it in the morning."

Frederic glanced at the stormy sky, and then shook his head.

"If they come after us, they will reach this place before morning. I don't believe that they will – Herr Schumann will delay them as long as he can, and the weather is as good an excuse as any, but there is no sense in chancing it. There is no rain, and if it comes later, we will pull into shelter. The carriage is dry, and we have blankets."

Johann nodded agreement. He hurried back into the inn, and moments later he returned, leading Barbara carefully by one arm. Rosina walked on the far side of her mistress and lent her support as well. They climbed up into the carriage, and once Johann and Frederic had unpacked a few of the blankets and they were all packed in as well as possible, they set off once again.

They proceeded carefully, remaining in the center of the road and not pushing the horses. It was going to be a long night's drive, and there was a river ahead. They would have to ford that river to reach Gesa, and the animals would need all their strength for that crossing.

They drove through the night, and though thunder rumbled and lightning lit the skyline in jagged streaks, the rain slipped past and they made good time. Just before morning Frederic pulled the carriage to one side of the road and came around to the door to speak with Johann.

"I'm going to get some rest," the young man said softly, not wanting to disturb the ladies. "I'll tend to the horses, tie them off and give them food, and then take one of the blankets back to the driver's seat. There's a small bed behind it. The sun will be up in a couple of hours, and we'll need the light to cross the river."

Bessler nodded. He climbed carefully out of the carriage, stretched his legs, and then helped Frederic with the animals, brushing them down and hanging bags of feed about their necks. It was fortunate that Frederic was a good driver, prepared for such a circumstance. They'd lain in a bit of extra supplies at the inn, as well, so there was no lack. The animals seemed content to munch quietly at the grain, tucked in out of the weather beneath the soaring branches of a huge oak tree.

Johann studied the sky for signs that the storm might yet come their way. He didn't want to tie the horses beneath a tree if there was lightning. He saw nothing but mist, and clouds, and after a few moments he followed Frederic's lead and climbed back into the carriage, wrapping himself in a blanket and settling on the seat beside Barbara. She stirred, but didn't wake, and moments later he felt her soft curls drop onto his shoulder. Warm, and safe for the moment, they slept.

Daylight was a hazy, vague illumination. Johann extricated himself from Barbara's embrace and stepped into the chill of the morning air. Frederic was awake and had a small fire burning beside the road. He had produced a cook's kit from somewhere on the carriage and was boiling water for tea.

"Good morning," he said cheerfully. "We'll be ready to move out soon. I thought the ladies would be better with something warm, and I could use something myself."

Johann nodded. He looked up and down the road, but visibility was poor, and it was impossible to see more than a dozen yards in either direction.

"It should lift by noon," Frederic said.

They stood together as the water boiled, and just before Frederic removed the pot from the fire, Rosina appeared. The girl appeared fresh, more rested than seemed possible, and despite the hardship of sleeping the night in the carriage, on the road, her eyes sparkled. Despite the stress of being uprooted from her home, the freedom of this sudden new life agreed with her.

A moment later, Barbara, looking a bit steadier on her feet, also appeared. Johann quickly prepared her a cup of the warm tea and held it for her as it cooled.

"We will cross the river before noon," he said. "Once we are on the far side, I believe we will have little to fear from any pursuit."

Barbara nodded, but she didn't answer. Johann caught her staring back down the road the way they'd come. As good as all of this was for Rosina, it was equally hard on his new, young wife, and he determined that he would make it easier in any way possible. She really was a beautiful girl, and though he barely knew her, his heart rushed, and he blushed, every time he allowed his gaze to rest on her for more than a moment.

They finished their tea in silence and clambered back into the carriage. Johann helped Frederic with the horses, and before the haze had fully lifted from the road, they were moving again. There was little conversation. Everything had happened very quickly for all of them, and each was lost in thought, contemplating an uncertain future.

Just before noon, Frederic reigned in the horses, and pulled the side of the road again. When he didn't continue, Johann climbed out and walked around to see what had happened.

The carriage rested at the top of a fairly steep hill. The ford should have been at the bottom of that hill, a narrow, shallow gap in the river. Instead the waterline had climbed halfway up the slope. White froth whirled and danced in slow circles on the brown, muddied surface. The river had swollen beyond its banks and was climbing steadily upward.

The sky was clear. The rain that had caused the flooding was long past, but the roiling waves below might as well have been a brick wall.

"We can't stay here," Johann said firmly. "We are caught against the river like a rat in a hole. If they come for us, they will find us here at the end of this road, and there will be nowhere to go."

Frederic frowned, and nodded. He knew it was true, but there seemed no way they were getting across the swollen waters of the river. There were three horsemen, two men and a woman, and one other carriage nearby, obviously having met with the same dilemma.

"We'll turn back, Frederic said. "If we turn up the river, away from the direction of the storm, we should be able to find another place to make our crossing. See how the trail leads along the bank?"

He pointed, and Johann followed the direction of that point. He saw that there was, indeed, another road winding along the side of the river. It wasn't as well worn as the main road, and it looked rough. Johann suffered a quick pang of guilt as he thought of Barbara being forced to bounce along on such a road, but there was nothing else they could do.

"Let's be quick then," he said, turning back to the carriage.

He climbed inside, and Frederic backed the horses, preparing to turn off to the side. There wasn't much room on the road itself, and the ground to either side was muddy, wet and treacherous.

He maneuvered the animals slowly and carefully, getting the carriage perpendicular to the road, and preparing to drive it up and over a small hummock and onto the secondary trail.

Then it happened. One of the men on horseback, suddenly disgusted with the wait, and the day, slapped his mount hard with a crop, driving it to a sudden gallop and heading back down the road. The sound of leather on the horse's flank cracked through the air like thunder, and despite Frederic's tight grip on the reins, their horses shied. The young driver fought them. He called out to the frightened animals, but it was too late. They bucked and the carriage slid sideways, up and over the rise at the top of the road and onto the slope.

Johann called out frantically, trying to climb back out of the carriage and help, but a sudden lurch drove him back inside, and he was forced to take a seat, bracing Barbara with his body to keep from pummeling her as he was tossed about. Rosina clung to the bench across from them, eyes wide. She gave a sudden terrified scream, and the horses shied again.

They were moving, sliding down the embankment toward the rough, muddy waves. Frederic cracked his whip and shook the reins, but the horses were off balance, and by the time they regained their wits enough to pull, they couldn't get firm footing on the road. The weight of the carriage slid down, gained speed, and the horses, straining and slipping, were dragged after it.

The animals lunged, valiantly tugging at the harness, but the weight, and the slope of the hill was too much for them. With a shuddering moan, the carriage slid sideways on its wheels, miraculously avoiding a snapped axle, and plunged into the water. The current caught the wood solidly and pulled, and as those seated above watched in horror, the carriage, horses and all, was swept from the bank and into the center of the river, whirling around as the terrified animals paddled and fought to free themselves.

They spun so that the horses faced downstream, and then, as the waters of the river swept around a bend, they were simply gone. Only the echo of Johann's and Frederic's hoarse shouts, and the screaming of the women, remained to echo in the cool, damp air.

TEN

Black locked his office carefully, turning each of the three keys in the proper order and nodding almost imperceptibly as each set of tumblers locked into place. The security was a ritual that he never shirked. He'd come too far in life to allow a moment's carelessness to undo it, and despite the fact that he stood on the top floor of his own complex, surrounded by those who either admired him, feared him, or both, he never took chances. Maxwell Black believed anyone could be bought. He'd applied that philosophy to his enemies, and he applied it to his own people, as well.

Satisfied, he turned and walked to the lifts. He didn't push any of the buttons lit up on the display to the left of the door. Instead, he pulled another key from his pocket and inserted it in a slot beneath the panel. He turned it until he heard a soft click, and then turned it a second time; the lift hummed to life. When it was moving smoothly down the shaft, he turned the key a final time and removed it from the slot. The lights above the door lit as always. He passed the main floor and continued on for what seemed a long time.

The doors slid open and he stepped out into a very large room. It was lit by gigantic fluorescent fixtures attached to a cage-like frame that encircled the room. The cage served as a brace for all sorts of equipment, pulleys, lifts, shelving units, and banks of computerized systems that whirred and clacked with a life of their own.

The huge area was blocked out into large cubicles by framing similar to that overhead. Each was outfitted with different equipment. Many of the smaller areas had their own banks of computers and monitors. Black walked past the first few and turned down a corridor that led off to his right. Ahead, a larger cubicle stood open, and through the wire mesh he saw what appeared to be a ten foot stone wheel. It hung from a metal framework that resembled the small cranes used to extract motors from automobiles. Two men stood beside the wheel. One made notes on a clipboard, and the other stood, hands on hips, staring at the structure.

It was motionless, and seeing this, Black frowned.

"What happened?" he asked.

The two men turned to him, startled. Black moved very silently, and with the machinery, computer equipment, and other assorted sounds of the huge chamber to filter it, they'd missed the sound of the lift.

"I..."the man with the clipboard started and then stopped.

The other man, shorter with gray hair, scowled at the large wheel, then kicked it violently. It thrummed with sound, like a giant stone tuning fork, but it remained motionless.

"It's not working," the man with the clipboard said. His name tag simply said Dan. He was thin with too-thick glasses that rode low on his nose. He pushed them back into place.

"We've tried every variation of the fields conceivable. We can set the wheel in motion. We can even keep the wheel in motion, but only for a time. The longest period so far is about a week, with a steady lessening of efficiency as the spinning slows."

"We've been able to manipulate the field on a continuous basis, keeping the wheel spinning," the gray haired man said, "but without the outside stimulus, it's just like all the others. It starts, it runs, and it stops."

Black stared at the wheel and scowled. It didn't' really surprise him. He'd seen hundreds of prototypes, big wheels, small wheels, pendulums, odd conglomerations of gears and pyramids. He's seen liquid metal used as the core, as well as superheated and super cooled gases, to no good effect. Nothing they did changed the solitary fact that perpetual motion was a myth, and would remain so until someone found Bessler's key. Black was no longer certain he believed that there was a key.

He knew what his intelligence reports told him of the progress Wright and his people had made. There was even a rumor that the complex where Elizabeth Kassel had been taken such a short time before created so much of its own power that it managed to sell some back to the city. When asked about the excessive energy, they claimed to be doing research in more efficient solar cells. Air reconnaissance had revealed what appeared to be a great number of solar panels on the roof of the building, but close examination showed nothing remarkable about them. It was all an elaborate sham. Black knew it, and they knew that he knew, but it was a standoff.

Without revealing himself and his intentions, he couldn't very well report them. If he wanted what they had, he would have to take it, and he'd have to do so without any help from the government, the police, or any entity likely to seize it once they found out what it was.

Black's own backing came from several large oil conglomerates. He had no illusions of their putting the secret of perpetual motion to use in the interest of mankind. If they used it at all, it would be most likely to power the pumps that drew oil from the crust of the earth. It might show up in some government projects – military transport, the space program. Of course, if it turned out that the secret involved gravity it wasn't likely to be much good for the latter.

That was the problem. Without knowing, it was impossible to plan. Without the key to the device, his hands were tied. He could report nothing of use. His people had discovered some amazing things. Some of the devices they had designed were much more efficient than anything currently in use, but that didn't matter.

"Keep at it," he said. Then, without another word, he turned and left the cubicle, its wheel, and the two men behind. He turned right and followed the center corridor to a bank of computers on the far wall. The setup was truly impressive, a network of supercomputers, tied together and working as one, solving complex mathematical problems so quickly that the weak link, the humans operating the peripherals and programming the software, couldn't keep up.

He turned, slipped through a small doorway and into a room formed of four fabric-covered walls, but without a roof. Inside there were several desks, two of which were occupied. Behind the first a small, mole-like man with thick glasses and heavy eyebrows sat hunched before a computer screen. His hand hovered over a mouse, and he moved his cursor across the screen with eerie precision, clicking now and then, waiting, watching, and then continuing.

Beside him a woman with long red hair clattered away at a keyboard. She was transfixed by a sequence of numbers pouring across the screen. Black knew the numbers were coming from the small man's console. The two worked in tandem, one varying an algorithm almost imperceptibly, and the other monitoring the output, comparing it against figures and formulae from previous experiments, discarding each as it failed some arcane test, and moving on.

Black didn't interrupt. If he stopped the flow of their tandem motion he knew from experience it could take hours, maybe days, to recover. They would work, just as they were now, for hours at a time. They'd been together for so long they could read signals in one another's performance. When one started to suffer fatigue, the other drew the work to a close.

On a third desk sat the folder Black had retrieved from Edgar Kline. The single page within had been carefully scanned, broken into sectors, and fed into the computer banks, which were designed to facilitate the breaking of complex codes. The combined IQ of the two working on the problem was staggering. They'd worked together on DNA sequencing, had designed algorithms still in use for corporate security across the globe, providing varying passwords that shifted every few seconds. Black had seen the printouts from the sessions that had created the system. They'd had to be carried out in boxes—reams and reams of paper—shredded and burned the minute it was no longer of use. The system itself had been purged, hard drives destroyed and degaussed. The work, in the end, had amounted to a circuit board the size of a dime.

Now they worked on the code. The Orffyreus Code, he called it. Bessler's code. How one lone man, centuryies dead, could have created something complicated enough to challenge his team Black could not begin to understand. There were complexities to the problem that added layers of difficulty. The secrets themselves were coded into allegory, and then back into code and again to mathematical symbols. There was a key, of course, something that Bessler had intended others to use to decipher his work, but he had inconveniently died without recording that key or passing it on. At least, if he'd passed it on, it had not passed into the world.

Black turned away. He didn't return the way he'd come. Instead he made a circuit of the warehouse sized room. There were compartments, workshops, and prototypes of all sizes and shapes along his way. Some were attended; others sat still and alone, or spun, whirled, swayed or pivoted their way through the most recent round of tests. A great deal had been learned here. Secrets had been discovered, and money was always being made. That was something he insisted on. If he found what he sought, he would turn it over to those who financed him – probably. Along the way, though, anything that was discovered was his. It was the one point he'd not been willing to negotiate on. No split, no compromise. It was money that drove him.

Footsteps sounded in the corridor behind him. He didn't turn. Moments later Jonathan drew up beside him, matched his pace, and held out a telegram.

"What is it?" Black asked. He made no move to take it.

"You'll want to see this one," Jonathan replied. "I think we've finally gotten the break we've been waiting for." Black stopped, took the paper, and scanned it quickly. He read it a second time, then glanced up and met Jonathan's gaze.

"Well, well," he said. "I believe you may be right, old friend. Pack, and bring the car around front. I'll be there in twenty minutes."

Jonathan turned on his heel, an about-face worthy of a marine, and was gone. He didn't run, but somehow he moved as quickly as if he'd sprinted. In moments Black stood alone in the corridor, the telegram clutched in his hand, his eyes gleaming.

Then he carefully folded the paper, stuck it in his pocket, and followed after Jonathan.

ELEVEN

The pieces of the ancient wheel were scattered over her desk like a stone puzzle. Some of the bits were metal and wood. These had been carefully wrapped, oiled, and preserved. There were no instructions, though the wheel showed up several times in Bessler's journal. From the basic diagrams she'd been able to piece most of it together, but the central mechanism defied her. There were at least half a dozen ways the interior pieces might fit. Of those two or three could be tossed out without much thought because of the way they'd make the mechanism bind up.

Something just outside the periphery of her thoughts played tag with her concentration. Each time the design began to come together in her mind, something intruded, or some crucial detail didn't fit. It occurred to her that both Benjamin and her grandmother could have intended this wheel as a test, even as a trick. Maybe it wasn't all there. Maybe there were pieces missing, or this wasn't the actual wheel that had worked, but one of the earlier failures.

Her education had included basic physics, but she remembered little of what she'd been taught. Since opening the crate, she'd spent a good deal of time buried in the books that filled her office shelves and lined the smaller cabinets in her apartments, but it was slow going. It helped that her grandmother was a note taker. The margins of pages were lined with scribbled text and figures, small tabs of paper protruded between pages, and in other places entire passages had been highlighted. It was like a long maze set out to lead her toward a solution, but she kept running into dead ends and questions that led to more questions, rather than answers. It should have been frustrating, but she found that the longer she spent on the problem, the more it fascinated her. Even the dead ends had lessons to teach.

She was lost in thought, an ancient metal spring in one hand, and the other propped under her chin, when she became aware that someone was watching. She turned quickly, nearly knocking the wheel from its precarious perch on the ancient stand, and Benjamin stepped in quickly, gripping it lightly and righting it.

"Sorry," he said. "I didn't mean to startle you. You were so intent on that piece that I couldn't bring myself to interrupt."

She stared at him for a moment as her mind slowly released the ancient mechanism and returned her to the present. She turned, glanced at the spring in her hand, and stared at it thoughtfully.

"Seems pretty simple, doesn't it?" he asked.

She nodded absently. "There's nothing simple about it, though. If it had been easy, Bessler would have succeeded much sooner than he did, and he wouldn't have been the only one. I've looked at this thing from every angle I can imagine, and yet there's something missing."

"A piece?" Benjamin asked.

She glanced up at him again. The notion that she was being tested returned, and she frowned. "I don't think it's a missing piece," she said. "There is something about the construction that is wrong. Something so basic that it eludes me. If anything, I'd say there are too many pieces, not too few. Everything seems to create new frictions, and every surface that contacts another surface becomes more a part of the problem than of the solution."

Benjamin chuckled. "You see the dilemma I've suffered with all these years, then," he said softly.

She frowned. "Surely you've seen this put together before?"

He nodded slowly. "Yes, Lily showed it to me several times. Once we left it in motion for three months before she took it apart and stored it. That was a long time ago. It's been in the crate ever since, waiting for you to carry it across the ocean."

"You never assembled it?" she asked.

Benjamin shook his head. "Never. I'll admit that I'd love the chance to try. I know that what we have done on a much larger scale is based on the principle behind that wheel, but I came on board later in the game. Lily had long-since cracked the secret by the time I met her, and my energy has been focused on the modern incarnations. With what I know I am still, very frankly, amazed that this wheel ever existed, and that it still works. Our own devices require machining and engineering to very strict specifications to operate. Bessler created his wheel with crude tools and the naked eye. He was a genius."

Elly's shoulders slumped. She'd been operating on the assumption that if she failed to figure out how the wheel was to be constructed, that Benjamin could walk in and show her the error in her thought process in a matter of moments. The thought that only two people in history had ever made the thing work, and that both of them were now dead, depressed her.

"I'm sure we can figure it out together, if you tire of the challenge," Benjamin assured her. "I know the principles behind the wheel, and that is something even Bessler didn't have going for him when he created it. "

Footsteps echoed in the hall. Someone knocked softly on the door. Benjamin opened it wide, and Cynthia stepped in. Her normally impeccable hair was disheveled, and a fine coat of sweat coated her skin. She'd obviously been running.

"What is it?" Benjamin asked, taking her by the shoulders. "What has happened?"

Cynthia glanced at Elly.

"If there is a problem," Elly said, catching the moment's indecision, "then I want to hear about it. I'm part of this now, for good, or for ill. In fact, unless I'm mistaken, I own it. What's wrong?"

Cynthia turned her gaze to Benjamin, who nodded impatiently.

"It's the plant in Pompano," she said breathlessly.

"Something is wrong with the plant?" Benjamin took a quick step toward the door, but Cynthia held him back.

"No," she replied. "Nothing is wrong. Everything is on

schedule, and we are ready for the test. It's not that."

"What then?" he asked.

"Black," Cynthia said. "Maxwell Black and some of his men have been seen in the city. They've been questioning natives. Reports say they brought enough supplies for a long expedition."

"How…"

Before Benjamin could continue, Elly dropped the spring onto her desk with a loud clatter and cleared her throat.

"Where," she asked, "is Pompano? What does it have to do with us, and what is Black after? I've been here a while now, but I still have very little idea what this place is all about. What do we do here? Where else do we have projects, and what are they?"

Benjamin took a deep breath.

"Send for coffee, Cynthia," he said softly. "I think it's time we brought Elly up to speed, and we could be in here for a while. If what you say is true, there is no time to be wasted."

When they were all seated, a carafe of hot coffee on the desk and three cups steaming before them, Benjamin began to speak.

Your grandmother and I determined long ago that, as secure as we might make this facility, it was a bad idea to keep everything cooped up under one roof. Maxwell Black is only one of the people concerned with our work. There are rumors even among government officials. The only thing in our favor is that if any one of them let what they suspect become public knowledge, they would lose the chance, however slim, that they could steal, twist, or warp what we are doing to their own ends. If they fail, or get too frustrated, the next best thing they could do would be to destroy us and send the secret with us to our graves, as it was thought to have gone with Bessler to his.

"If they can't have it, nobody can?" Elly asked.

"Exactly," Cynthia said. "Maxwell Black should not be underestimated. He is a very smart man, and some of those working for him are smarter still. We keep as close a watch on them as they do on us – that way if they actually break through our defenses; we'll know right away and can begin damage control. The problem with people like Black is that they have a very narrow view of the world. There are two kinds of things for Black, those that advance his personal interests, and those that do not. A large, relatively free source of power becoming readily available to the world does not, but control of such a resource does. For him, it's that simple."

Elly nodded.

"We spread our work as widely as we can without risking exposure," Benjamin continued. "Over the years we have picked a handful of locations around the world that we feel are secluded enough and safe enough – both from outside intrusion, and from their own governments – for large-scale experimentation. We also choose the locations where our work can serve the greatest good. That was a stipulation of any project your grandmother considered, and we have honored her memory in that regard."

"So where is Pompano," Elly cut in, "and why is Black there? What is he after?"

"Pompano is a small city in Ecuador," Cynthia explained. "We've had an operation down there for about five years now. We have another in the southern corner of the Andalusia region of Spain. There are plants operating in several hard to reach mountainous regions, including the Andes and in Tibet. It takes a lot of time and effort to find such a location, populate it with personnel who can be trusted, and then bring in the proper equipment. Anything accomplished too quickly sends signals that can be tracked, economic markers, local officials taking notice, the chance of infiltration. We have levels of security in place that would have made J. Edgar Hoover smile, and still your grandmother worried."

"I worry," Benjamin added, "and it seems that the worry isn't too far off base. There is no way that Black could have learned of the operation in Pompano without a leak."

"We don't know what he knows," Cynthia countered. "He may have just gotten a hint, a sight of someone who was recognized, or a shipment that wasn't masked carefully enough. We can't assume he knows everything."

"You are right, of course," Benjamin said. "We can't assume

anything at all. We have to get down there, and quickly. It won't take us long once we are on site to ascertain the scope of the problem. We may have to shut it down, but better now, before it goes into full operation."

"I'm going with you," Elly said.

The other two, who seemed for the moment to have forgotten that Elly was there, turned to stare at her.

"That's out of the question," Benjamin replied. "There will be too much danger, Black..."

"Has already tried to take me once, and I didn't appreciate it," Elly finished. "I also don't appreciate being told on one hand how all of this is mine now," she waved her hand to indicate the office, the hall beyond, and the complex surrounding them in a single sweeping gesture, "and on the other hand ordered about like a schoolgirl. I'm either in charge here, or I'm not, Benjamin, which is it?"

"I ..." He fell silent.

Cynthia started to speak, then bit off whatever it was she was about to say.

"This will be a dangerous operation," Benjamin said softly. "No one is trying to cut you out of anything, but there is training involved. We have been dealing with Black and his ilk for many years now, and we know, basically, what to expect. It would be tragic if he got his hands on you again, or if something went wrong and you were hurt. I would never forgive myself."

"Then it's a good thing," Elly replied, eyes flashing with barely controlled anger, "that it isn't up to you. I will take full responsibility for my own safety and actions, but I will be going on this trip. I will not be coddled or babied through this, pushed aside when something important happens and spoon fed a company line about my grandmother's wishes. Her wish was that I inherit her work, and that I continue it.

"When I first heard that, I wasn't happy about it. I had a life, a quiet, happy life, with no Maxwell Blacks or hidden mercenaries chasing me about. My grandmother knew that, and still she thought to trust me with her life's work. I intend to accept that trust fully. Tell me, Benjamin, would she have stayed quietly behind while you ran off to defend her secrets?"

Benjamin glanced at Cynthia, who returned his stare. They held that gaze, and their silence for only a moment, then the two of them burst into laughter so sudden, and so infectious, that Elly was completely taken aback. She stood, her hands on her hips, watching the others convulse, beyond speech, for a good five minutes, trying not to be drawn into their mirth.

Wiping his eyes to clear the tears, Benjamin spoke at last.

"No, Elly, your grandmother would not have stood quietly by. In fact, she'd have been as likely to throw something at me – something hard and painful – if I'd even suggested it.

"I apologize. I tend to look at our work, and our projects, in a very insular fashion. Lily…your grandmother, was a very integral part of every operation. It was her drive and energy that made most of what we have accomplished possible. Now that she is no longer with us, much of that burden has fallen on me – until now. I suppose I'm having difficulty transposing things. You are very different from her, and yet, at times – like just now – you remind me of her so clearly she might be standing in the room."

"We need to get going," Cynthia cut in. "There will be plenty of time to talk on the flight."

"You go and pack," Benjamin said, laying a hand on Elly's shoulder. "Bring boots if you have them, and light clothing that covers well. No dark colors if you can help it. We'll be in a lot of bright sunlight, and the insects can be pretty bad. You want to cover as much as possible, while adding no weight. Light colors reflect the heat."

Elly nodded. She was already on her way to the door.

"I'll pick you up on my way out," Cynthia called after her. "We can meet Benjamin in the garage, and ride together to the airport."

The next hour passed in a confusion of activity. Elly grabbed what clothing she had that seemed appropriate, including a pair of hiking boots she'd never had much use for, but was suddenly glad she'd brought along. She knew she could pick up some items when they reached their destination, but being unfamiliar with Ecuador, she didn't want to take any chances.

She tucked a couple of books and her own journal into her bag, but carefully avoided packing anything of her grandmothers. She'd already come close to handing over too much information to Maxwell Black. If she met him again, she wanted to be sure she was prepared.

Cynthia arrived just as Elly snapped the cover of her suitcase closed, and the two of them hurried down the hallway together. They took the lift to the ground floor, and as they did so, Elly realized with a start that it was the first time since coming to America that she'd left the area of the complex. She'd been out in the city a couple of times, shopping twice and once for dinner with Benjamin, but this was the first time she'd walked away from the safe, cocoon-like depths of her grandmother's building.

And she wasn't just going across the city. To Elly, who had grown up in a small town in England and never traveled more than was absolutely necessary, a place like the Ecuadorian jungle was like a fairy-tale land. It hardly seemed possible that such a place could exist, let alone that she would see it up close, rather than on a television screen.

Benjamin was waiting for them in one of the dark sedans they always used. It was identical to the one that had rescued Elly her first night and it brought back the memory of that time with a clarity she could have done without.

"Ready?" Benjamin asked? He slid her bag, and then Cynthia's into the trunk and slammed it tight.

Elly nodded. "As ready as I'm ever likely to be."

Benjamin nodded. He held the door, and after the two women had slipped into the back seat, he climbed in beside the driver, and they rolled out of the parking garage and onto the streets of the city. They rode in silence. Benjamin flipped through papers in a briefcase in his lap, Cynthia laid her head back as if she intended to nap, and Elly was left to watch the streets and cars flash past her window as they roared through New York and on toward the airport. Despite her earlier bluster, the huge city, the dark night sky, and the silence made her feel very small, and very alone.

TWELVE

The jet was sleek, comfortable, and very quiet. Once they passed the initial surge of G-force on the runway, Elly felt as if she might as well have been on a boat or a train. They experienced a couple of mild pockets of turbulence, but nothing alarming. Coffee and tea were served as soon as they leveled off, and when the seatbelt light went dark, Benjamin called Elly and Cynthia to sit with him around a polished wooden conference table. The seats were soft leather and cool to the touch.

Benjamin's briefcase was open on the seat to his left. Elly sat on his right, and Cynthia slid in across the table from him. He thumbed through a small pile of folders, and then handed one to Elly.

"You may want to go through this before we touch down. I'm going to give you a quick overview of what we have in Pompano. I want you to know what we're up against, everything that's at stake, and to understand the level of ruthlessness Maxwell Black and his men are capable of. There are others who have grown curious over the years, but he is by far the worst – and the most dangerous."

Elly nodded. She pulled the folder closer to her, laid her hands on top of it, and met Benjamin's gaze.

"What you'll see shortly after we land," he began, "is one of Lily's greatest accomplishments. It's one of the times when we had the chance to do some testing, and to do some good, and though there is a great risk anytime we actually put the technology to work in the real world, we've been very careful. I think you'll agree, once I'm done, that it's nothing short of eerie how Black and his people find our trail. In any case, our

Pompano project began with ancient tribal ruins."

"Ruins?" Elly asked.

Benjamin nodded. "Very old ruins. The jungle has buried more secrets than many civilizations ever develop. I think, maybe, it reminded your grandmother of Bessler and his wheel. Anyway, the ruins in question are extensive, winding down into a mountain a few miles outside of Pompano. They were discovered almost ten years ago, but at the time only the uppermost levels were available for study. The rest of them were underwater.

"One of our people found an article on the Internet asking for assistance, and we started to look into it. There were pumps available that could do the work, but they were expensive, and keeping them in operation was even more expensive than acquiring them, not to mention the risk to workers if the motors failed, or the fuel ran out at an inopportune moment.

"You'll remember from the journals that one of the first uses Bessler imagined for his wheel was to power pumps that might keep miners dry and safe?"

Elly nodded. "But this isn't a mine…"

"No," Benjamin agreed, "But the premise is, basically, the same. The ruins were once a city built partly on the surface, and partly dug into the side of a mountain. Over time land shifts, and there have been some earthquakes. Our best guess is that the damage happened during the latter. There are underground streams, and on the far side of the mountain, there is a very large river. We believe some dividing wall broke away beneath the mountain's surface and allowed water from the river to rush in and fill the city, backing up the tunnels to the level of the water in the river on the far side. The initial flood washed away a great deal of the evidence of the ruins, or I'm sure they would have been discovered sooner."

Elly frowned. "But, if there is a river on the far side of the mountain, and the wall between is broken, or damaged, what good would pumps be? Surely you can't mean to pump the river dry?"

Benjamin's eyes twinkled. "You are exactly right, and that was our initial reaction, as well. We sent an expedition to Ecuador, and they checked the base of that mountain from both sides. On the river side, they found crevasse beneath the surface – a long crack in the stone. It took time, and a lot of effort – not to mention considerable funding, but we were able to seal that crack. In fact, we reinforced the entire base of the mountain along that stretch to help prevent a recurrence. It's always possible, of course, that another earthquake could re-open the break, but with proper safety measures in place, we believed – and still believe – that the gain will be worth taking the chance.

"We've already lowered the water level considerably, and we've been able to temporarily seal off some sections from the remainder of the flooding, so even if the river side of the mountain gave way again, what we've gained wouldn't be lost. It's amazing. You'll find some pictures in that folder, along with more detailed explanations of how we've accomplished what we have."

"And you powered the pumps with my grandmother's wheel? Bessler's wheel?"

"Not yet," Cynthia said. "As Benjamin said, we have to exercise a great deal of care in bringing even the hint of our technology to the public. Fortunately, our research has led to breakthroughs in a number of other areas – not as remarkable as free energy, or perpetual motion, but enough to make our operations very profitable. One of the things we've developed is a very efficient pumping system. For the upper levels of the excavation we used modified diesel engines, and our own design of pump. The site is designated for research in that area."

"Then, why does Black want to go there? And even if he does, what does it matter?"

"We only used the conventional methods at first to cloak our true intent," Benjamin replied. "We will still use our pumps to clear the water from the lower levels of the ruins, but the diesels will become no more than a smokescreen. They will continue to run – there is no way to avoid the loss of sound and labor involved with the process, but when we are sure that everything is operational, we'll shift the pumps over to the Bessler generator below."

Elly glanced up sharply. It was the first time she'd heard the term used, but it was fitting. She'd sort of figured her grandmother would attach her own name to the project. After a moment's thought, though, she realized that the notion was contrary to all she'd learned of Lilian Kellam, and of the project. Selflessness was a rarity in the world, but this seemed to be one small pocket of it; of course credit would be given to the man who'd deserved it.

"Do the locals know?" she asked, fingering the folder. She was itching to open it and see the photos, but she kept herself under control.

"No, not really," Cynthia answered. "They know we are financing the pumps, and they know we are experimenting on the pump technology itself. All they care about, really, is the ruins and what we can discover in the caves. We also employ a great number of their people in the upper levels of the complex, running the diesels and working with the pumps. They don't understand the technology, but they are hard workers, and what we've done, along with helping them uncover their past, is to improve the local economy. Even if those in charge thought we were up to something, I doubt they'd complain."

"We were very careful," Benjamin said. "We brought in generators in very small parts, packed in with other supplies and only moved down to the lower levels when the plant was abandoned. We kept the locals out during the initial construction, told them it was for safety, and to maintain the confidentiality of the new pumps. They were eager to help in any way they could, so I'm fairly certain they have no idea about the lower level, or the Bessler generators.

"The diesels are operated largely by local labor. We keep personnel at the plant to a minimum, and there is no one there but a small security force when the pumps are shut down. Right now they are excavating the first levels we uncovered, and though we have the pumps in standby, in case there is a rupture and the water rises again, they are leaving us alone for the most part. I doubt that they'll even take notice of our arrival, except to stop by and thank us again."

"Black will notice," Cynthia said. "If he is there, you know he'll have people watching the landing strip and reporting back to him the minute we're spotted. I wish we'd had more time, and that we were going in with more force."

"It's not our country," Benjamin said flatly. "We are already breaching etiquette by coming in armed."

Cynthia didn't answer, but she also didn't look convinced. Elly turned her attention to the folder and its contents.

"I'm going to think about all of this, and I'm going to catch up on this reading," she said. "If I have my own private war going with Black, I don't want to push it off on any unsuspecting people."

"Of course not," Cynthia replied. Her voice didn't carry conviction.

"First we have to get there," Benjamin said, rising and turning toward his seat. "I'm going to get some rest before that happens. When we get there we'll need to find Black as soon as possible and figure out what he's up to. We won't even visit the plant unless we're sure there's a danger. He might be trying to lure us in and get us to lead him to what he seeks. If he's already been there, then he's seen the diesels, and the pumps, but nothing more. We'd have gotten a report if he'd infiltrated further."

Elly nodded, but she had already flipped open the folder and was lost in the reports, photographs, and correspondence filed within. Everything was in meticulous order, but it still took her a few minutes to separate the fluff from the important parts and arrange the two separately and efficiently. For the first time since she'd entered her grandmother's great, strange world, she felt like her training as a clerk was coming in handy.

Ecuador, it seemed, was prone to indulgent numbers of carefully designed missives, stamped and sealed and validated at every level of government before being passed on to whomever they dealt with. Her breath caught when she saw the first document bearing her grandmother's bold signature, but she bit back the emotion that threatened to overwhelm her and flipped through the pages quickly.

It was all pretty straightforward. The ruins were those of a city. There were extensive excavations underway outside the caverns, as well as within. The city itself had stretched into the jungle; the rear wall had been the mountain itself, and the city extended well within. What had once apparently been a network of natural caverns and tunnels had been carved, expanded and modified so that, rather than stopping at the face of the mountain, the ancient settlement had moved in and down. There was evidence that those who had lived there had made arrangements to seal the outer doors in case of attack, and there was even speculation that, rather than a natural disaster, it had been excessive digging by the citizens of that ancient world that had caused the flooding. The story behind it was fascinating, but Elly skimmed through quickly.

There would be plenty of time to bone up on her Ecuadorian history once they were home. She stopped, laid the folder on the table and glanced up in shock. Had she just thought of the complex as home? She glanced at Benjamin, and then at Cynthia, but both were leaned back in their seats with their eyes closed, resting. She knew she'd have to rest, as well, but there was time.

She returned her attention to the folder. The pump house was a long, squat building manufactured largely from local materials. On the surface, there was nothing odd about it. Elly didn't understand all the symbols and diagrams, but she got a good overview of where the pumps were situated and how the piping had been run into the mountain, draining the water and pumping it back around the far side of the nearest peak, where it ran down a slope and back to the river.

Also included in the folder were spec sheets on the pumps themselves. They started with an overview, showing the previous pumps that had been used in such operations, comparing and contrasting power consumption, efficiency, reliability and several other parameters. Anyone reading these documents would see exactly what they were meant to see, a modern, efficient pumping system using diesel engines and experimental pumps – nothing more.

When she flipped to the next page, she saw that it was a cutaway of the building. The diagram resembled the first one, except that the top had been sliced off cleanly, and beneath it a similarly designed lower level was revealed. There wasn't as much equipment on the lower level. There were two panels, and two large boxes, shaded with diagonal lines, and marked with the labels BG #1 and BG#2.

Elly scanned the text on the sheet. Nothing was recorded in detail. She nearly turned to ask Benjamin about this, since the upper level had been described in such minute detail, but then it hit her. They wouldn't record that sort of information in a folder that was being carried out of the complex. It would, in fact, probably be in their best interests to shred or destroy the diagram before they touched down.

The full realization of her situation began, at last, to crystallize in her mind. This was deadly serious. Things she'd seen in films were coming to life all around her, secret codes, access passes, even thugs with weapons and no qualms about their use. It terrified her, but at the same time it thrilled her.

The work they were doing was important. Instead of puttering away in her small apartment, planting flowers and shopping, she'd been given an extraordinary gift. Her inheritance was larger than life – not the money – but the chance to make a difference in the world, to help people who desperately needed the help. How many others got such an opportunity?

She quickly scanned the rest of the material in the folder. When she looked up, Benjamin was awake, watching her.

"We need to destroy this." It was a statement, not a question. Benjamin nodded.

"I wondered if you'd realize that," he said. "Do you have any questions?"

"If the Bessler Generators fail, what happens?" she asked. "I do not doubt their effectiveness, but if there are lives at stake, then I want to be certain they aren't under any more risk than necessary."

"There is a failsafe," Benjamin said. "We keep the diesels operating at full efficiency, and, of course, they are on line at all times to prevent the curious from wondering just what it is that powers the pumps. The system we have in place can clear twice the water in the same amount of time as the diesels can, and without as much as a gallon of fuel, but the diesels are sufficient to keep the level steady, should something fail. We even have them on a cascading system, so that if one diesel fails, the other kicks in and takes over. It's as safe as it can be, under the circumstances."

Elly nodded. She rose and handed the folder over to Benjamin, who took it to the far end of the small cabin. He hit a switch, and the sound of grinding blades whirred to life. Benjamin fed in the papers one after another, then the folder itself. Then, satisfied, he returned to his seat.

"You'd better get some sleep, if you can," he said. "It's going to be hot, and humid, and if you aren't used to the weather it can drain you pretty quickly."

She nodded, leaned back in her seat and closed her eyes. She was absolutely certain she wouldn't sleep, but moments later, with flickering visions of Black's face, the driver Jonathan's cold, empty eyes, and a huge, stone wheel playing against the backdrop of her eyelids, she dozed, and eventually fell into a fitful sleep.

They touched down in late afternoon sunlight so bright it glittered off the tarmac. The airfield was surrounded on three sides by jungle, held in check by tall chain link fencing. There was only a single, long runway and few aircraft visible on the field.

Elly sat up and shook her head gently to clear her thoughts. Benjamin and Cynthia were up the second the aircraft touched down, bustling about the cabin, collecting cases and light luggage. Elly wasn't as certain of her footing, and she remained seated until they coasted to a halt. She heard the clang of metal and knew that large chocks were being attached to the wheels. A sudden shift in air pressure marked the opening of the main hatch.

"Here we are," Benjamin said, grinning. "They aren't much in the technology department, but this is one beautiful country."

Her bags consisted of a single briefcase, and a duffle bag she could sling over her shoulder. Elly grabbed these and followed Benjamin forward. She hadn't been prepared for the sight that met her eyes when she stepped into the small jet's hatchway, but she managed not to step back, or to cry out.

The thing that struck her immediately, besides the overwhelming heat that had already caused a thin sheen of sweat to coat her skin, was the color. Everything was green. There were bright greens, darker greens, lighter greens, and all of them shimmered in an aura of rising heat and glittering sunlight. Elly steadied herself on the handrail, closed her eyes for a second, and then stepped forward. She kept her eyes on the steps beneath her, exaggerating the effort it took to keep her balance to avoid glancing back at the trees and overgrowth beyond the fence.

She'd never seen anything like it. It was vast, and coupled with the heat, seemed dangerous and oppressive. She felt its weight. The damp air plastered her hair to her neck and cheeks, and she had to squint against the sheer brilliance of the sun. It was impossible to shake the notion that, standing as they were in the center of an almost empty airfield that was surrounded on all sides by heavy foliage and impenetrable vines, they were being watched. She felt eyes on her, and her skin crawled, but she said nothing.

"Amazing, isn't it?" Cynthia stepped up beside her at the bottom of the rickety metal stairs they'd just descended. "And this is the civilized part."

Elly shivered.

"It's weird," Cynthia went on. "As many times as I've been here, I've never felt...right. It isn't the same as visiting California, or London. It's like we've stepped onto the surface of some other world – tolerated, but not really part of it."

"More like another time," Elly said. "It reminds me of movies I've seen of prehistoric times."

A choking roar sounded to their left, and the two women spun to see a bright yellow jeep crossing the runway and heading straight for them.

"Our ride," Benjamin observed, joining them. "I radioed ahead, and they sent someone out from the plant. Black and his men are all over the town, so we aren't going to stop there. I don't want to risk being spotted before we have a chance to get a look around and see if we can assess the danger."

Elly glanced at him in alarm. She'd assumed they'd go to the town first and get rooms.

The jeep screeched to a halt, and the driver grinned at them. He pulled off his hat, showing off long dark hair that rolled back over his shoulders in waves. He seemed unaffected by the heat, though his khaki shirt was open at the top.

"Welcome to Ecuador," he called out.

"Elly," Benjamin said with a grin of his own, "Meet Sanchez. I know he must have a first name – but I've never learned it. In fact, I don't know a living soul who calls him anything else. He's the plant foreman." Elly stepped forward, and Sanchez took her hand briefly, meeting her gaze.

"It is an honor to meet you," he said. "I knew your grandmother…I am sorry for your loss."

"I never really knew her," Elly said.

Sanchez nodded. He turned to Benjamin.

"We should get going. It could rain any time."

"Were you followed?" Cynthia asked.

"Absolutely – I believe we are being watched now, in fact." Sanchez gestured at the surrounding jungle. There was no way to know who – or what – might be standing among those trees.

"I assume you arranged things as I asked?" Benjamin said.

Sanchez nodded and grinned. He didn't reply, but Elly felt as if there were words hanging between the driver and Benjamin that she couldn't read.

Once their luggage was firmly tied in place, they climbed into the jeep, Elly up front with Sanchez, and Benjamin and Cynthia climbing into the rear.

"Buckle up," Sanchez called out as he revved the engine. "The road is pretty rough. We'll stop at the office," he pointed across the tarmac to a glistening white stone structure, "and then we'll head for the plant. We have quite a ways to go."

Elly nodded, but she'd barely clipped the worn belt across her waist when the Jeep lurched forward, spun and raced across the tarmac. There were several other vehicles parked near the office, but there were no drivers or passengers in sight.

"Don't we need to show our passports?" Elly called out.

"It will only take a moment, and it's a formality. It's been taken care of," Sanchez called out over the engine's roar. "We have an agreement with the local government that allows for the bypassing of some regulations. It will be a different thing when it comes time to re-enter the US."

They parked between two similar vehicles outside the single-story combination office and air tower. Benjamin climbed out and helped Elly down as Sanchez performed the same courtesy for Cynthia. Leaving the luggage on the Jeep, they entered the building, which was not air-conditioned, but which thankfully sported large ceiling fans that dried the perspiration on Elly's neck and gave her a quick shiver. The chill was replaced by sudden shock once the door had closed behind them.

From a short hallway, three figures emerged. The first, who bore a striking resemblance to Benjamin, stepped forward with a grin.

"Good to see you again, Ben," he said. "It's been too long since we had this sort of entertainment."

Eyes twinkling with amusement, Benjamin took the offered hand and turned to Elly.

"Elly, I'd like to introduce my cousin Edgar. His companions are Jennifer and Phoebe."

Elly stared outright. The resemblance between Cynthia and Jennifer, and Phoebe and herself, was uncanny. Their builds were the same, their hair was worn identically – it was like staring into an odd fun-house mirror that only changed the appearance of your clothes.

"We have to hurry," Benjamin said, taking her arm and leading her toward the hall where their three new companions had exited. "You'll need to change and give your clothes to Phoebe. We need to get them visible and on the road to town."

Elly's confusion gave way to wonder. It was a simple plan, but in its own way, brilliant. The three they had just met would go into town, register at the hotel, and settle into comfortable rooms. Once they were safely on their way, hopefully taking any prying eyes along with them, Elly and her companions would slip off through the jungle to the plant, hopefully undetected.

Caught up in the moment, she smiled. She wondered how many times her grandmother had gone through similar charades in the name of safety. She also wondered about the girl, Phoebe, where she'd come from, and how long it had taken them to find such a close match. Surely not on the spur of the moment?

Cynthia grinned at her as the two of them stepped through a doorway with Jennifer and Phoebe.

"You get used to this kind of thing," she said. "I'll tell you more about it on the way to the plant. We thought it might be less pressure on you to act naturally if we didn't tell you about this until we were on the ground."

Elly nodded.

There wasn't much time for talking, and even less for thought. They stripped out of their clothing and traded it for clean sets of dark green fatigues. They even had a set of comfortable boots in Elly's size waiting for her. Everything, it seemed, was planned on and prepared for. The level of attention to detail drove home, yet again, the importance of secrecy, and the danger in what they were doing. Elly found herself wishing they'd brought more people with them. Her memories of Black and the cold, calculating gleam in the man's eyes hadn't even begun to fade.

When they were done, the three surrogate travelers shook their hands, smiled, and were gone. Elly stood, dressed in the unfamiliar jungle gear, staring after them in bewilderment.

"They love this," Cynthia said. She laughed. "I guess I do too. It's necessary, in any case. If Black knew we were headed straight to the plant, he'd follow us or worse yet beat us there. If that happens we won't be able to check on the equipment at all – we'll have to abort and spend our time fiddling with the diesels and the pumps."

Benjamin joined them, and together they stood at a window and watched as Edgar, Jennifer and Phoebe climbed into the yellow Jeep with Sanchez, laughing as they buckled in, and roared off out the gates.

A well-dressed man in a light suit approached them, standing respectfully to the side, and Benjamin turned to him.

"Is everything in order, Raoul?" he asked.

The man nodded. "Yes, Senor Benjamin. You are all cleared. Your driver will be ready shortly, but I recommend you give it an hour or so to be certain your – friends – have taken the bait." Benjamin nodded, and then turned to stare out at the jungle. Elly followed his gaze, wondering if Maxwell Black and his men were out there, waiting. This time the chill didn't fade.

As the Jeep rounded the corner and was lost to sight, the man in the trees on the far side of the airship lowered his binoculars. Balancing easy in the crook of two branches, he reached to his belt and grabbed a small two-way radio.

He depressed the microphone button and spoke softly.

"They are here and headed for town." he said.

There was an answering grunt ... then static. He replaced the radio on his belt, slid the binoculars into their case and lowered them to his side, where they dangled from a leather strap. Then, without hesitation, he grabbed a nearby branch, swung out and around, and found his footing on the trunk of the tree. He climbed quickly and easily. Moments later, a second engine started, and he roared off away from the airfield, the knobbed tires of his bike gripping the jungle floor easily.

Soon he reached a road, and throttled back. A truck rolled out of the surrounding jungle, and he gunned the bike, spinning around behind it and up a ramp that had lowered from the rear. Once he was inside, the ramp was pulled in quickly, and the truck disappeared down the road.

In a tent deep in the jungle, Maxwell Black slid the radio back onto his belt, rose from a canvas chair, and smiled. He strode through the door toward his Jeep and called out to his men.

He stood, just for a moment, staring through the jungle toward the pump plant and the ruins beyond, as though his gaze might penetrate the greenery and find what he sought.

"It won't be so easy this time, Miss Kessler," he said softly. "This time I'm the one with the surprise."

He climbed into the passenger side of his jeep, and Jonathan, who'd been waiting in the driver's seat, fired the engines. There was still some daylight left, but the sun was dropping fast. By the time they reached town, it would be dark, but Black knew this worked in their favor. His plan rested as much on stealth as careful planning – a single misstep and they wouldn't get within a mile of that place, and so, there could be no misstep.

They drove into the jungle, and the lengthening shadows swallowed them whole.

THIRTEEN

They waited at the air field for nearly an hour. There was tea, and Raoul was a gracious host. He regaled Elly with stories of other such arrivals, and of how they'd managed to slip the supplies and equipment through customs that had facilitated the creation of the Bessler Generators. Elly was surprised at how much the man knew of their secrets, but, seeing her consternation, Benjamin explained.

"Raoul is our liaison with the local government. Someone 'in country' had to know what our plans were, and Raoul came highly recommended. Not many in the world enjoy the level of trust we place in him. He and your grandmother were very close."

"Indeed," Raoul said. "I owe your family, and your country, a great deal. My education, for instance, and my career."

"Raoul was one of your grandmother's 'projects'." Cynthia explained. "She visited Ecuador many times, and not just to work on the complex. When she was here, Raoul caught her attention, and held it. His family was in a bad state, and she helped."

"Meeting your grandmother was the turning point in my life," Raoul agreed. "When it came time to arrange this with my government, it was the least I could do. Besides," his eyes twinkled, "what man doesn't have a bit of James Bond in him? I have to admit there is a certain energy that surrounds this work. I enjoy the intrigue."

"I hope we'll have a chance to get acquainted, once this is over," Elly commented. "I have the feeling the story is a long one."

Raoul nodded. "It is, indeed, and you are correct – it is better saved for another time."

At that moment, a young man in a green camouflage pants and an olive t-shirt entered the room. He wore a straw hat back on his head, and very dark sunglasses. Elly guessed he was in his late teens, until he removed the sunglasses. His eyes were deep, lined with small creases at the corners, and she saw that his youthful frame carried more years than it seemed to.

"This is Pedro," Raoul told them. "He will get you through the jungle as quickly as possible. They are waiting for you at the plant, and the alternate entrance will be open when you arrive."

Raoul stepped forward then and took Elly's hand. As she watched, blushing, he bowed and brushed her fingers with his lips. "I hope we will get the opportunity to share stories soon, Ms. Kassel," he said.

"Elly," she murmured.

He rose, and nodded. "Elly," he agreed.

Then they were moving again, and everything blurred. They hurried out a side door, where their new vehicle pulled up quickly. Their baggage had already been transferred, quickly and efficiently packed into the rear of the Jeep. The canvas roof had been snapped into place to obscure the passengers. With a deep breath, Elly stepped up onto the running board and felt strong hands draw her into the back seat, where she sat, sandwiched between Benjamin and Cynthia. Pedro, the driver, sat alone in front, and he didn't turn to them or talk as he roared away from the airport and turned onto the jungle road beyond.

They were quickly swallowed in what seemed to Elly to be a tunnel of deep green and lush brown. Though the Jeep was loud, she still caught snatches of the cries of large birds. The trees overhead teemed with life. She saw butterflies larger and more colorful than she'd ever seen, was nearly smacked in the face by a huge dragonfly, and every time she nearly caught her breath enough to speak, they bounced around another curve, or turned suddenly onto a road she hadn't even seen coming. Eventually she gave up the idea of communicating during the ride and just sat back to enjoy the scenery.

She felt vaguely uneasy, as if they were being watched,

or followed, but she knew it was unlikely. Benjamin and the others had been doing things like this for so long the deception and secrecy were ingrained in their thought patterns and their actions. Every time a question sprang to mind, she realized it had already been answered in one way or another.

They rode for at least an hour. The roughness of the road and the stiff springs of the Jeep combined to numb Elly's back and legs. She hoped they wouldn't have to do a lot of walking immediately after their arrival, because she wasn't certain her legs would support her. She had expected adventure, but hadn't really understood the totality of what that meant. This was a real jungle, and Black represented a very real danger. They were a long way from her new rooms, her office, and the protective network her grandmother had worked so long to build, and they couldn't even expect much help from police or the local government because of their own need for secrecy. It was thrilling, but at the same time frightening, and she couldn't decide which emotion was stronger.

The Jeep slowed, at last, and as Elly leaned forward, stretching her back, she saw that the road opened ahead onto a larger clearing than any she'd seen since the airport. She couldn't make out anything in the clearing except what appeared to be a tall, chain link fence. Frowning, she leaned forward a bit more. They rolled free of the trees onto a winding, dirt trail that led around the perimeter of the fence. At the top, above the diamond-shaped links, rolls of razor-sharp barbed wire snaked in and around, forming a very imposing barrier to anyone foolish enough to try climbing into the complex.

In the distance she saw a squat, rectangular building. It was made of white stone, or possibly concrete. There didn't appear to be any windows. Smoke stacks rose at either side, giving it the general shape of an old paddle-wheeled steamboat, and Elly saw that a second fence, not quite as tall, but also topped with razor wire, ran around the edge of the building itself. No one moved, and she saw no sign of vehicles, or workers.

"It looks like a prison," she said.

Benjamin nodded. "It's not very pretty, I'm afraid. This place was built for efficiency, not esthetics, and the simple design makes it easier to watch – and defend."

The Jeep rolled to a halt facing the fence, and Elly turned to Pedro. She was about to ask what he was doing, and why they didn't follow the road to the right, or left, when the vehicle shook – not violently, but enough to catch her attention. She glanced to the side and saw that they were descending – and not slowly. Within seconds the Jeep was completely beneath the ground – and then it was rolling forward again, much more slowly, down a concrete ramp. It slanted downward for about a hundred feet, and then leveled off.

Red fluorescent bulbs hung in fixtures that jutted from the dark, solid walls. Behind them, the bit of sandy earth where they had been parked moments before rose into place and cut off the last of the sunlight from outside. When the mechanism fell silent, there was a quick, bright flicker, and the lights shifted from red to brilliant white.

The Jeep started forward again, and Elly turned to stare at Benjamin, whose eyes were bright with delight at her consternation.

"This was Cynthia's idea," he said with a chuckle. "Any traffic that comes in via the normal route is too likely to catch someone's attention. We pay our workers well, and we screen them carefully, even though they aren't privy to any information on the lower levels, but it's impossible to be certain of everyone. Black isn't beyond threatening their families. The less information we provide, the less likely they are to divulge it.

They rolled around a long, looping curve and the floor beneath them slanted downward again. This time it seemed like several minutes before Elly felt the Jeep level off. Moments later they came to what seemed to be a solid stone wall, and Pedro stopped again. He got out of the vehicle, approached the wall, and pressed a spot in the stone. When he did so, a panel flipped up. He stepped closer, leaned in, and some sort of very bright light blinked on – flashed over his eye – and then dimmed again. Pedro returned to the driver's seat, and a moment later, with a hiss of hydraulics, the wall split in two, allowing them to drive into a very large, well-lit chamber.

Elly gasped at the enormity of it. The wall closed behind them, Pedro killed the engine on the Jeep, and they sat for a moment, taking in their new surroundings. On the other side of the room there were a couple of windows leading to further rooms. A man stuck his head out of a doorway beside one window, caught sight of them, and waved. Elly heard him call out, and a group of men and women gathered, standing together and waiting.

"Shall we?" Benjamin asked.

Elly took a deep breath, and then nodded.

They met the other group halfway across the huge chamber. Foremost was a tall man with dark, disheveled hair, thick black framed glasses and a schoolboy's grin. He stepped forward enthusiastically, shaking hands with Benjamin, hugging Cynthia, and stopping in front of Elly. He reached out and she allowed him to take her hands in his, though she blushed and squirmed inwardly at the sudden attention.

"So you are Lily's granddaughter," the man said softly. He had a nice voice, deep and resonant, and he didn't have to raise it to draw the attention of those nearby. "I've heard quite a lot about you," he said, "though they didn't warn us you were so attractive."

Elly's blush deepened and she pulled her hands away. All of them laughed, then, and Benjamin spoke up.

"No time for that now," he said. "Elly, I'd like you to meet our finest field engineer, Marvin Goldblum. He's been on site here from day one. He oversaw the initial design, and supervised construction. He's been here ever since, making sure things run smoothly."

"And a dreary business it's been," Goldblum cut in. "If it weren't for occasional visits from Benjamin and his crowd, we might have believed that the outside world had ceased to exist."

"You don't go into town?" Elly asked.

"We don't go – period," a short, stocky blonde woman piped in. "We sit, and we monitor gauges. We play Pinochle and read books. Antoine," she gestured to a man on her right with long, graying hair and deep, chocolate brown eyes, "is writing a memoir, though it reads more like the romantic fantasies of a teenage boy to me."

Elly turned to Benjamin, who nodded. "It's true," he said. "We can't afford for those above to start wondering where the extra workers come from, or return to, and we can't take the chance that Black's spies will pick up on a face they know. Marvin is well known in certain scientific circles, and Anne," he pointed at the blonde woman, "is a researcher of some repute. We maintain utter secrecy here. The plan is to bring in a new crew after a few months have passed, give them a two week period to orient themselves, and get this motley crew back to civilization before they go stir crazy. This lower level is totally self-sustaining. We have food and water stored here, a fairly extensive library, computers, and research facilities."

"It's comfortable enough," Marvin conceded. "And in any case, where else in the world could we spend our time contemplating those?"

He indicated a pair of large domed metal casings. They stood about three times the height of a tall man – cylindrical on the sides and rounded at the top. Very little equipment was attached directly to the casings. Long encased tubes ran across the floor, also sealed, and disappeared through one side wall. Though there was no sound, Elly "felt" something – a vibration? A hum?

"Are those...?"

"The Bessler Generators," Cynthia affirmed, "the first two in the history of the known world to be applied to such a task. We use them at the complex, of course, but only to supplement existing systems. This is a use that Bessler himself foresaw."

The blonde woman, Anne, stepped closer to Elly and pointed at the tubes that ran into the wall.

"Those shafts conceal pistons attached to a system of gears in the wall. About halfway to the floor of the surface chamber is the coupling that allows us to either make use of the power created down here, or shift over to the Diesels upstairs.

Elly stared at the twin domes. She was slightly disappointed not to see two large, stone wheels, rolling with constant force. Benjamin caught this in her expression and chuckled ruefully.

"We'd all like to see them work," he said softly, "but it isn't safe. Those domes are rigged to blow if they are tampered with in any way. There is an emergency fallback system that will engage the diesels, and this chamber is designed with the worst possible scenario in mind. We can blow those generators into dust and all they'll feel upstairs is a slight tremor."

Elly bit her lip. The generators entranced her, but she hated the intrigue, the slipping around in shadows and worrying at every turn if they were being watched, or worse, if they were about to be attacked. She couldn't imagine how her grandmother had survived an environment like that for so many years, and still managed to build something like this. That the same responsibility now rested, at least in part, on her shoulders was both frightening and irritating at once.

She stepped out of the group and walked over to the generators. The others stood back and watched her. She moved slowly and deliberately, expecting to feel – something – through the floor, or in the air. She had envisioned Bessler's wheel in her mind, building it from the schematics and diagrams in his journals, embellishing it with her own imagination. She hadn't foreseen anything like this. She made a mental note to require Benjamin to show her one that was not sealed as soon as they returned to the complex. If there was no such wheel, she would have one built.

She placed her hand on the outer surface of the dome and her face lit with sudden surprise. She flinched, as if she would pull away, but then changed her mind and pressed her hand firmly to the metal. It wasn't so much a motion as an aura that teased her fingers. She felt as if all the hairs on her arm had stood on end, though when she glanced down, she saw this was not the case. Elly closed her eyes, and just for a moment, she felt that sensation shift through her body, tingling to the roots of her hair. She opened her eyes and stepped back.

"Amazing, isn't it?"

Marvin's voice, so close beside her, startled Elly, and she spun.

"I'm sorry," he said with a smile. "I didn't mean to sneak up on you. I wish we didn't have to keep them locked away, but every time I wish that, I think of Maxwell Black, and I change my mind. If that man, or anyone like him, ever got their hands on one of these wheels, life as we know it would be over. Battleships could roam the oceans at will, no fuel necessary to keep them moving and endless power to spin their gun turrets and their radar. They would be silent, and deadly, and I believe I would die inside if I knew I'd contributed to such a thing."

Elly stared at the man. His frank, impassioned comments, which eerily mirrored part of what she herself had just been thinking, caught her unaware. She hadn't been thinking about Black, for that one instant. She'd been thinking about the wheel, obsessed with it. Suddenly, the metal domes and the sealed shaft seemed paltry protection.

"I hadn't thought it through so far," she admitted. "I guess I have a hard time understanding a person like Mr. Black. I've lived a rather... sheltered life. The worst I've seen are irritated litigants in property disputes yelling at one another across a solicitor's desk while I took notes – that is, it was the worst I'd seen until I came into my inheritance. I've already met Mr. Black, you see, and his man Jonathan as well."

"I'd heard as much," Marvin nodded. He held out his arm, and Elly took it with a smile, allowing him to escort her back toward the group.

"Let's get the three of you settled in," Marvin said. "We spruced up three of the empty apartments. You can get cleaned up, rest a little, and then over dinner you can tell us what Black is up to, and why, exactly, you are here. Once we know what we're up against, we should be able to plan a proper welcome."

"That sounds perfect," Benjamin agreed, "but for the time being, let's get everything running on the diesels. I don't expect any real trouble, but then, that's the sort of trouble that tends to catch one by surprise, isn't it? Better we're ready ahead of time and pleasantly surprised."

Marvin nodded. He glanced at Anne, who grabbed Antoine by the shoulder and hauled him off in the direction of the control rooms. The rest of them followed Marvin through an office and into a hallway beyond. From the interior of the main chamber, this had appeared to be a solid wall, but now that they were beyond the office, Elly saw that the complex actually extended a good way beyond. There were several hallways, some leading to either side. Rooms opened off a few. One was the dining room, and Elly heard the bang and clatter of pots from within. They passed a glass fronted library, its shelves lined with books of all sorts. A young woman seated at one of the reading tables glanced up, startled, and watched as they passed.

"Not everyone knew you were coming," Marvin explained. "Even down here we maintain levels of security, all based on the old 'need to know' scenario. Trust one person too many, and it all falls down around your ears. When you live underground," he winked at Elly, "you tend to take old clichés like that more seriously."

They rounded a last corner, and Elly saw that this new passage was wider than the others. It extended what must have been the full length of the wall she'd seen from the outside, and about every twenty feet or so there was a cluster of four doors, two on each side of the passage. Marvin led them past the first cluster, and then the second. He stopped at the third set of doors. There were numeric pads outside each, and he quickly pressed a sequence of numbers on the nearest. A soft click resonated in the empty hall, and Marvin pressed the door inward.

Elly and the others stepped into a small, neat chamber. It was long and rectangular, sliced in half by a small half-wall topped by a counter. Behind the counter they saw a bed, neatly made, a dresser, and two or three shelves lined with books. The front of the room sported a small wooden table and four chairs, a TV/DVD combination with a stack of plastic movie sleeves to one side, and a small coffee maker with cups, sugar, and sealed creamers. A short refrigerator hummed softly in the corner.

"It's not the Hilton," Marvin said, "but it's home. This is your room, Elly. Benjamin will be across the hall. I've put Cynthia directly next door, because the two rooms share a bathroom. If you don't need anything else immediately, I'll leave you two ladies to sort out who showers first, and to get some rest.

"One more thing," he said, turning before he stepped out the door, "These locks are programmable. Right now they are set to 123456 for simplicity. I recommend you take a moment and change them now. While the door is open, just press this button – the one that says 'set' – and punch in any six digit sequence you like. We never expect to have any trouble down here – certainly none of us would invade your privacy, but again – it never hurts to be ready."

Elly stepped over to the lock and examined it while Cynthia disappeared out into the hall and opened her own room. Elly frowned at the lock and tried to think. She had no idea what numbers to use, never having had to choose a security code, and the inability to bring anything to mind frustrated her. It was such a simple thing.

Finally, more out of irritation than any real fear of a need for secrecy, she pressed and held the 'set' button and punched the original code sequence in reverse, starting with six and counting back to three. A sudden, impetuous urge made her shift the one and the two so that the number was slightly more complex. She released the set button, stepped into the hall, closed the door and punched in the new code. The mechanism operated flawlessly, and she grinned at it as if great things had been accomplished.

Just then, the bathroom door swung open, and Cynthia poked her head through.

"I need to check a couple of things with Benjamin before I settle," Cynthia said. "If you want to use the shower first, I'll be back in about twenty minutes."

"That's fine," Elly agreed. She stepped back into her small apartment and closed the door. Cynthia offered a mock salute and disappeared though to the adjoining room.

Elly saw that somehow in the few moments between meeting Marvin and the others, her bags had been spirited off to this room. She found clean clothes, checked the shower, which was fully stocked with shampoos and soaps, and stripped quickly. She'd sweated more than was usual, and the jungle clothing was rougher than she was used to. She stepped under the hot, stinging jets of water and closed the door to the shower, luxuriating in the warmth. She took as much of her twenty minutes as possible, toweled herself dry, and returned to her room, closing the door after her.

She intended to take Marvin's advice and get some rest,

though the days' activity, and the things she'd learned on the flight made her want to get back to the journals. She'd left the classified documents behind, but she'd brought one; Bessler's account of his life. She had no intention of leaving that story at the point she'd reached in her earlier reading. She didn't believe in cliff hangers, and she hadn't yet reached the part in the story where he actually built a working wheel.

Despite the evidence in the complex in New York, and the presence of the two domed structures within a short walk's distance of her, she still couldn't quite bring herself to believe the devices were real. She remembered her lessons in physics and mathematics, and tossing those years of education aside, even faced with something as wondrous as Bessler's wheel, wasn't something she could do lightly.

In the end, despite her efforts to keep her eyelids up, fatigue took over. She lay back on the bed, wrapped a warm cotton blanket around herself, and drifted off to dreams of bouncing Jeeps, huge, deep-green leaves, and the cold, snake eyes of Maxwell Black.

FOURTEEN

In Pompano the Jeep carrying Edgar, Phoebe and Jennifer was picked up by Black's spotters the moment it edged out of the jungle. The three figures kept low in the back seat, exposing their features only when necessary, and at first the sentries were fooled.

"They have arrived," the leader said, holding the radio transceiver as he watched over the windshield of his own vehicle. They were parked in a deserted alley, half-concealed behind a broken down cart and drenched in shadows. The alley gave a clear view of the road leading in from the air strip, and only a minor shift allowed an equally good view of the one relatively nice hotel Pompano boasted. The Jeep pulled up in front of the place, but only the driver climbed out.

The man disappeared into the front of the hotel, and Black's man hesitated. He could see no reason why the entire party wouldn't disembark to book their rooms, but he didn't want to seem overeager in his reports. Black was a good leader – from a distance. The closer the man came, the less comfortable association with him became. This would be a poor time to be deemed unworthy.

The driver reappeared, slipped into the driver's seat, and pulled back into the street. An access road circled the hotel, and he turned into this. There was parking in the rear, and easier access to certain of the rooms, but less light. The deepening twilight made it difficult to keep the group in sight from a distance. They had assumed that, bringing the Kassel girl to Pompano for the first time, only the best suites would be adequate, and these were in front. The sentry cursed.

"They are pulling around to the rear of the hotel," he reported. He waited, and the radio crackled softly. He nodded once, then clipped the radio back on his belt and tapped his driver on the shoulder. He leaned close, whispered his orders, and the driver pulled out slowly. Glancing both ways to be sure they were not spotted, the two turned left and made the sharp jog to the right, following the other Jeep toward the rear of the hotel.

No one noticed their passing.

Outside of town Maxwell Black jounced and rattled about, standing on the passenger side of a second Jeep and staring ahead through the swaying leaves and shimmering heat. Visibility lessened with each passing mile as the daylight gave way to early evening. They weren't far behind the sentry, and he wanted to get there before Wright could pull some new trick, or give him the slip. His patience was nearly exhausted by the heat and the constant droning buzz of insects.

Black didn't mind trouble – lived for it, in fact – but he hated the jungle. He hated anything that caused him physical discomfort or that interfered with the luxury he felt he had earned. He'd spent his time in jungles, and he'd come through it with a taste for soft leather and warm brandy. Every moment he remained in Pompano increased his desire to be somewhere else – anywhere else.

The Jeep hit a particularly large pothole and his head smacked hard into the Jeep's roll bar. Cursing, he dropped into his seat. He half-turned toward the driver's seat, where Jonathan sat, grim and concentrated on the road, and then thought better of it. It wasn't the driver's fault the road was rough, and they were in a hurry.

Moments later they began to catch light through the thinning trees and brush. They rolled out of the jungle, and Jonathan downshifted, sending up a huge cloud of dust. He cursed softly and rolled ahead more slowly. They didn't want to roar into town and draw unwanted attention to themselves, but now they had to worry that the dust would serve the same purpose. The growing shadows should cover it, but there was no room for chance. If the three in the hotel were watching, they'd just been spotted.

The radio crackled. Jonathan, who was wearing a headset to block the noise from the Jeep's engine, nodded once, grabbed the microphone and spoke into it quickly. He turned to Black.

"Hernandez is in position. They are in rooms on the third floor. Their vehicle is parked in the rear."

"Have him send someone around front until we get there," Black snapped. "They could be planning to ditch the Jeep and sneak out the front. If they've seen him, they'll try and give him the slip."

Jonathan nodded and returned to the radio, then to his driving. They curved in at the near end of the small town and rolled slowly past squat buildings. There were animals in the streets, some chickens and one goat. Few people were about – the heat of the afternoon hadn't faded, and the air was thick and muggy. The town didn't come to life until the cooler night air had time to leech the warmth from the roads and sidewalks. Black knew they would appear like swarming vermin once the sun was completely gone. He wanted to be long gone by then. The time for intrigue and long drawn out mind games had departed about a dozen mosquitoes in his past.

They drove past the hotel once. Jonathan spoke to Hernandez on the radio and verified that their quarry had not departed the building. They circled back and turned into the drive leading behind the hotel and disappeared from the street.

"They're here," Phoebe announced. She stood just to the left of tall, curtained windows, glancing out over the winding drive that led to the rear of the building. "Black and his man just pulled in."

"That makes four in all," Jennifer said. "Do you think the drivers will come?"

"Jonathan might," Edgar replied. "He and Black work as a unit; they'll be more comfortable that way. He may split the others, though, leave one in each Jeep. Depends on who they are, and how cocky he is."

"You think they know we've spotted them?" Phoebe asked.

"Probably," Edgar said. "My guess is that they'll assume it, even if they don't know. Our advantage is that they won't expect us to stand and fight. They probably think we're planning some secret escape out the front, or a side door. All hell is going to break loose when they realize they've cornered the wrong prey."

Faces grim, they waited. Each of the three held their weapons ready. It was going to be difficult to explain a fire fight to the hotel, and to the local authorities, but when it came down to it, they would have less trouble explaining than Black would - they all lived locally, he was the stranger.

Black's Jeep pulled in beside the other, poorly concealed near the rear of the parking lot at the back of the Hotel. Black jumped down, walked to the driver of the second vehicle, exchanged a few words, and then turned to stare up at the very window through which they watched him. Phoebe pulled back around the corner of the sill instinctively, as if he could see right through the curtain and into her mind.

"Christ," she said softly, "that guy gives me the creeps."

"Don't let him spook you," Edgar advised. "He's just a man."

Phoebe glanced around the corner, and stiffened.

"They're on the move. Only two of them are coming. But..."

She hesitated, and before she could say whatever it was she'd intended to say, there was a loud pop from the rear of the building.

"Get down!" Phoebe cried, diving to the floor as the glass of the window shattered inward. She rolled to the left, out of sight, but before any of them had gathered their wits, a loud hiss filled the room.

"Gas!" Jennifer screamed. She moved to try and cover the canister with the bedspread, but her knees buckled before she was halfway there. Edgar, keeping his mouth closed, charged the door, hoping to catch Black and Jonathan in the open, but he faltered, and as he hit the door, fumbling for the knob, he glanced back at the two girls. He managed to form the single word "Sorry" on his lips before he tilted to the side, staggered, and fell heavily into the wall. By the time Black and Jonathan reached the door, the room's three occupants were out cold.

Black stepped in, his gas mask already in place, and took in the situation quickly. When he got a good look at Edgar's face, he cursed.

"It's not them," he snapped. He turned, and was halfway back out the door when he stopped. Jonathan watched, waiting for instructions.

"The small one, get her," Black said harshly. The two of them dragged over the bedspread, already half-draped across the floor, and wrapped it quickly around Jennifer's still form. When she was concealed, Jonathan lifted her easily, tossing her over one shoulder like a sack of grain, or a roofer with a square of shingles.

Without hesitation the two slipped back out the door, closed it behind them and took the stairs at a jog. There was still no one in sight, but the broken window would probably draw some attention before long. They crossed the parking lot, and as they did so, Jonathan lowered Jennifer's unconscious form to his side, carrying her like a carpet and shielding her from the hotel with his body as well as he could.

Moments later they slid her carefully onto the back seat of one Jeep, and both vehicles started off around the building. The rear door of the hotel opened, and two men hurried out. One appeared to be a baggage handler, or a maintenance man. The other wore a pale cotton suit, and though his hair was slightly disheveled, as if he'd just woken up, Black figured he must be the manager.

As the Jeeps rolled slowly past the rear corner of the building, the manager turned and stared at them, suspicious. Instead of speeding up, Black motioned for Jonathan to idle slower. He stood and waved back in the way they'd come.

"Back there!" he called out. "Two men with guns. They shot out a window and ran."

The man turned toward where Black pointed, then spun and shot rapid-fire words in Spanish to the maintenance man, who took off inside at a run.

"Gracias," the man called, waving to Black, who was no more than a shadow against the growing night. The man saluted and sat back down. Jonathan drove out the looping drive and onto the main road, heading back in the direction of the jungle and keeping his speed down as long as they were in sight. No one followed.

Black spun and lifted Jennifer's limp form, unrolling her roughly onto the back seat. She didn't even moan. He checked her pulse, found it strong, if a bit slow, and fished behind the seat for a length of rope. Once he had her hands securely tied behind her back, he ignored her, turning back to face the jungle.

"To the camp?" Jonathan asked.

"No, take us straight to their complex," Black replied. "I want them to see what we have here," he reached back to pat Jennifer's arm. "It will give them something to think about when the time comes to negotiate."

"We're negotiating?" Jonathan asked, surprised.

"No, but they don't know that. We'll do whatever we can to get them to let us in without a fight before we resort to more force. Our presence here is a lot more tenuous than theirs is, and we don't have a lot of friends in local government. We can bribe some of them, but not all, so we have to watch our step."

Jonathan nodded and turned down the road toward the flooded caves and the pump complex. They rode down the shadowed road in silence, punctuated by the roar of the Jeep's engine, and the high, keening cries of jungle birds.

The hotel manager shook Edgar nervously. It was impossible to tell how badly he and the woman might be hurt. Footsteps sounded on the stairs outside, and the maintenance man, out of breath and wild eyed, entered the room. He stared at the bodies passed out on the floor and the shards of broken glass from the windows in shock.

"Give it to me," the manager said. His eyes flashed his impatience, and the other man stepped sheepishly forward, extending his hand. He held a small bottle of smelling salts, and the manager took it, quickly untwisting the top and holding it under Edgar's nose.

Edgar snorted, rolled to the side and away. His eyes snapped open and he stared at the man huddled over him. Instinctively, Edgar lashed out with the palms of both hands, pushing the manager back.

"Wait," the smaller man cried.

Edgar was on his feet in seconds, staring about the room

and trying to reorient his senses.   He saw the maintenance man, cowering against the wall. He caught sight of Phoebe, still on the floor beneath the window, surrounded by the broken glass. There was no blood.

The manager was on his feet again, and Edgar spun on him. Then, as his mind cleared, he shook his head and took a step back.

"Christ," he said at last. He searched the room frantically, but there was no sign of Jennifer.

"What time is it?" he asked the manager.

The man glared at him indignantly. "What has happened here, Senor? There is much damage – the window is ruined, I..."

Edgar grabbed the man by the lapels of his jacket and hauled him up to until only the tips of his toes brushed the ground.

"What time is it?" he repeated. The man grunted in surprise, then glanced at his wrist. Edgar beat him to it. He glanced at the wristwatch, saw that only about ten minutes had passed, and let the man go.

He pointed at Phoebe.

"Take care of her. She may need a doctor."

"But..."

Edgar grabbed his bag from the small table and was out the door before the manager finished his thought. He took the steps as quickly as he could, dizzy and disoriented, and loped across the parking lot to their Jeep. He didn't know where their driver had gone, probably for a drink, or some rest. It didn't matter. What he needed was the radio, and he needed it quickly.

He reached the jeep, grabbed the transceiver, and flipped to the emergency channel. The dial remained dark when he toggled the power switch. Nothing. Frowning, he worked the controls, turning any knob he could find, but getting the same result. It was dead. He turned and noticed that, though lowered, the hood wasn't fully latched. He yanked it up, stared inside, and cursed loudly.

The battery and carburetor had both been smashed, probably just before the gas had been shot into their room. He felt helpless, frustrated, and more than a little foolish for being taken in so quickly and completely.

He headed back to the Hotel at a run, slipped in the back door and took the hallway to the main lobby. He found the payphone, lifted the receiver and dug into his pocket frantically. He pulled out a handful of change and started feeding it into the coin slot. At last he got an operator, who put him through to the airport. As he waited for the line to connect, he cursed himself over and over. Behind him he heard the manager and the maintenance man, and he knew he had only a couple of minutes before he'd be forced to confront them and answer questions.

Finally, Raoul picked up. Edgar wasted no words.

"Black took Jennifer," he said tersely. "They destroyed our Jeep, and our radio. Warn Benjamin...Black is coming."

"I understand, "Raoul said briskly.

The phone went dead and Edgar slumped against it, replacing the handset. Then, resignedly, he turned to face the irate manager. He heard a siren, and wondered if it was an ambulance for Phoebe, or police for him. It didn't matter. All that mattered was that he'd failed, and now everything rested on his cousin and Lily's granddaughter. He hoped his warning arrived in time, and that they were able to do something. He thought of Jennifer, and then of Maxwell Black.

Then he glanced at the manager, tried a half-hearted smile, and said, "I need a Jeep."

FIFTEEN

Elly woke suddenly. Something was buzzing and she couldn't place it. Then, rising to one elbow, she saw the room, remembered where she was, and oriented herself. The buzzing was her door. She rose from the bed and stepped across the room to open it.

Anne, the blonde woman, stood outside holding a tray. The tray was covered in dishes with steam rising from each, cups, glasses and silverware tucked in neatly beside the food.

"I thought we were eating in the dining room?" Elly said, letting the woman enter.

Anne placed the tray on the one small table and turned quickly. Her features were drawn into tight lines of worry, and her expression was tense.

"There's been a problem," she said softly. "Benjamin and Cynthia went with two of our people to investigate. Someone is at the main gate, and we have a message from Raoul."

"A problem?" Elly repeated. "What kind of problem? I didn't think Raoul would contact us here...isn't that dangerous for him?"

Anne nodded. "It is not common that we hear from him directly. We have people in and out all the time, of course – deliveries, supplies, and reports flow in and out of the complex daily. This was different, though. It was a short broadcast on a secure frequency. Very little information was passed."

"But enough to make Benjamin rush out to see what was wrong," Elly said. She frowned at the food.

"I should have been informed," she said. "I know I'm new to all of you, and I know Benjamin is likely trying to protect me, but that is irrelevant. I inherited everything from my grandmother, and if part of that inheritance is danger, that's mine too.

"What am I supposed to do, just sit here and eat and pretend like nothing has happened?"

Anne blushed, and Elly put a hand on the woman's shoulder.

"It's not your fault," Elly said. "I know that. I just wish I could get through to them that I didn't' come here to stand around and watch. If there is something – anything – that I can be doing, I want to do it."

"Of course," Anne replied. "Eat this," she indicated the tray, "and I'll go check to see if there's been any report of progress. I'll come straight back here, and when you are done, I'll take you to the control center. We can monitor what happens upstairs through the security system."

Elly nodded. "That sounds reasonable," she said. Her stomach rumbled, reminding her that it had been several hours since she'd eaten. She sat down and lifted the covers from the plates, reaching for the fork. She was halfway through a large chunk of steak and reaching for a drink before Anne was fully out the door. The food was delicious, and she'd have loved to enjoy it, but she couldn't quit thinking about Maxwell Black. If he was out there somewhere, looking for her, then she needed to be part of whatever they did to stop him. She'd been in the man's power once, and she never intended to repeat the experience.

By the time Jonathan pulled the Jeep to the edge of the tree line and shifted to neutral, Jennifer had reached a groggy, half-consciousness in the back seat of the Jeep. Her head ached horribly, and her throat felt as if someone had poured sand through a funnel until it was full. She wasn't gagged, but when she opened her mouth to speak, her lips stuck together and separated with a soft pop, and despite her efforts to moisten them with her tongue, she was unable to make a coherent sound.

She moaned, and Black turned, just for a moment, watching her. She saw the movement as a blur, caught the ice-chips of his eyes, and closed her own. She knew she was in trouble, and the binding at her wrist told her it was deep. That was enough to silence any further attempts at speech, for the moment. If whoever was in the front of the Jeep believed she was unconscious, or too weak to put up any kind of struggle, they might make a mistake. She took advantage of the momentary stillness to slide back a little on the seat and slowly flex the muscles in her arms and legs. This brought more pain, but the pain helped her focus her thoughts.

"Do you think they've spotted us yet?" the driver spoke first. His voice was low, filled with a quiet, controlled menace.

"They knew we were coming before we made it halfway," was the response. Something in that voice itched at Jennifer's mind. She closed her eyes, and memories of Phoebe and Edgar flashed through her mind. She remembered Phoebe, standing at the window and looking out over the parking lot, remembered Edgar's warning that they should be ready ... and then Phoebe screaming at her to get down.

Where were the others? Had they been harmed? She knew it had to be Black and one of the others who'd accompanied him. No one else would have the audacity to launch such an attack in a foreign country in broad daylight. She hoped there hadn't been time to do anything other than grab her and be gone. If Edgar wasn't hurt, and he was out there, then she had a chance.

She tried opening her eyes slowly. At first all she could make out was the back of the seats. She needed to shift if she was going to figure out where they were, but she couldn't do that without giving herself away and drawing their attention. She caught the heavy scent of the jungle, and a couple of quick glimpses up through the windshield showed only a dark, cloudless sky. A clearing, then, she thought. Either they'd taken her to their own camp, or to some other place where the road ended. That didn't leave too many choices near Pompano.

"Move closer," Black said. "It's dark out here, and I want to get in close enough that we can show them what we have, just in case they aren't aware. We aren't going to try and get in with only two of us here, but I want them to know what's at risk. Then we'll let them simmer a while."

The Jeep rolled forward slowly, bumping and bouncing, and Jennifer gritted her teeth against the pain that shot up her arms and into her shoulders. If she cried out, they would know she was listening. They'd know soon enough anyway, but anything she could keep from them might work in her favor. She needed to find out where they were, and where they were taking her.

She tested the rope binding her wrists, but her fingers were weak from low circulation, and the knots were sound. She wasn't going to free herself, at least not quickly enough to make a difference.

"There," the driver said. He ground to a sudden stop and flung Jennifer forward. She tumbled half off the seat and cried out in dismay. Black turned like a snake and grinned at her, flipping her back onto the seat easily with one hand.

"So, you've rejoined the living," he said.

He turned away and stared off in the direction his driver pointed, squinting into the gloom. After a moment, he grunted.

"Yes, that's them," he said. He stood in the seat of the Jeep then, and waved.

"What if they shoot?" the driver wondered.

"They won't," Black assured him. "You would, and I would, because it would be the wise thing to do, but they aren't ruled by wisdom. They have their scruples, and their morals – it handicaps them every time."

No shot was fired, and Black turned to Jennifer again.

"Sit up," he commanded.

Jennifer didn't move, and he was on her like a snake. He gripped her hair so tightly it felt like the skin would separate from her skull and lifted her face off the seat. His lips brushed her ear as he spoke again.

"Sit up now, or I will haul you up by your hair. I am strong enough to do it, I assure you and tall enough to keep you on your toes. It isn't necessary if you slide up onto that seat and sit pretty. Do you understand me?"

She couldn't breathe or speak, and her silence infuriated him. He shook her by the grip in her hair and she gasped.

"Yes," she said. "Okay."

Clumsily, still shaky and weak, she turned and let her feet drop to the floorboard. Her vision spun crazily as vertigo took hold, and the tingling, searing pain where Black still gripped her hair stole her concentration.

"Stand up," he commanded.

She tried. She pushed on the floor with her feet, and leaned forward, trying to win her balance, but she had no strength in her legs, and she tumbled forward. He held her easily, placing his free hand beneath her chin and drawing her up until she stood on her toes, dangling from his grip in her hair and supported by his palm under her chin.

Hot tears spilled down her cheeks, but she bit her lip to keep from crying out. It hurt like hell, but she wasn't going to give him the satisfaction of knowing it.

Black paid no attention to her struggles. He turned back toward the front of the Jeep. Jennifer blinked and shook her head, trying to clear her vision. Finally, a blurry image coalesced in the dim twilight, shimmering silver through her tears. It was the pump station. She saw the tall fence, the squat building, and she squirmed in his grip. If Black planned to use her to get in there he wasn't going to do it without a fight.

He shook her and her eyes stung with instant, salty tears. She gave a soft cry, and with a last shake, he flung her down into the back seat. Her arms collided with the back of the seat, bending them back painfully and she cried out again, but he paid no attention to her. Stunned, Jennifer toppled to her right, landed on her side on the seat, and lay very still, unable even to breathe at first. She heard the two men talking, but her ears were ringing, and she couldn't make out the words. She heard the Jeep's engine roar and nearly fell to the floor again as it was shifted into reverse. They backed, spun, and tore off back into the jungle.

As the fog in her brain cleared slightly, Jennifer noticed that something was different. At first she couldn't wrap her mind around it, but gradually she realized that her hands were much more loosely bound. The rough treatment, and the fall to the seat had stretched the knot. She worked her wrists back and forth, the rope chaffing her skin and her hands numb, and began to very slowly inch her way out of the bonds. She didn't know where they were taking her, but if she could help it, they wouldn't be keeping her there. She knew the jungles, all she needed was a couple of free moments to get to her feet and be gone.

It was dark, but the moon provided enough light to run by. Somewhere out there she knew that Edgar could be looking for her, probably frantic with fear. She hoped she'd find a way to him before all hell broke loose. She hoped he was still alive.

Elly leaned over Anne's shoulder and stared intently into a security monitor. They saw the Jeep whirl and speed back into the jungle, and Elly pounded the top of Anne's chair in frustration.

"That was Jennifer," she said. "I'm certain of it. If I hadn't known better, I'd have thought it was me. And that was Maxwell Black who had her by the hair. Why didn't Benjamin stop them? Where are they?"

Anne turned and rose, flipping off the monitor.

"They'll be here any second." She turned to a panel of colored lights. They were color coded like a stop light, red, yellow, and green. Two that had been green went to yellow, then to red, and then flashed back to green.

"That's them now," Anne said. "These lights indicate whether the entrances and exits are secure. That row," she indicated the lights that had just shifted color, "is for the internal lift. When it's green, it's sealed from sight. When it's yellow it's being accessed, and when it's red, the doors are open. Now it's green again – that means they have sealed the wall behind themselves and are on the way down."

Elly nodded distractedly. She'd already turned away and was pacing up and down the room. The thrill had gone out of this adventure, and she couldn't clear the image of Jennifer, dangling from Black's clenched fist, from her mind.

There was an excited babble of voices, and footsteps sounded in the hall. She spun and yanked the door open before a startled Benjamin could get his hand wrapped around the handle.

"Why didn't you help her?" she said. Her eyes blazed, and Benjamin actually took a step back, bewildered, before the others crowded in behind him and glanced over his shoulder to see what prevented his entrance.

"Why didn't you go out there and get her from him?" Elly insisted. "You drove miles and miles to save me from that same man, and you just let him haul her around by her hair and drive away."

"We couldn't breach security to..." The words died on Marvin's lips as Elly spun on him.

"No security is worth that girl's life," she said hotly. "Not worth any of your lives, or mine. What are we doing here, trying to help the world, or to become another part of the problem?"

Another question occurred to her and she turned back to Benjamin. "Where are the others? Edgar? Phoebe? Does he have them all?"

Benjamin took her firmly by her shoulders and pushed her gently aside so they could all enter the room.

"No," he said softly, "they are fine. Edgar is the one who called Raoul, and Raoul warned us they would come here."

"You knew they had taken her, and that she was coming, but you didn't even think it was important enough to wake me up?" she asked incredulously. "Did I miss something, or did my grandmother not leave this to me? I thought I made it clear that I came here to be part of this – to learn, yes, but because I need to understand what I've gotten into. The more I understand of it, the less I like it. We are supposed to be the good guys."

"They won't harm her, Elly," Cynthia said, stepping around Benjamin. Her face was grim, but she was in control, and Elly – not wanting to appear less adult or mature – held her tongue.

"Edgar is out there now, and Phoebe. They have others with them. Unless they search her very carefully, and soon, he'll find her. They are more familiar with the area, and they know what to look for. Jennifer wears a small homing device, very well hidden. Once they track her down, they'll find a way to get her out of there safely, if one exists. All that would have happened if we rushed out there was that we'd have been vulnerable, and they would have turned tail and run. If we compromise our own security, then word will leak to the government, and not only our people, but the entire project will be in danger."

"So what can we do?" Elly asked, unwilling to let it drop.

"We fortify this place," Benjamin said, "and prepare for

every eventuality we can imagine. The worst case scenario is that we evacuate this lower level and blow the generators. The diesels will continue to operate the pumps, and the secrets will be safely beyond Black's grasp. We're going to have to dismantle anyway, now that he knows we are here."

Elly's head pounded. She'd only just seen this place, the amazing technology, the excited group who ran it, and now they were going to have to shut it down because a small-minded man with no soul wanted the secret for his own. It was too much to take in all at once, and she backed away from Benjamin, coming into contact almost immediately with one of the chairs and falling into it heavily.

"How long will it take?" she asked. "And what about the workers in the caves? Will they be safe without our support? I know you said the diesels can handle operating the pumps, but what if the diesels fail?"

"We'll bring in more," Benjamin assured her. "For now, they'll be fine. We'll contact the local government and arrange to move in two more diesels as a safety backup procedure. If it gets out of hand, we'll bring the Bessler Generators back on line and take the consequences."

Elly remained unconvinced. No matter what they did, things were going to be worse in a few hours than they had been the same number of hours in the past, and she found it unacceptable.

Before she could say anything further, there was a loud beep from a corner of the room, and Marvin hurried over to a dark computer monitor. He shifted the mouse to bring it to life and quickly typed in his credentials. The screen flashed white with text across the face, and he read intently. When he turned back, he was smiling.

"Edgar has picked up her signal," he said. "They are tracking her now, keeping well back and as quiet as possible. We can't risk too many of these satellite messages – don't want to alert anyone – but he'll check in every hour."

"All we can do, then," Benjamin said with a sigh, "is to wait."

Elly stood and headed for the door. She didn't look at any of them, and she didn't trust herself to speak at first. When she reached the hallway, she turned back and glared at them, one at a time.

"We are going to get her back without anyone getting hurt," she said with quiet authority. "We are going to find a way to take care of Maxwell Black so that we can keep this plant running and the people in those caves safe. I will be in my room. The minute we know anything, I want to be informed."

Without waiting for an answer, she turned and walked away. By the time she reached her door, she was shaking, not sure where the burst of anger had come from, or if she could sustain it for any length of time. It took three attempts to get the security code right on her door, despite its simplicity. Once inside, she went to her bed and sat, staring about herself in frustration. She wanted to help – to do something, but there was nothing, and she knew it.

Her bags caught her eye, and she rose, retrieving the journal. She went to the refrigerator, saw that it was well stocked with drinks, and chose a cold can of beer. She felt as though she needed it to calm her nerves, and the first sip was both refreshing, and calming.

With no other way to spend the time, she sat back, flipped open Johann Bessler's journal, and began to read. She thought of deep green jungles, and Maxwell Black, but soon the neat, even letters of the journal dragged her away into rushing water, screaming horses, and endlessly spinning wheels.

SIXTEEN

The swirling current canted the carriage over on one side as it slid downstream, then, possibly from the frantically screaming horses finding momentary footing, it swung back and rushed straight ahead. The image of the horses' manes with waves crashing over their backs and spray sparkling in the sunlight was surreal.

Frederic clung to the reins and drove his feet into the boards at his feet, pressing himself tightly in place against the front of the carriage. He couldn't afford to be tossed free – he was the only hope of regaining control. He heard Johann behind him, crying out in fear, and then shouting something. He couldn't catch the words, and it wouldn't have mattered if he could. There was nothing he could do but cling tightly and pray.

The hill where they'd sat what seemed only seconds before disappeared as they were swept around a bend in the river. Rocks and fallen trees jutted from the water here and there, water rushing over and around them at terrifying speed. One of the horses screamed, and then another. They were keeping their heads above the water but barely. The carriage itself had settled lower and grew heavier with each passing second.

Then, just as Frederic was certain they would drop too low, that the water was too deep and they would be swept under and drowned, the wheels struck the river bed beneath them with a sliding, grinding lurch. The horses were slowed, pulled up short by the sudden weight behind. After a moment's panic, their hooves met the riverbed as the carriage wheels had done.

The rushing current threatened to spin them again, and Frederic cursed. Johann leaned out the window behind him, screaming into the roar of the water and fighting to be heard over the terrified horses.

"At an angle," he cried. "Don't try to turn them to the shore; we'll be overturned in the current. Use the current to push from behind and try to get them to climb out at an angle."

Frederic understood immediately what Johann was telling him, and it made sense. He gripped the reins tightly and pulled, leaning to his left as he did so. The horses fought him. They stumbled as he applied pressure, uncertain whether to ignore him and continue to fight the river, or to be directed. The water momentarily grew shallow, and their shoulders rose above it. They tried to break for shore, but Frederic hung on grimly, keeping them angling slowly and preventing the sure disaster of a quick turn.

He spotted a break in the brush ahead, and he aimed for it. When it seemed they might slide on past, he took a risk and pulled harder on the left rein, angling them a bit more steeply into the bank. The horses scrambled. He saw one up, and then down on its knees...then up again. They lunged, and the carriage canted to the right, shuddering as if the water might pound the wood and metal frame to powder. The carriage shuddered, and then rolled forward. The wheels dug deep into the mud of the bank, and for a moment the horses foundered, but their terror carried them on, and up, and out, and with a last bouncing shiver the carriage broke free of the mud and rolled up over the bank.

Frederic clenched his teeth and shook the reins, and the horses pulled. The bank wasn't particularly steep, but there was no road beneath their wheels, and the vehicle was soaked with heavy river water and caked in clinging mud. They moved up, inch by inch. The carriage shook, and Frederic saw Bessler drop to the ground and move behind to push. He didn't know what help it would be, but there was no time to argue. He only hoped the horses would not fail, allowing them to slide back to the river and burying Bessler beneath the weight.

As suddenly as it began, it was over. At the top of the short slope, the riverbank leveled, and a few hundred yards away Frederic saw a worn path running parallel to the water. He pulled the horses up short, and they stood, blowing and snorting, stamping their feet in nervous fear, and trembling. The carriage stopped and a moment later Bessler appeared around the side, eyes wide and hair flowing wildly about his face.

"My god," he said simply. "My god, we are alive."

Johann fell heavily against the side of the carriage. There were muffled sounds from within, and moments later the door opened again. Rosina stumbled out, turning barely in time to grab Barbara's hand as she stepped free of the carriage and nearly slipped in the slick mud. Johann gasped and staggered around to help. He and Rosina helped Barbara away from the carriage and to a large stone, where she sat and leaned back.

Frederic calmed himself, and then forced the reluctant horses to pull the carriage a bit more, tucking it in beneath a small grove of trees beside the road. He climbed down and went to them, calming each, whispering in their ears and rubbing their muzzles. Johann watched from where he knelt beside Barbara, holding her hand. He was amazed at how the animals reacted to the younger man's ministrations, and made mental notes to question the driver when they arrived at their destination and learn what he could.

No one spoke beyond the whispering of the driver to his horses. No one approached down the stretch of the road. The sun continued across the afternoon sky, and they sat, drying their feet, the mud drying on the flanks of the horses and the sides of the carriage.

Frederic retrieved a pan from the carriage and climbed down to the water. When he returned, he began rubbing down the animals, washing away the mud as well as he could, brushing and soothing them. He fed them and brought water for them to drink, and eventually Johann joined in the work. The two women remained seated in the sun, gratefully accepting a drink when Johann brought it to them, but seemingly unable to rise.

Finally, Rosina wobbled to her feet.

"I will fix food," she said.

Barbara, pale, frightened, and looking weak again, only nodded. Rosina built a small fire a little way into the trees. She gathered wood, staying carefully away from the side of the road closest to the river. When she had the fire going, she unpacked more of the pans and some of the dried food they'd carried. They hadn't intended to spend the night on the road, so they had little with which to prepare a meal, but she did what she could.

She made tea, spread jam on slices of hard bread, and fried salted pork into crisp strips of bacon. The scent of the cooking meat drew Barbara to her feet, and after a couple of wobbling steps, Johann caught her arm and helped her across the road. She stood, staring ruefully at the filthy, nearly ruined carriage.

"I wouldn't want to be the one to explain this to Father," she said.

Frederic glanced over at her and grinned.

"I'm sure he'll willingly trade his carriage for his daughter's life," the driver said. "It's a miracle we're standing here talking about it. If Johann hadn't directed me to angle up that slope, we'd be a sight wetter and less well off, I think."

"It was nothing," Johann said, waving his hand. "It was you who drove the horses up and out of the water, and you who calmed them once we were safe. I owe you a great debt, and eventually the opportunity will come when I can repay it."

They fell silent again until Rosina turned and called to them.

"There is tea," she said, "and bacon. We should all eat, and then we must rest."

"Yes," Johann said, taking Barbara's arm and helping her nearer to the fire. "We will rest for a while, and then get on the road. This trail must lead to the main road, and we cannot be so far from Gesa. Once we arrive, we will get the horses tended to, and Frederic and I will see about repairing the carriage. We won't send it back in this condition, and we will all need a few days rest before anyone attempts the return journey."

"They will be worried," Frederic protested.

"They will worry, yes," Johann replied, "but they will wait. Dr. Schumann cannot afford to search too long or too hard for you. He will tell a story that explains your answer, and he will wait. To do otherwise would be to show that he knew of our departure, and that he condoned it, and he has gone to a great deal of trouble to avoid that circumstance. In any case, there is no other option. This carriage may get us to Gesa, but you cannot drive it all the way back in this condition."

Frederic stared at the carriage a long moment, and then nodded. "You are right," he admitted. "It would be dangerous, and far too difficult for the horses, to which we owe our lives."

"It is settled then," Johann said with a smile.

The four of them drank their tea I silence, and when they had eaten what there was the two women retired to the carriage and made what sleeping arrangements they could. Frederic and Johann unhitched the horses and tied them off where they could rest and graze, and then settled in to the driver's seat and the small sleeping compartment behind it, which the driver relinquished cheerfully.

The night passed in quiet silence. The heavens did not open to rain on them, and when Johann awoke, he found that Frederic had risen early and was ready to hitch the animals and be on the road. They stirred the coals of the fire, shared tea, and were off on the road to Gesa.

Johann's cousin received them warmly. He had a spare room, where Johann and Barbara were made at home. There was space for Rosina in separate servant's quarters, and Frederic, for the few days he was in town, bedded down in the stable with the carriage and the horses, which he tended with studious care. Johann assisted with this work, despite Frederic's protestations that he could manage, and before long the carriage looked not only as good as it had on the day of departure from Dr. Schumann's residence, but better. It was polished and painted, all traces of the near disaster in the river patched and repaired, and soon the day came when the driver proclaimed it ready for the return journey.

Johann would have held him a few days longer, but he knew the young man was worried over what his employer would think and do over his absence, and eager to be on the road. Barbra wrote a long letter to her father that Frederic promised to deliver personally, or destroy if he were detained, and Rosina, surprising even herself, leaned up on her toes to kiss his cheek before he climbed up into the driver's seat.

"Be well," Johann said, shaking Frederic's hand. "Give my regards to the good Doctor."

"I will," Frederic replied. He smiled at Barbara fondly and patted his jacket where he had tucked her letter into an inside pocket. "The weather looks good, and if I can make the crossing early enough, I should be home by this evening."

"Go with God," Barbara said softly.

Then he was gone, and Johann, his bride, and Rosina turned to thoughts of Gesa, their new home, and to the work and days to come.

Johann's cousin was a generous man, but his home was not large. Johann missed his large, airy workshop and determined that before he could set about his great work, he would need a suitable space in which to complete it. While Barbara completed her recovery, he wandered Gesa, speaking with merchants, making contacts and renewing old acquaintances. Eventually, he came to the baker, and he found what he needed.

On the edge of town, not far from his cousin's home, there was a vacant house. It had belonged to the baker's parents, and they had passed on during the winter, leaving the home vacant. Gesa wasn't a large town, and there was little market for a place so old and small. Johann went with the baker to look at the place, and was pleased.

It was a single large room with only a small kitchen and a bed chamber carved from the open space. As a home, it left a lot to be desired, but as a workspace much of the work a more modern home would have presented to him wasn't necessary. He paid the first two months rent from the money he'd gotten from Dr. Schumann, and within only a few hours he had managed to find a local boy with a cart to help him carry the tools and materials he'd brought with him to the new workshop.

After arranging for the remainder of the materials he needed, Johann brought Barbara to see the place. They walked slowly through the town, arm in arm, and more of Johann's enthusiasm leaked into his bride with each step. By the time they arrived at the small house and he had escorted her across the threshold and into the central workspace, she had almost come to believe, as he did, that he could create his wheel, and that it would work. How could it not, with such a man behind it?

"It is so empty," Barbara said, staring at the main workshop area. "Such a tiny little place."

"We won't be living here," Johann reminded her.

She nodded thoughtfully. "It just seems a small, insignificant place for such a grand enterprise."

She turned to him then, her eyes sparkling.

"It will work, won't it Johann?" He nodded.

"You have never once said, 'I think,' or 'maybe,'" she said. "You have always been so sure of yourself, and so certain of success."

"I have failed at this more times than I could count," he told her gravely. "I had a vision, just before I met you. In that vision, I saw what I had done wrong. I learned the secret to completing my task, and I have no doubts. I could have completed this at any point, but I wasn't ready – the time wasn't right. Now, I have you – and I will have my work to share with you, and to make you proud."

They embraced, standing in the empty room of the old house. Johann hummed, and they danced slowly, circling the room. Barbara giggled.

"So this is your great wheel," she said softly, laying her head on his shoulder. "You and I, whirling round and round. I will be dizzy soon, and you will have failed again."

"You will see," Johann said, slowing and pulling back so that his hands rested on her shoulders. "I know how it sounds...I know that everyone, including your father, believes I am a fool, but I saw what I saw, and I know what I know. When I build this wheel, it will spin, and it will keep spinning. It will never grow dizzy or stop unless the parts simply wear out.

"Because a thing has never been done, and is considered impossible, does not make it so. There would be a great many things in our lives that would be harder and less amazing were this not true.

"I will start tomorrow. I should have all the materials that I need by the afternoon. Within a month, you will see. Everyone will see; then our future will be certain."

"What would such a thing be worth?" she asked, eyes wide.

"I would not like to put a price on it," he said, "but a fortune, to be certain. We won't be living with my cousin for long."

They embraced again, and turned, leaving the cottage workspace, the tools, and Johann's dreams to wait. For the moment, they had one another, and it was more than enough.

SEVENTEEN

Herr Richter, the owner of the house that Johann had leased, stopped by regularly. He was very curious about his new tenant, as were the town elders, and just about every citizen of Gesa. Johann obviously had money, though they could not fathom its source. His new wife was beautiful, and friendly, and though she professed to know little of what her husband was working on, it was obvious that she adored him. The couple was a curiosity, and the house on the edge of town was a mystery beyond any excitement Gesa had known in recent years.

Johann was unfailingly polite, when Herr Richter stopped by, but just as adamant in his refusal to allow the man entry. Despite protestations that it was natural for the owner of a home to want to inspect the premises now and again, Johann would wink, ply the man with beer, and end up leading him away to walk down some country lane together, or into town, where they shared many meals and talked of many things.

In fact, the only thing they didn't talk about was the work being completed. If the subject came up, Johann would just wink, pat Herr Richter on the shoulder and grin.

"Soon, my friend," he would say. "Very soon I will be ready to show you and anyone else who will look. I promise you it will be a marvel, and that it will be worth the wait. You will have a very famous tenant before you know it, but for now I must keep my work, and my secrets, to myself."

"But why?" Richter asked in exasperation. "Why must it be a secret? Surely your fame will grow more quickly if we know what we are expecting to see?"

Johann only shook his head at this.

There were rumors, of course. Rosina, for all her good intentions, tended to talk more than was prudent. She knew very little, but she'd overheard the term Perpetuum Mobile used, and she mentioned once or twice to other servants around the village. No one took it too seriously. It was preposterous, after all. No sane man, and Herr Bessler seemed eminently sane, would attempt such folly. It was fool's gold, and most thought Rosina was only using the story to draw attention.

Throughout it all, Johann worked.

He set up a stand in the center of the great room he'd chosen for his workspace. The framework for his wheel stood only about a meter in height. The wheel itself was about half this in diameter, suspended at the top. Johann had given a lot of thought to how his work would be perceived, and in order to lessen doubts the ensuing accusations and arguments that would follow, he'd chosen this central point in the room as perfect.

When you entered the room, you could walk all the way around the device – it was open on all sides. There was no way that a secret mechanism to control it could be concealed in a wall. There was no way for a thread, or a wire to be strung between the device and the wall, the device and the ceiling or the floor. It wasn't tall enough to prevent onlookers from running a hand through the air above it, and in the open room it could be viewed from every angle.

This was a feverish time for Johann. He rose before the sun, his mind whirling with the details of the day's work. He often woke from the same dream, or a similar dream, to that which had brought his revelation. The glowing light and the inner workings of the old organ were so familiar to him and so ready to his mind that he found himself, more than once, sketching idly on the margin of his plans and rendering the exact workings and mechanisms behind the organ he'd helped to construct. Each time, he carefully marked through these designs.

He wasn't worried that another would see what had inspired him – he doubted that any set of experiences or memories other than his own could provide that. He just didn't want people drawing the wrong conclusions. He very simply wanted to present his wheel for what it was, make his statement, and then sit back as they inevitably attempted to stab holes in it, discredit it, or him, and eventually failed to do so. He wasn't worried about being discredited, because he was absolutely certain that he was right. The wheel was going to spin, and spin, and spin, and there was no more chance of them finding otherwise than there was of them finding a way to stop the world spinning on its axis, or the sun from rising, and then setting each day.

He created the wheel itself with its simple mechanism on a bench that had once been the dining table. During the time of assembly, he didn't leave the work area at all. He saw no one, not even Barbara, though she came to visit him at the doorway several times to check and be certain he was eating, and that he watched his health.

He had pulled dark curtains across all the windows and barred the shutters. The door was latched and then locked with a wooden bar he'd installed. Until the wheel was assembled and closed – a sealed unit containing his secret – he was taking no chances.

Johann had a plan. He intended to make the working model of his wheel, show it to the world, and then to sell it. He had a price in mind, and he knew that it was steep, but he knew, also, that his work was worth every penny. What he was going to provide was the impossible – a perpetual source of energy that could be harnessed for any number of uses. His mind had already taken him so many directions with the implications that he grew dizzy if he thought about it too much.

He wanted the money so that he could make a home for Barbara. He wanted to be able to write about what he'd discovered, and he wanted to be involved in the research that would follow. He also wanted to pursue medicine, and the numerous other fields of study and endeavor that he'd embraced throughout his life. As consumed as he was by the concept of a Perpetuum Mobile, Johann did not see himself caught on this one concept for the rest of his life. He had already conquered it; all that remained was to present it to the world, be paid for his genius, and then to move on to the next challenge.

Finally, it was done. He'd taken the wheel, once sealed, and suspended it in the center of its frame. There was a notch on one side of the wheel where he was able to hold it still by sliding a short dowel through, and he engaged this immediately.

Next he checked his curtains, and his shutters. He walked slowly around the perimeter of the house and studied the roads in every direction. There was no one in sight. Barbara wasn't due to come for him for another hour. Taking a deep breath, closing his eyes, and mouthing a short prayer, Johann stepped back inside and turned. He latched and locked the door behind him.

The room was very dark. He lit a pair of candles, one on either side of the wheel. Just as in his dream, time seemed to have slowed. After all his months and failures, he felt an odd reluctance to pull the dowel free. It wasn't that he doubted the wheel would work – he was certain it would. It would turn, and turn, and until he stopped it and re-engaged the brake, it would continue to spin throughout his lifetime if nothing changed or wore out in the mechanism. It was the ending of a period of his life, and the beginning of another. It was a death, of sorts, and he felt the reluctance of the moment clouding his reason.

Then as suddenly as it had come upon him the fog that lay over his mind lifted, and he stepped forward to stand beside the wheel. He didn't hesitate. He took the dowel firmly by its cross-piece handle and slid it free of the wheel. Nothing happened, of course, it remained stationary. Johann closed his eyes, reached out with the tips of the fingers of one hand, and spun the wheel gently.

He kept his eyes closed for a long moment, picturing it in his mind as it had stood, silent and waiting. Then he opened his eyes, and Johann Bessler smiled. The wheel spun smoothly. There was very little sound, and this lent the motion of the wheel an eerie, otherworldly quality.

Johann turned away and walked to the wall beside his workbench. He felt along the third plank from the door frame until he found a small notch. Prying at this, he freed a short section of the board and reached inside. A moment later he held a leather-bound book in his hand. He laid it on the bench and glanced over his shoulder at the wheel. It spun as it had spun moments before, oblivious to him, to the world, to gravity or the impossibility of its motion.

Johann pulled out a quill and a bottle of ink. He flipped the book open to the mid-point, where he found the first blank page. At the top of this page, he carefully penned the date, and the time. In close script, very small and precise, he recorded the moment. The last words he wrote in that entry were:

"The wheel is spinning, and I can't help thinking it spins me forward into something new."

He capped the ink, cleaned his quill, and replaced the book in its hiding place. He'd been keeping this journal for a very long time. All of his previous designs and theories were recorded there. Ideas he'd had for the improvement of the organs, clock mechanisms, and watches he'd worked on were there, as well. He kept a more public journal, one that he left where others might see it to distract them from the possibility of the existence of this second, more personal log. Everything of importance that he'd learned in the last decade of his life he's written in this book, and he intended to draw up on it heavily when the time came to write his memoirs. For now, the secrets were his alone.

He might have shown it to Barbara, but he felt that it would be an unintended burden to do so. Johann had always been a combative man, and he'd made enemies everywhere he'd stayed more than a few weeks. When he made new ones, he didn't want Barbara to be in a position where she could be taken advantage of. He didn't believe she would give him away purposely, but what she didn't know she couldn't reveal, and so the book remained sealed away.

Johann returned to the wheel. He drew one of the room's two chairs closer, sat, and watched. The spinning motion was monotonous. He saw that there was a small spot of something dark, grease, or oil, on the side, and he watched as it traced a dark circle in the air. The longer he stared, the odder it felt, and the longer the trailing shadow of that spot became. He was still sitting there when Barbara rapped gently on the door.

Johann started. He stood quickly, stepped to the wheel and reached for the brake, then thought better of it. He drew his watch from his pocket on its gold chain and glanced at it. The wheel had been in motion for over an hour and showed no sign of slowing, changing, or acknowledging the world around it. He smiled, closed the watch and slipped it back into his pocket.

Stepping to the door, he called out softly.

"Is it you, love?"

"Yes," Barbara replied. "You are locked in again – are you well?"

"You have come alone?" he asked, ignoring her question.

After a hesitation, she answered. "Yes. Just me, Johann. What is it?"

He pulled the wooden bar from the door, unlatched it, and peeked through the doorway. Barbara was alone, as she'd said, and he took her by the arm, drawing her gently into the room. She stepped past him, and he latched the door. He was fitting the bar back into place when he heard her gasp, and his smile broadened.

"Johann!" she cried softly. "You have…is it?"

"It is," he nodded, stepping to her side and watching the slowly but steadily spinning wheel plow its course into eternity.

"It works," she breathed.

"I never doubted that it would work," he said. "Didn't I tell you that I knew? That I was certain?" his voice was softly chiding, but his eyes sparkled with delight at her reaction.

"Yes, but…" her words trailed off. She stepped closer, and then walked very slowly in a circle around the frame. Johann watched her. She stepped closer still and examined the frame, her expression quizzical. She reached out and ran her hand through the air above the machine, as if to confirm what her eyes had already told her. There was no wire. There were no secret threads or tricks dangling in the air and fooling her senses.

She turned back to him, stood for a long moment of baffled uncertainty, and then flew across the room into his arms. Her sudden embrace nearly threw him off balance, and he caught her, laughing in delight as she pressed into his embrace. He kissed her on top of the head and stroked her back.

Barbara turned in his arms so that she could see the wheel. She watched it in silence for what seemed an eternity, and then she spoke.

"What is next, Johann? What will you do? Who will you show it to?"

"I will show it here, first," he said. "I will open this place and let the people of Gesa see what I have created. I will let the wise men of the village investigate it. I will answer any questions that I can answer without giving away the secret of my wheel, and I will announce that the secret is for sale."

"For sale?" she asked, turning to look into his eyes.

"Of course," he replied. "It is a secret that can do great good, but not if I keep it to myself. It can also do great harm, I fear, so I have to choose carefully. I will set a high price, and I will screen who attempts to meet it. The best I can do is to present the wheel to the world and to try and steer it in the direction where it can do the most good.

"As for us, there will be new secrets to discover, new places to visit. I have carried the burden of this task for too long. I want to learn things for the sake of learning and to share what I know with others who know things that I would learn. I want to travel, and to write."

He winked at her and drew her closer in his arms.

"I want to have children."

Barbara blushed, and turned back to the watch the wheel, but not before he caught the smile that twisted the corners of her lips. As he held her, he imagined he heard her heartbeat grow more rapid.

"There will be time enough for fame and fortune," he said.

Letting her go and stepping around her to the wheel, he rested his palm against the wheel and brought it to a stop. He slid the dowel carefully into its slot, and drew the cover over the entire framework so that all they could see in the flickering light was a shrouded, mysterious form.

"It is time to eat," he said. "And for some wine. In the morning I will tell Herr Richter to spread the news that we will display the wheel this Sunday. I won't tell him what it is, only that the thing that has occupied my time since my arrival in Gesa has been completed, and that I want all who are interested to share in the moment."

Barbara nodded. She put out one of the candles, and Johann snuffed the other. They removed the bar from the door and laid it aside, then stepped out into the night. Johann locked up behind them, and they walked off toward the central square of Gesa, arm in arm.

As they walked, Barbara leaned on his shoulder. In a soft voice, tinged with awe, she said.

"It works. I wish my father were here. I wonder what he would say?"

Johann laughed, kissed her on the side of the head, and replied.

"He would say, my love, that it is impossible."

She laughed and nodded. They walked on in silence, their passage traced in shadows through silver moonlight.

EIGHTEEN

Johann hired the same group of local children who had helped him move his tools and supplies into his new workshop to spread the word about the big unveiling. He had flyers carefully hand-printed and these were distributed among the local businesses and hung on the sides of buildings where they were clearly visible from the street.

As excited as he was to reveal his creation to the world, he was equally nervous about keeping it secure. This was no parlor trick or simple invention. It would revolutionize science. Precepts long considered inviolate would have to be cast aside, and entire technologies would crumble to be replaced by other, more efficient branches of science. The string of events leading into the future, beginning at the base of his wheel, ran through Johann's mind in a constant stream, and he fought to contain them long enough to remain calm and protect his investment of time and energy. It would serve no purpose if he opened the wheel to the public and the secret was immediately stolen.

The flyers proclaimed only that a miraculous new invention would be unveiled, and that all who were interested were invited to attend the unveiling. Special invitations went out to the mayor and other officials of the town, as well as to Herr Richter, who was arguably the only person in the entire village more excited by the unveiling than Johann himself.

Of particular interest to Johann was the attendance of the doctor and several teachers from the local school. He wanted reactions from all walks of life, and he welcomed investigations and intelligent questions about his work. It was one thing to convince villagers you had done something miraculous, but an entirely more difficult prospect to convince men of learning and science. Without the belief and backing of such men, he'd never be considered more than a clever trickster.

The night before the unveiling Barbara had to drag him physically from his workshop. They locked up carefully, and she led him away to get food and rest, listening all the while as he rambled on about security, and his theories, worrying over who he had invited, who he had not invited, what he might have done to present the wheel better, and where he might be giving too much away.

The two had talked about a price, and though it was high, both agreed that, given the miraculous nature of his invention, it was a pittance. Too many times history had left great men beside the road with a rotten apple and a tip of the hat while lesser men took advantage of their genius and reaped the rewards. Johann was convinced that he would have to fight to keep his secret, and was determined to hold fast to his price. He wanted £20,000. He also wanted some assurance that the knowledge would be put to good use – pumps for the mines, irrigation, the grinding of grain.

He had given long thought to the practical side of the wheel. He knew that the extent of its practical applications would be one of the first things brought into question. If all it did was spin, and it couldn't generate enough force to perform any real labor, then it would be nothing but an oddity – a toy for physics students to experiment on, but of no use to the world at large, and of very little value. It was important that he establish early on that a larger version of his wheel could, indeed, sustain a sizeable output of energy over a conceivably endless period of time with no more expenditure of energy than it took to set the thing in motion.

He strung a rope fence around the house to keep people from crowding too close. Arriving early, he opened the shutters and removed the dark curtains so that light invaded the room for the first time since he'd taken up residence. There were both front and rear doors, so he determined that the best course of action was to meet those arriving out front and escort them in, then through in groups to prevent the place from being absolutely overrun.

Despite a bottle of strong wine and Barbara's best efforts, Johann had been up most of the night. He'd stood for a long time at the window, staring down the road toward his workshop. When she'd urged him to come to bed, he'd lain very still, trying not to disturb her, but though his eyes were closed, his mind raced. In the world between sleep and reality, he wandered fretfully from memory to memory. He lived out endless scenarios, split halfway between horrible failure and the adulation of his peers.

He'd considered inviting Dr. Schumann, and several others he'd met during his travels, but had decided against this for the moment. Better to see, in a semi-contained environment, what people would make of it, and what the general reaction might be. He expected to be called a madman, a fool, to possibly run into claims of witchcraft from the clergy, and then, eventually, to be vindicated as the wheel continued to spin, day after day. Truth, if left to its own devices long enough, inevitably managed to find a way to draw notice.

When the sun had risen and Johann at last stepped out the front door of his workshop, he found that most of the town had gathered there. Word of his revelation had spread quickly, and had apparently reached even the most outlying farms and families. He'd never seen so many gathered in Gesa. He hadn't even known there were so many people nearby. He'd been too caught up in his work to pay any real attention.

Johann stood in the doorway and blinked in the sunlight. Several men stepped forward, and he recognized Herr Richter, Mayor Lichstein—a short, red-faced man with a large nose and tufts of gray hair at his temples—and the local Priest, Father Steinmetz. There were others, but Johann concentrated on the three who led the way. He shook hands with each.

"Welcome," he said. "I'm glad you've come."

"How could we not?" the mayor asked. He smiled, but the expression was somewhat forced, as though he were unconvinced this outing was really worth his valuable time. The Priest, thin and hawkish, made no pretense of a smile. Only Herr Richter, who was beside himself with anticipation, seemed genuinely happy to be there or to hear what Johann had to say.

"I have created something unique," Johann told them. "If you will follow me, I believe it is suitable that the three of you be the first to see – and to know what I have done."

None of them answered, so Johann turned and entered the workshop. They followed close behind. The crowd hovered, moving closer, but Johann closed the door behind Herr Richter after calling to those gathered that he would soon open the door and admit them all.

The wheel was covered by a dark cloth, so all that was visible in the center of the workshop was an amorphous shape. Johann wasted no time sliding the cover free and revealing the wheel, stationary in the center of its framework.

"A wheel?" the mayor asked. "You have brought us here to see a wheel?"

Johann nodded, but the smile that curled his lips and sparkled in his eyes kept the older man from asking more. Johann pointed to the dowel.

"Father Steinmetz, if you would be so kind as to pull that dowel pin free of its slot?"

The priest eyed the wheel skeptically, and then shrugged. He stepped forward and pulled the brake free. The wheel remained stationary, and the three turned once more to Johann. Even Herr Richter was beginning to wonder at the wisdom of enmeshing himself so deeply in this unveiling without a better idea of what it was that would be presented. His early enthusiasm would seem ludicrous if there was nothing worthwhile to be seen.

Johann stepped forward, and with a soft flick of his wrist, he set the wheel in motion. It spun lazily as the three of them watched. There was no reaction at first. The wheel spun easily, but it could have just been remarkably smooth bearings, or specially weighted. First the mayor, then Father Steinmetz, and then Herr Richter started to speak, and stopped themselves just short. The wheel spun. There was no slowing of the motion, nor did it speed up. There was no change whatsoever.

Finally Herr Richter could stand it no longer.

"What is it, Johann? What are we watching?"

"The same thing you would be watching," Johann said

softly, "if you came back to this room in a month, or a year – or even a decade. You are watching a wheel that, once set in motion, remains in motion with no further requirement of energy from an external source. You are witnessing the first..."

Father Steinmetz spoke into the moment's hesitation, his voice muted, "Perpetuum mobile." He watched for a few moments longer, and then turned to Johann. "Impossible."

"And yet," Johann shrugged, "here we stand."

"Is it like a clock?" the mayor asked. "Is there a mechanism that must be wound, eventually, to set it in motion?"

"There is no such mechanism," Johann replied. "Lay your hand on the wheel."

The mayor looked uncertain, but he stepped forward at last and did as Johann asked. The wheel stopped easily and sat motionless, making no attempt to swing one way, or the other.

"Turn it again," Johann instructed.

The mayor gave the wheel a spin, and it turned, continuing its earlier motion as if it had never been disturbed.

"But how long will it run?" Herr Richter asked. "How long is it possible?"

"It will run until you stop it," Johann replied. "If you do not stop it, it will run until some component physically wears out. Nothing else will change its motion. It will spin perpetually without external stimulus."

The three stood in silence for what seemed a very long time. Finally, as though determined to disprove the moment and return his world to its former stability, Father Steinmetz began a slow circuit of the wheel and its framework. He examined it carefully. He ran his hand over the top as Barbara had done. He knelt beside the framework and studied the floor beneath, even going so far as to run his hand along the floor in search of some very thin wire, or some clear component he couldn't easily spot with the naked eye. He found nothing, and rose to his feet, moving very slowly.

"But," Herr Richter said, as confused as ever, "how does it work? If nothing is wound inside – if nothing pushes it into motion, why doesn't it stop?"

"I would be a poor business man indeed if I shared that

secret with you," Johann chuckled. "It is what it appears to be – a device capable of maintaining perpetual motion. What I have accomplished here has never been done before, nor do I consider it likely that others will do it without my assistance. In fact, until this wheel began its first revolution, it was thought to be impossible by all but a few true believers."

There was a clamor from outside the window, and the three suddenly became aware of the world around them. The mayor shook his head in wonder and stared at Johann.

"I don't pretend to understand how such a thing is possible. If this is some sort of fraud, I will see you ruined. If not..."

"It must be fully investigated," Father Steinmetz said. His voice was stiff, and it was clear he was uncomfortable having the reaction of the church on his shoulders. Though his eyes never left the spinning wheel, he kept his expression as neutral as possible. "While you would indeed be foolish to share such a secret openly, Herr Bessler, I would be just as remiss if I let the evidence of a few moments convince me that of all the brilliant men God has placed on this earth, most of whom would say that the task you set yourself was impossible, you alone have succeeded. I will have to return, and I will have to bring others."

"Bring any and all who would see the wheel," Johann replied. "I am not afraid of their inspection or their doubt. I have done what I have done, nothing changes that. I expect much worse than honest investigation will arrive at my door before this is done. The wheel, and its secret, will be available for sale when that verification is complete, and once my price has been met I will willingly explain and instruct any who care to learn. Until then, I will have to be careful."

"I believe you are right," Father Steinmetz replied. "I wish that it were not true, but there are those who will not be happy for you. The men who have proclaimed this impossible will not lightly suffer being proved so fundamentally wrong, and those who would have created it themselves, but have lost their chance to your own efforts will be equally bitter. Guard yourself, Herr Bessler. Guard yourself, and care for your wheel."

Johann nodded. He had begun to glance over his shoulder distractedly, and the mayor nodded.

"You must open the doors," he said. "We will leave final proof for another time – for now you have promised them a show, and I do not believe they will leave until they have had it."

"I have been locked in this workshop for a very long time," Johann replied with a smile. "I welcome the chance for the fresh air, the sunlight, and the conversation. I will gladly show them all, twice if they like, and explain what they are seeing over and over."

"Word will spread quickly," Mayor Lichstein warned. "We are not so far from other villages and towns, and I expect riders and pigeons will go out before evening, explaining what has been seen. I believe you will have more than your share of company and conversation over the days to come."

The three visitors slipped out the back door and after only a few steps beyond the rope barrier, they split and hurried off, each in a different direction. Johann watched them for a moment, then turned back, crossed the room, and opened the front door.

The crowd had swelled, nearly doubling in size since he'd last seen it, and Johann blinked, a little dismayed. Controlling his nerves, he beckoned the first group to come with him into the workshop. He took them twenty at a time, crowding them in around the wheel. He allowed one in each group to stop and restart the wheel, and another to run their hands over and under the framework to assure those who watched that no trickery was involved.

He answered question after question, most of them repetitious and trivial. Occasionally one of the local merchants, craftsmen, or better educated citizens asked specific questions about the power output he believed such a device capable of, or about particular practical uses. These were the moments that kept Johann's mind keen and his eyes bright. These were the issues he wanted to address – needed to address – so that the full scope of what He'd created could be better understood. No one believes in anything so much as what they can witness.

The crowd remained through the day and into early evening, and even when the light had begun to fail and Johann lit candles to cut the deeper shadows of the workshop, there was a small group huddled together in the workshop, watching the wheel spin. Barbara appeared as the sun set behind the skyline, and Johann escorted the last of his guests out the door, answering final questions and accepting the accolades and praise of all who had seen.

There were skeptics, of course, and many of them were loud and adamant. Johann knew it would be a bad night to visit the local Inn unless he wanted to be dragged into endless drunken debates and possibly end up in a brawl. It was a lot to take in, and the village would need time to cope with this surprising new situation. Nothing was going to happen overnight.

Johann carefully closed the shutters once again and drew the dark curtains back into place. He locked the back door and dropped the large, wooden bar across it before moving to the front. Barbara stepped out ahead of him, and he stood for a long time in the doorway, staring back into the dark shadows of his workshop. There was still no sound – the wheel was silent – but he knew it was spinning. He wished, just for a second, that he had a light of some sort to illuminate it, but he wasn't about to leave a lit candle unattended in the same room with his invention. A fire could destroy it or, worse yet could destroy enough of it to reveal the workings within.

That was his biggest concern, now that the secret was out. That someone would break into the workshop and disassemble the wheel, or steal it outright. He knew it was unlikely – the wheel was a meter tall and the framework that suspended it was heavy. It would take several men and a good, solid wagon to cart the wheel away, and before they could do so thieves would have to break down the doors or smash through one of the shuttered windows.

"It will be fine," Barbara told him, leaning her head on his shoulder as they walked slowly away. "Everything is going to be fine. You are going to be very much in demand now, so I've decided that tonight is mine."

Johann glanced at her and smiled.

"Every night is yours," he replied absently."

She shook her head, and then laid it back on his shoulder.

"I know you too well already, husband. You will always think about your work first. You can't help yourself – it is how your mind works. If it was not…"

"There would be no wheel," Johann concluded.

They walked away, and left the workshop locked and bathed in darkness. Already riders had been dispatched, letters written, and even a couple of carrier pigeons had taken flight. News of this magnitude was rare, and everyone wanted a chance to be the first to spread the word. It was the last quiet night in Johann Bessler's life for many weeks to come – and possibly the last truly happy one.

In the darkness, untouched by time or the long tendrils of impossibility, the wheel spun, endless circles rolling into a shadowed, uncertain future.

NINETEEN

Trees flashed by far too quickly, but Edgar ignored the danger and focused on the road. It was dark, but he kept the lights dimmed. He knew the road as well as anyone, and he couldn't afford to be headed off by one of Black's patrols. Too much was at stake. As he drove, he tried not to think of Jennifer, or of Black. The one image filled his eyes with tears that blurred the little light available, and the other threatened to paint the world a bright, hatred red.

He knew the others would be doing what they could, but it changed nothing. He had a head start on them. He knew where Black was going, and Jennifer had been taken on his watch.

His head throbbed from the after effects of the gas, and his throat was dry. He knew they'd been careless. After so many years of playing cat-and-mouse with Black, they'd relaxed too much. It was easy to play spy and forget the danger, but he should have known better. He knew Black better than most – knew what the man was capable of – and the stakes had changed with Elly's arrival in America. Her abduction should have shaken loose the cobwebs, but he'd shrugged it off – and now Jennifer was gone.

The road curved sharply to the left and Edgar narrowly avoided slamming sideways into a tree. The tires shot dirt and he gripped the wheel so tightly it felt like his knuckles would press out through his skin.

He knew the moon shone bright in the sky beyond the overhanging blanket of trees, but only tiny silver flickers penetrated as far as the road. He swerved again and jammed on the brakes. There was a glow ahead, and he knew he'd come too far. Black's camp was close – very close – and there was no way they hadn't heard his approach. The Jeep slid on the soft dirt surface. Edgar fought the skid, spun the wheel, and without giving himself time to consider his actions, he shot off the road into the trees. Behind him lights flickered off the branches and leaves overhead. Voices called out from the shadows, and another engine sputtered, then fired.

With no time to think, Edgar killed the engine, let the Jeep roll to a stop, and waited. He heard the sound of voices pass behind him, and saw lights flashing. It was only a matter of time until they realized where he'd left the road and came after him. He had no intention of letting them catch up. The nose of the Jeep rested between the trunks of two trees with plenty of room to pass. Edgar counted silently to himself to still his nerves. He heard Black's men crash through the brush. He heard their voices rise in excitement as they discovered the point where he'd driven into the jungle. Still he waited.

Then, with a silent prayer to the gods of spontaneous combustion, he turned the key. The Jeep roared to life, and Edgar flipped on the headlights. No room left for stealth. The second his eyes acclimated to the sudden glare, he shoved the gear shift forward and rolled around the first tree, spinning on a tight axis so his headlights cut a bright swath through the jungle.

At first it seemed there was no way through, that he'd driven himself into a dead end. Then he saw it. Ahead and to the left the dense leaves and soaring trees gave way just enough. He gunned the engine and shot forward into a small gap, leaves slapping at the windshield and scraping the paint as he shot through, hit the road and skidded around to face Black's camp.

He had no way to know what lay ahead, but he knew most of those in the camp were behind him now, back on the road looking for him. The last thing they'd expect was a frontal assault by a single man in a Jeep. At least that's what Edgar hoped.

With the headlights illuminating the road, he made the last turn in a spray of gravel. Faces appeared from the shadows, staring blankly into the sudden assault of light and sound, and he roared past them. One man in fatigues was too slow, and Edgar clipped him, sending him flying toward the tree line.

The camp was laid out in a semi-circle of low-slung tents drawn back to either side of the road. There was a larger, more permanent structure mid-way down the left side, and Edgar focused on it. There was a canopy out in front of this larger tent held up by poles, and to the right of this what appeared to be a fire and a makeshift galley. Black had dug in, and it looked like he intended to stay a while.

Edgar bore down on the main tent. Voices rose all around him, screaming commands and curses. A bullet whined past his shoulder, and Edgar swerved. His throat was dry, and his head pounded. A second shot rang out and then more curses. Edgar grinned fiercely, imagining Black, or whoever he'd left in charge screaming at his men not to fire across the road at one another.

There were trucks and vehicles parked around the camp, but it was impossible to tell if Black had come back to the camp. For a crazy instant, Edgar thought he'd just ram the command tent and be done with it. They'd get him, of course, but before they did he'd take a shot at Black and see if he could send the man back to hell. Then his senses kicked in and he thought of Jennifer.

Wherever Black was, she was there too. If they were in the camp, they'd be in the tent directly ahead, and he was as likely to take her out as Black, or one of his men. He cut the wheel to the right and snapped the poles holding the awning like toothpicks. One of the ropes staked to the ground caught on his rear-view mirror and the Jeep lurched, just for an instant, as poles, stakes, and ropes gave way. The twang of broken fiber ripped through the night and Edgar heard a man scream. Then he was past, and free of ropes and canvas, roaring down the road on the far side of the camp.

Behind him more engines fired. They'd be after him soon, and though Edgar was familiar with the jungle, he hadn't been down this road as often as they had. If it didn't lead him somewhere familiar soon, he was going to be in serious trouble. He spun the wheel hard, felt the tires slip just a bit, then grip the packed dirt and he rounded another long, slow curve.

He glanced over his shoulder, saw nothing, and turned back to the road just in time to catch the reflection of headlights on the trees to his right there was another curve ahead – someone was coming down that road, and coming fast. With no time to think, Edgar spun the wheel hard and spun off the road again.

His left fender glanced off the base of a tree and the Jeep lurched right, veering back toward the road. Cursing, Edgar floored the gas and shot across toward the trees on the far side of the road. As he crossed, he glanced left into the wild, shocked eyes of Maxwell Black. At Black's side, Jonathan clung desperately to the wheel and yanked to the right. The two vehicles came so close the passengers could have reached out and touched one another.

Edgar spun the wheel back again, sent the Jeep into a skid, and came up against a tree with a sickening thud. He sat, just for a second, in stunned shock, then he hit the gas again and the Jeep died. Cursing, he turned the key. The engine coughed, but didn't catch. He heard approaching engines, and shouts. Then the engine caught, and he remembered to shift gears.

Across the road Black's engine revved crazily. Edgar didn't wait to see what had happened. He shot back out of the trees, skidded around the corner and concentrated on road.

From the floor of the back seat of the Jeep, Jennifer's world was darkness, the roar of the engine, and a series of pounding jolts to her ribs as the tires found ruts and dips in the road. Her hands were nearly free, but she hesitated. If Black or Jonathan looked back and saw her chaffing her wrists, free of her binding, they would stop, truss her up like a pig, and it would be over.

She was dazed, and her sense of the passing of time was skewed, but she knew they'd been driving for quite a while. There was only so much jungle between the city and the complex, and it didn't make sense that they would have made their camp in any other direction. Whatever she did, she'd have to do it soon, or it would be too late.

She rolled to her side, and at that moment a flash of light whipped across the trees. She blinked, tried to focus, but as she did she hears Jonathan cry out. The Jeep's brakes squealed and the tires gripped the road, sending them into a fish-tailing spin.

There was no time left to think. Jennifer slipped her arms from the last, loose wrap of the ropes. She rolled to her stomach, brought her knees up, and without a sound she pressed her cramped, aching muscles into service and dove forward. She cleared the side of the Jeep and went diving headlong into the shadows. The Jeep careened on down the trail.

The night erupted in sound. Metal ground, men screamed, and there was the sickening crunch of something crashing heavily. Jennifer's shoulder smacked painfully into a tree. She cried out, but her voice was lost in the cacophony. She fell heavily and lay face first in the grass, gasping for breath and gritting her teeth against the pain.

For just a second her vision swam, and she was certain she'd pass out, but a sudden cry of pain from the darkness behind her pierced the fog and she forced herself to rise. There was no time to think about where she was going, or what she'd do. She staggered to her feet, lurched away from the road, and started off through the trees at an uneven trot. Her legs were on fire from the long, cramped ride, and her shoulder throbbed. She flexed her hand and was relieved to find she could move her arm.

She didn't think about Black. She didn't worry about whether or not they were behind her, spreading out methodically to bring her back. She moved in as straight a line as she could, keeping quiet and concentrating on each step. After a while, the lights and the sound behind her faded and she heard nothing but the scrape of her shoes on the jungle floor, her ragged breath, and the pounding of her heart. When she could go no further, she found a large, fallen tree, curled up behind the base of the stump, and leaned her head on her knees.

She fought the fatigue, and the pain, but it was no use. Within moments she drifted into fitful sleep with the loud, rhythmic call of insects droning all around her.

Black's head throbbed. Blood ran down his forehead into his right eye, and the night was oddly unfocused. A shimmering halo of light surrounded anything that wasn't clouded in shadows. All around him the night was alive with sound. He was vaguely aware that the Jeep's engine had died, but he couldn't sort through the voices, the screams, and the rushing buzz in his head.

His face pressed into soft, moist grass, and with a colossal effort he slipped his hands beneath him, flat on the ground, and rose to his knees. He shook his head, realized his mistake as pounding, throbbing pain assaulted his temples from the inside, and grew still.

He heard the crunch of boots. There were voices, and lights. Black closed his eyes, gritted his teeth, and stood. He wavered, just for a moment, and then turned slowly toward the approaching sound. His eyes snapped open and he glared at the three men, who stopped dead in their tracks.

Black swung his head slowly from side to side and took in the scene before him. He saw the road about twenty feet away. He saw the Jeep. It was canted to one side. The fender was bent inward toward the driver's seat, where Jonathan's still form slumped forward, unmoving. Black's thoughts grew clear and very cold in that instant. He closed his eyes again, just for an instant, and saw the other Jeep skid around the corner. Trees and faces and lights flashed through his mind, and then grew silent. He opened his eyes.

"Where is she," he said.

The men gathered before him stood and stared in dumb silence.

"Where is she?" Black repeated, taking a step forward. "The girl. There was a girl in the back seat of the Jeep."

One of the men turned and sprinted to the wrecked vehicle. The others watched Black a moment longer, then broke and followed. He stood and watched them for a moment, then took a tentative step. His back was sore, and the cuts on his face and arms stung, but nothing seemed broken. He'd been thrown clear, somehow. As he approached the wrecked Jeep, anger began to build.

His men scrambled around the Jeep, finding no one in the back seat. They spread out quickly, one barking orders and pointing. Others joined them and scattered into the jungle. Black ignored them. They would bring him the girl. He stepped up to the Jeep, stared at it, and then walked around to the driver's side. Jonathan was unconscious, possibly dead. The man's head slumped over the steering wheel, and blood ran down his arm. The front of the Jeep was caved in, and steam rose from the broken radiator, hissing in the already moist air.

"Get up," Black grated.

Jonathan didn't move. Black stepped closer, reached out, and slapped the man hard across the face. Jonathan's head snapped to the side, but his eyes remained closed. There were no signs of life. Black clenched his hands into fists. He closed his eyes and tried to bottle up his fury, but it was too much. He'd had them. He'd had the girl. He'd been on the verge of winning the biggest prize in history, and this idiot – this sniveling weakling, had failed him. The other driver hadn't run into a tree.

And who in hell had that other driver been? Where was the girl? His head throbbed, and his thoughts whirled.

Just then, Jonathan groaned. He rolled his head to the side slowly, but he did not sit up.

Black launched forward and rained blows on the injured man's head. He struck him in the face, the shoulders, ripped at his hair and his clothes. It was only moments before two of his men grabbed him from behind and pulled him away. He fought with an all-consuming rage, but they held him tightly. One of his lieutenants poured water from a canteen over Black's head.

He grew very still then. The men released him and backed away. He glared at them, but said nothing. His eyes were clear and deadly cold.

"Get another Jeep," he barked at the man with the canteen.

The man turned to without question and leaped to obey.

"Get everyone ready," Black snapped. "We're going to have to move more quickly now."

"What about the girl?" one of the men asked.

"They'll find her," Black replied. "We don't have time to wait."

"What about…"

Black spun on the man before he could finish his thought and gripped him by the neck. The man grew pale as Black tightened his grip.

"Forget him," Black said. "Leave him there. We'll deal with it when we get back."

He released the man and turned slowly to face each of them.

"Are there any more questions?"

There were none. Moments later three Jeeps pulled up and Black swung up into the passenger seat of the first. He raised his arm and then dropped it, pointing down the path and into the darkness.

"Get me to that complex," he said curtly, "and hurry."

When the sound of departing engines had nearly died in the distance, Jonathan stirred. His finger twitched, and he groaned softly. No one heard. Insects had gathered to buzz and crawl through the blood running down his arms and his face. One eye was closed completely, but the other slowly opened, blinked, and then focused. Numb fingers gripped the bent remnant of the steering wheel.

With a sudden surge of adrenalin-fueled rage, Jonathan sat up, dropped his head back, and screamed into the pitch-black sky. The sound echoed, and then faded. Moments later, he was gone.

TWENTY

Black called a halt at a cross in the road. He stood and stared toward the complex, momentarily lost in thought. His head still pounded from the crash, but his mind was clear. He considered calling back to check on the girl, but he knew it didn't matter. The fools at the complex had seen her with him, and even if she was free and wandering in the jungle, she could never reach them in time to make a difference. As far as Benjamin and his little protégé were concerned the girl was Black's prisoner. It wasn't perfect, but it was enough.

He turned to the driver of the Jeep on his left.

"Get to that complex," he said. Make as much noise as you can. Ram the gate. Make it look real, but you'd better catch their attention. I need some time, and you're going to get it for me."

The man nodded. He gestured to the back of his Jeep, and when Black turned to look, the man in back lifted a bazooka to his shoulder, patted it lovingly, and grinned. Black nodded, and the driver shoved the Jeep into drive and took off with a roar. Black turned to his own driver, and that of the vehicle on his left. "We're going to the caves. Radio ahead and tell them to get those charges set. I want them ready to go on my word."

Black sat down, and both drivers gunned their engines. The moon had dipped slightly toward dawn, but there was plenty of darkness left to conceal them. In moments, the road was as dark and silent as if they hadn't passed at all.

Benjamin stared at the banks of security monitors that showed the perimeter of the complex and frowned. Motion detectors had picked up an approaching vehicle, but there was nothing in sight. He wasn't sure if he should be expecting Edgar to come careening out of the jungle with Black and his men in hot pursuit, or Black himself, breaking out of the trees with some type of cannon.

"What is it?" Elly asked, stepping up beside him. There was a new edge in her voice, and when he turned to meet her gaze, her eyes flashed on the edge of anger.

"Someone is coming," he told her. "I can't tell yet who it is." Elly frowned.

"No one has heard from Edgar," she said. "Jennifer is still out there somewhere; the entire world's gone crazy, and we just sit here."

"We..." Benjamin never finished the sentence. Elly's eyes went wide, staring over his shoulder at the monitor screens and he spun quickly, taking in the situation at a glance.

"My God," he said softly.

Then he spun away again.

"Get the others," he snapped. "Quickly. There are workers out there, men who have nothing to do with any of this. We have to get them under cover, and we have to stop ... that." He pointed over his shoulder at the screen, where a Jeep with three men in fatigues bore down on the main gate of the complex. The men were belted in and hunkered down, and though they drew nearer and nearer to the metal fence, they showed no sign of slowing.

"Look!" Elly cried.

Benjamin stopped and glanced back. One of the men had come up to a crouch in the back seat. A bazooka rested across his shoulder, the business end aimed straight ahead, directly at the gate and the small guard shack to one side. Before he could spin away, he saw barrel spit fire, and seconds later the gate blew off its hinges and inward toward the walls of the complex. He saw the stunned guards stagger into the road, and then dive back behind the remnant of their shack as the Jeep bore down on them.

Benjamin spun, and was gone. Elly started after him, and then remembered what he'd said. She wasn't really in the mood to be taking more orders, but in a situation like the one she was in, she had no experience to fall back on. She remembered how Benjamin and the others had freed her from Black her first night in America, and she knew she had to trust him. For the moment.

She rushed down the short hall, rapping on every door she passed. She didn't know where the others all were, but she knew she had to get them moving.

Cynthia met her in the hall, drawn out by the explosion at the gate. Elly told her what had happened as they hurried down the hallway together. Before they reached the end, a low, droning siren rose, pulsing and shivering through the entire structure in low, resonant tones. Red lights up and down the sides of the passageway blinked in time.

"What is that?" Elly asked.

"The generators," Cynthia replied, raising her voice to be heard. "Someone initiated the sequence that transfers the complex over to the diesels."

"But..." Elly stopped. "The caves. Can the diesels handle the load?"

"The alarms will be going off there too – at the caves, I mean. The crossover takes about twenty minutes. There's plenty of time for them to get clear in case something goes wrong. The generators will stay live until the diesels are at full strength"

Elly glanced over her shoulders toward the gate. She thought about the Jeep bearing down on them and wondered just what one of those bazooka shells could do to a diesel generator.

"We can't let them shut it down," she said.

Cynthia stared at her.

"We have to stop them," Elly insisted. "How do I reverse the shutdown?"

"We have to shut them down," Cynthia said hurriedly. "There's no time to waste. If we leave them powered up and security is breached..."

"I don't care about security," Elly screamed. "I don't care about secrets, or Maxwell Black, or this whole stupid little war. There are lives at stake. Those men and women in those caves are depending on us to pump the water out and keep them safe, and that is what we're going to do."

A low, whining alarm sounded, and Cynthia held up her hand.

"The caves," she said. "That's the signal that someone is on the radio."

Marvin joined them, wild-eyed and the three of them sprinted to the control center. There was no sign of Benjamin.

"Where's Antoine?" Elly asked.

"I'm not sure," Marvin replied. "If I were to guess, I'd say with Benjamin, or ahead of him. Antoine is not one for sitting back and waiting for things to happen."

The red lights continued to strobe slowly. Marvin keyed the microphone on a large console and spoke quickly.

"Base to Cavern One, Base to Cavern One. Do you read, over?"

After a few seconds of static, a voice crackled over the speakers.

"Base, this is Cavern One. We have a situation here."

"Go," Marvin said instantly.

"We have company, and it doesn't look like they're planning on allowing the evacuation. We have men in position, and we're ready to move on this, but I'm requesting a delay on the crossover. I don't know who they are, or what they want, but my men are down in the cavern, and they're scared, over."

Marvin started to reply, but Elly grabbed the microphone and pushed him aside.

"We will comply," she said sharply. "There will be no crossover. Hold your men in position until we can get you support, or until we know the situation." She hesitated a moment, and then added more hesitantly, "Do you read...over?"

There was a moment of silence. Marvin gently eased the microphone out of Elly's hand and keyed the microphone.

"Cavern One, this is base. We repeat. There will be no crossover. Hold position."

"Cavern one, copy."

The line went dead. Marvin turned to Elly, started to speak, then caught her expression and decided against it.

"I hope all the time I've spent down here without sushi has been worth it," he muttered.

He rolled his chair to the left and his hands flew over the controls. Elly watched, uncertain whether she should say something, or do something. As she waited, the red lights slowed and then blinked out. Marvin spun the chair to face her. His expression was half amused, half excited. Cynthia stood to one side. After a moment, Elly realized they were waiting for her to instruct them.

"Bring up the gate on the screen, if you can," she said. "That's where Benjamin was headed. If we can find him with the cameras, maybe we can find a way to help."

Marvin turned and went to work, and in moments the bent, broken ruin of the main gate had come into view. There was no sign of the Jeep, but its path was clear enough. Marvin panned the camera until he saw the Jeep, abandoned, and three figures furtively moving from cover to cover toward the entrance to the upper floor of the complex.

"Can they get in?" Elly asked.

"The doors will be locked," Cynthia said, "but they aren't guarded. All personnel on the upper floor are associated with the generators, and the project at the cavern. They understand the security we have in place, but none of them will be armed. Their instructions are to secure the doors in case of an emergency and take cover. There are safe rooms for their protection.

"Look," Marvin said.

One of the intruders had knelt in the dirt, partially shielded by a parked truck. He held the bazooka to his shoulder again, and brought it to bear on the front door of the complex.

Before he could fire, the door opened, and Antoine slipped out.

"What is he doing?" Elly cried.

As if in answer, Antoine dove to his left, rolled up onto one knee and brought a rifle to his shoulder. He aimed and fired without hesitation.

Elly let out a little cry as the man with the bazooka slumped suddenly to the side. As he crumpled, the weapon fell uselessly from his hand. The other two dove for cover.

"It's a tranquilizer," Marvin said.

Elly stared at him, but Marvin never looked away from the

monitor. "I know you have somehow gotten the impression that we don't care about the people involved here," he said, "but we have taken a lot of precautions to be certain we never go too far – that we never become those we are protecting…" he waved his arm in the direction of the generators, "all of this from. We have no lethal weapons here, but we are prepared to defend ourselves. The man Marvin shot will be fine, but he's going to have a hell of a headache."

Elly would have replied if there had been time. She was relieved to hear that they were taking no lives, but she was no less certain that the secrecy, and the intrigue, were leading them all in a very wrong direction.

"They're turning!" Cynthia cried.

The two remaining intruders were pulling back slowly. Antoine made a half-hearted move to follow them, but he and Benjamin held back. The two men reached their Jeep and slipped back in behind the wheel, leaving the bazooka beside their fallen companion and backing slowly out of the complex. The man on the passenger side kept his gun leveled on the door where Benjamin hunkered just out of sight, but no more shots were fired.

"What was that all about?" Cynthia growled.

"What do you mean?" Elly asked.

"They blew their way in, chased the guards into hiding, made a half-hearted shot at the front doors – and then just left? Why would they do that? Even with Benjamin and Antoine out there, their odds of getting inside were good, and they must have backup on the way. I don't like it."

Marvin didn't say anything, but he nodded agreement.

Elly frowned. It hadn't occurred to her, but now that Cynthia brought it up, she was worried too. Maxwell Black was a lot of things, but stupid didn't seem to be one of them. This pointless attack had to be a distraction, or part of a larger plan – but what?

"Forget the gate," she said suddenly. "They won't come back that way, watch the jungle. How many roads are there leading in?"

"Four," Cynthia replied hesitantly. "But what makes you think…"

"It's a trap," Elly said decisively. "You're right; no one in his right mind would attack the gate the way they did and then just leave. And they didn't even take their weapon for a second assault...they could have gotten it out of there without much effort, but they didn't even try.

"We just got a call from the caverns to tell us that something was happening there. We should have paid more attention. Whatever it is, these three were sent to distract us from it. Can we get them back on the radio?"

"We can try," Marvin replied. "We have to keep broadcasts to a minimum, and be careful what we say. If there is something going on, you can bet they're monitoring any frequency they think we might use."

Elly nodded impatiently.

Marvin shrugged and turned back to the microphone. He flipped several numbered dials, keyed the microphone three times, and then spoke clearly into the microphone.

"Cavern One, this is Base, over."

Nothing but static answered. Frowning, Marvin keyed the microphone again and repeated his call. There was no answer. He flipped the numbered dials and tried again. On the third frequency change they heard a weak signal. Marvin very carefully adjusted his controls, and the signal strengthened, just for a moment.

"They are closing us off. I repeat – they are closing us off. I don't know what they want, but all standard escape is shut down. Initiating emergency egress. Requesting backup. Base, if you read this, going to one niner five, over."

The signal went dead. Marvin followed the frequency. The signal returned, weaker still.

"Cavern One, this is base," Marvin said sharply. "How many are there?"

"Base, this is Cavern One. I have about forty-five workers in here, men and women who'd like to get home to their families. There are only about ten intruders, but they are heavily armed. I repeat, request backup. Egress points Charlie and Oscar activated. Over."

"Roger, Cavern One," Marvin replied. "We'll do what we can. Hang in there."

The signal died, whether from another quick frequency change, loss of power, or something worse.

"What can we do?" Elly asked.

"I'll stay here," Marvin said. "You two find Benjamin, and Antoine. Get into a Jeep and get over to the cavern. That last was code. We have emergency evacuation routes. They'll get the workers out, and then they'll return and hold their ground.

"There are a few of the locals I trust; I'll bring a couple of them in here with me, and the rest I'll send home. We'll do what we can to fortify the front doors, and we'll seal off the lower levels until this is over – one way or the other."

Cynthia looked as if she was about to protest; Elly cut her off.

"Fine. Make sure that anyone who stays with you knows what they are getting into. We may have no lethal weapons, but from the look of the front gates, they suffer no such weakness."

Before Elly could turn to go in search of Benjamin, Marvin cursed under his breath, and she swung back to stare at the monitors. Two Jeeps nosed through the trees near the edge of the jungle, very near the point where she'd seen Black with Jennifer earlier that day.

"It's Black," Cynthia said.

"Do you see Jennifer?" Elly asked.

They strained to see closer, and Marvin worked frantically at the controls, trying to zoom in on the passengers in the two Jeeps, but there was no sign of the girl. Black came into sharp focus.

"Damn him," Elly snapped.

"I don't know about that," Marvin said, "But it looks like something ran over him. Look at his face!"

Before they could comment further on Black's battered appearance, there was a crackle on the radio, and they all turned to it, staring. A signal came in, then out of tune with a whine of feedback. Then it grew clear, and an ice-cold, all-too-familiar voice hissed through the speaker.

"Benjamin, what am I to do with you. You really have led me on quite the chase these past few years. Don't you think it's time we talked?"

Marvin stared at the microphone as if it were a snake that might strike at any second.

Footsteps pounded down the corridor behind them, but none of them turned. They were riveted on the tall, slender form leaning forward over the windshield of one of the jeeps, a microphone in his hand.

Elly reached for the microphone.

"Where is she, Black," she said. She wanted to scream at him, pound the microphone on the monitors and the control console until nothing was left but a bent, ruined pile of metal, but she kept her temper in check. Too much depended on the next couple of moments.

"Your little friend?" Black asked. "Oh, she's being well taken care of, I assure you. I really wouldn't concern myself over it, to tell the truth. You have other problems – bigger problems than a single girl."

"What do you mean?" Elly asked. She cursed herself inwardly for reacting as he expected her to, and she bit off the rest of what she'd intended to say.

"You got the message," Black said. He chuckled, but there was no humor in the sound. "Very clever of you to shift frequencies so rapidly, but it's been several years since a simple ploy like that would really work. Modern electronics are marvelous, don't you think?"

Elly remained silent, and after a moment, Black continued.

"There are a great number of workers in those caves. Most of them were on their way home to their families, another day's work behind them, and without a care in the world. Very sweet. Idyllic, even. It's too bad we had to...delay their departure.

"But why?" Marvin said. His face was white with tension, but his eyes were clear. His fingers flew over controls, and though Elly didn't know what he was doing, she was suddenly very glad to have these people on her side. She might, or might not agree with their philosophy on what was at stake, but they were good people, and they were brilliant, where Black was only vicious and clever.

"I thought you'd never get around to asking," Black replied. "I have something planned that I believe they will get a charge out of…so to speak. I like to end things with a bang."

Black broke into a chuckle, and the voices of those in the Jeep with him made an eerie backdrop.

Elly took the microphone in her hand grimly.

"What do you want, Black? What do you think you are going to gain? Will you walk in here, put my grandmother's secrets on your shoulder and carry them out? Will you explain to the government why you endangered the lives of their citizens? Will you kill us all and try to make a break for it?"

There was a momentary silence, and then Black's laughter became more genuine.

"I wish that you had met your grandmother," he said, "because two women more alike I cannot imagine. This is truly a moment.

"No, I do not expect I can carry what you conceal in your cleverly built complex away with me, nor do I think the local government would think well of me if I were to slaughter the lot of you, as much as the prospect might amuse me. My plan is much simpler, and to the point.

"There are a number of explosive charges set at strategic points along the inner and outer wall of the caverns that depend on your pumps to keep them dry. My men have closed the exits – every man and woman who works beneath that mountain is trapped. Their lives depend on your next words, and you have no time left for bargaining. Turn over Bessler's secret to me, or the charges will be detonated, and those people will be trapped. It will look like an accident, of course, and all witnesses will be tragically lost.

"Wondrous as your pumps may be, I doubt they are up to the challenge of pumping the entire river out of the caverns in a matter of moments."

Elly released the microphone to shield her words from Black and turned to Martin.

"Can he be serious? You've known him longer than I have, and you know the caverns. Is what he threatens possible, or is he bluffing?"

"I'd love to tell you it's a bluff," Martin replied grimly, "but I'd be lying. What he claims is very possible. No one ever considered sabotage. And Black?"

When Martin hesitated, Cynthia cut in.

"He's a monster. He's killed, and he'll kill again – if not today, some other time, and some other innocent person. I don't know if he's telling us the truth about the explosives, but even if he isn't, we can't take the chance. He's capable of anything, so that's what we have to expect."

Elly nodded grimly. She turned back to the monitor and reached for the microphone, but at that moment, the decision and the breath were snatched from her as she watched in horrified fascination. A second Jeep careened out of the jungle about twenty yards from Black. It nearly rolled as it turned; then the tires caught and it roared ahead. Behind the wheel a man hunched grimly, keeping low to make a smaller target.

Black heard the vehicle as well. He spun, startled, and barked orders. The men in the back of his Jeep fumbled with their weapons, trying to spin and target the madman bearing down on them, but they were too slow.

"It's Edgar," Cynthia cried.

At the moment she called his name, Edgar rammed nose first into Black's Jeep, knocking the man sprawling and canting the vehicle onto its side. The men in Black's second Jeep came to life. They jumped to the ground and rushed Edgar's Jeep as he slammed the gear shift into reverse and shot loose dirt into the air, trying to disengage from Black's ruined vehicle.

Two of the men aimed, and Elly let out a short scream, but then, moving as if in slow motion, both men spun. Something had punched each of them hard on the shoulder, and they reeled, crashing into one another and falling to the earth. Black rolled to his feet, glanced back at Edgar, who had finally freed himself and was backing away hurriedly for a second run on Black himself.

From the direction of the complex, Benjamin and Antoine raced toward the scene. They held their weapons at the ready, and Elly realized they must have fired once already, saving Edgar's life.

Black didn't hesitate. He dove past his men, slid in behind the wheel of the second Jeep, and before anyone could make a move, he ground the gears into reverse and was moving back toward the jungle. Benjamin and Antoine stopped, taking aim, but they were too late. By the time they fired, Black had nosed back into the trees toward the road. Edgar started after him but Benjamin waved him down.

Meanwhile, Marvin frantically keyed the microphone on the transmitter, trying to get the attention of anyone below. Finally, Benjamin pulled a hand-held radio from his belt and replied.

"Benjamin, go."

"Black is headed to the caverns," Marvin almost screamed the words. "There are explosives. Benjamin, he threatened to kill all those workers if we didn't give him the secret of the generators. Now I think he's gone to make good on his threat!"

"Damn," Benjamin said. "Does he still have a radio?"

"I don't know," Marvin replied. "If he does, we're already too late."

"Marvin, you keep those pumps working," Benjamin said finally. "Cynthia, get down here; we have to try and catch him."

"What about Elly?" Marvin asked. He turned then, and saw that both women had already gone.

Below, the Jeep rushed to the main entrance. They would be able to take the main road, which was a little shorter and smoother, but it was going to be a race.

Marvin turned from the radio to the dials, controls, and meters that had become his life. The generators hummed steadily, the only sanity left to the night.

TWENTY-ONE

The caverns were accessible only by a central passage, carefully shored with beams and framed with an intricate weave of conduit, wiring, plumbing and machinery. The lights near the entrance had been cut off, but a glow emanated from the chambers below and seeped out into the shadows.

Deeper in the mountain, the central passage opened into several smaller chambers, leading to passageways winding in and down. Black's men had sealed each of these, taking up positions where the passageways crossed. They'd hit the lights first, throwing the workers below into confusion, then, as emergency power was brought on line and panic set in, shots were fired. They weren't fired at anyone in particular, just into the darkness. Into the tunnels. The bullets ricocheted off of walls, nicked wires and sent echoes reverberating deep into the mountain.

In the moments following the shots, the invaders spread out into the shadows. The charges had been in place for weeks. A careful series of bribes, late night infiltrations, and luck had planted six explosive loads at crucial locations along the tunnel walls. The weak point of the caverns had always been the wall that held back the river. All it would take was a single large breach in the integrity of that wall.

There were murmurs, then shouts of confusion and fear from the caverns, but they only lasted a few moments. Not all of the workers below were simple archaeologists. Some had been hand-picked and planted by Benjamin for just such an emergency, and even as Black's men jockeyed for position in the outer passages, these men and women went to work. They hurried among their co-workers, calming them and pulling them to the relative safety of store-rooms and other cover. When the shots from above ceased, several of those below broke off and slipped down corridors that didn't show on any of the maps. Each of these was checked as quickly as possible to be certain there were none of Black's men watching their exits, and then, moving carefully and keeping the others as quiet as possible, they began an evacuation. Men and women slipped into shadowed passageways they hadn't even known existed and hurried into the jungle beside the mountain. Their exodus went undetected, and then, the few who'd led them to safety turned, making their way back through the passageways into the mountain.

On the return trip they stopped, arming themselves and establishing communications via a small, integrated network imbedded in the stone of the cavern walls. The signal was encrypted, riding on an RF carrier, and indecipherable by any non-proprietary receiver. To Black's men, it might appear as a crackle of static, if they were scanning. All of this took only a matter of thirty minutes. During this time, Black's men heard only silence. They saw only shadows, and they began to make mistakes.

In the main passage, a two man team had begun to work their way deeper into the cavern. Their orders were to hold the workers below ground, but the lack of any response, and the silence, had made them edgy. They moved slowly, covering one another and keeping close to the walls. The first of the two reached a left-hand turn and waved his partner around.

A second later, that partner disappeared into the shadows with a grunt. Before the first man could flee, a dark form slipped around the corner, raised a gun, and fired. The dart made a direct hit on the man's thigh. He slumped to the ground without a sound.

Two figures melted from the deeper shadows and peered cautiously up the passageway.

"Two down," the first said. He was a thin, swarthy man with a deep, piercing gaze. The other was a woman with long hair tied back in a ponytail. She didn't smile.

"How many more, do you think?" she asked.

"No way to know for sure. They came up pretty suddenly. If their point is just to keep us in here, then probably not more than a dozen."

"Ten," she corrected, nodding at the two fallen men. They pulled back around the corner again, and the man spoke softly into the microphone he wore just over his chin.

Others had met with similar success. Six of Black's men were down, and Benjamin had gotten a short burst transmission through. He was on the way with others. If they could hold out a few more minutes, the tide would turn.

"We need to spread out," the woman said. "We don't know how many of them there are, but we can't assume we've stopped them."

"If there are any left," the man replied, "they may still believe the workers are trapped below. They may think it's more important to complete their mission than to worry about getting away. If they fail, they'll have to face Black."

The two stepped into the passage and moved carefully toward the front of the cavern, sweeping each and every nook along the way. They moved quickly, but they spotted nothing out of the ordinary. When they reached the main entrance, the woman turned left and began following the mountain around toward the river a half mile away. Her partner followed, and the shadows closed in behind them.

Black could only see through one eye. Blood had trickled over the right side of his face from a gash on his forehead, and was caking on his skin. Every time he slowed for a turn, or a dip in the road, insects swarmed him, but he ignored them. When he hit a straight stretch, he grabbed the radio from his belt.

There was no time for electronic trickery, and in any case, it was too far into the game for it to matter. He flipped the power switch, pressed the talk button. "Red five, Red seven, this is Red one; report."

The radio crackled, but remained silent. The road curved toward the mountain, and, cursing, Black gripped the wheel with one hand and the fingers of the other, fighting for control of the radio. The Jeep canted up on one wheel, slammed back onto the road, and leaped forward. The radio crackled again, and then a voice cut through.

"Red one, this is Red five, copy, over."

"Roger. Red Seven, report." Silence, and then the first voice returned.

"I've heard some shots, sir...I think I'm the last."

Black swayed, and nearly lost control. Anger shot through him so hot and hard it nearly incapacitated him. If the road ahead had not been straight at that moment, he'd have driven into the jungle, but he recovered.

"Goodman?" he grated. No call signs now and no hesitation. "Goodman, is that you?"

"Yes sir, Mr. Black," came the immediate reply.

"Goodman, things are going to hell – do you understand that?"

"Yes, sir," Goodman replied, "I believe I do. There are voices getting closer sir. What should I do?"

"Blow it," Black grated. "Blow it to hell, Goodman; blow the whole damned mountain down on their heads if you can. Can you do that one thing for me?"

There was a slight hesitation, and then Goodman's voice crackled over the line a final time.

"Roger, boss...see you in hell, then."

The radio went silent. Then, despite the blood, the insects, and the pain, Black dropped the radio on the floor, gripped the steering wheel in both hands, and smiled.

James Goodman was a man with a mission. Black would have said the same thing, but there were things he didn't know. For the three weeks, since the day Black's instructions reached Goodman in his dingy, New York apartment, a single image had filled his head.

He saw walls of stone bursting inward. He saw raging water, rushing down passageways they'd been denied for centuries. He saw men and women washed away in a deluge they could neither control nor defend against. When he dreamed, he stood in the center of a giant, hand-carved stone passage. A roaring sound rose, starting as a small buzz in the back of his brain and rising to a throbbing, rushing flood.

He woke each night, bathed in sweat, his head pounding with adrenalin. He sat up in his bed, eyes closed and heart racing until the images faded. Until he realized there was no water to wash him away.

Black provided the explosives, and Goodman supplied the skills. He'd crawled tunnels for Uncle Sam, for several third world nations with the right amount of money, and he'd crawled back out of every one of them. The same could not be said for others; friends had been left in those dark, damp places. Enemies had died there. Snakes had slithered over his leg and rats had clambered down his back. He'd felt the earth tremble as tunnels collapsed, and felt the muffled power of the explosives he left behind closing in on entire underground worlds.

They haunted him. He saw them, but they slid away into crumbling, sifting funnels of earth and water and shadow. He heard their voices. Some talked to him, told him stories to remind him of the darkness. Some screamed at him, and others hummed and sang and chanted in languages he didn't understand.

Until Black.

Until now.

Now he had a new mission, and the biggest tunnel he'd ever crawled...a tunnel so tall he could walk through it, hit it with a pickaxe without risking a cave-in, so large it could whisper its own secrets and tell stories from a past so far removed and so alien he couldn't even conceive of the world that spawned it.

Black saw this as just another job, but Goodman knew better. It was destiny – his destiny – and even without the orders he'd just heard, he'd have seen it through. He had to do it – it was his last chance. All the other tunnels had been the warm-up acts for the final dance, and the minute he'd hung up the phone ... the minute he'd told Black he'd called the right man...everything had become focused on what came next.

The explosives had been in place for two weeks. Goodman had other skills than crawling with the rats and killing. His eyesight was good in the dark and he suffered no claustrophobia.

He was good in the mines, and he'd learned to speak several languages in his years as a mercenary. Spanish came almost as easily to his lips as English. Sometimes in his dreams, it was the language that took control.

He wasn't as close to his detonator as he'd hoped to be when Black's call came. He'd been checking in with the others, keeping the lines of communication open. He wanted the mission to succeed almost as much as he wanted his own part to be final. He didn't want a small breach in the walls – he wanted the entire mountain to come down. He wanted to stand in the center of the passageway below him and wait for the stone and the water to crash in on him and blot out the world.

Now he feared he'd waited too long. He dropped the radio in the dirt and turned toward the cavern. His station was about two hundred yards out, concealed in the brush. It had been too long since the last message had come through, but he'd held his ground. His orders were to report in on the half hour, and that is what he'd done. The problem was that the last report had gone unanswered, and he'd had no immediate orders beyond the last report.

All that had changed, and only the finale remained. The last act. Goodman walked slowly toward the cavern. Then he stopped.

In the distance he heard the sound of an engine. Then another. One had to be Black, but the other? He stared into the trees as though he might pierce the darkness, but it gave up no secrets. With a shrug, he turned his back on the jungle, on Black, and on the world. Only one thing remained – only one thing mattered. This was his night, and the tunnels were calling his name.

Black reached the main entrance to the cavern and skidded to a halt. The lot was full, but no one was in sight. He was leaping to the ground even as the Jeep's engine died, and he hit the ground in a roll. The jarring impact sent sparks dancing across the backs of his eyes, but he gritted his teeth and shook them away. He scanned the sides of the cliff to either side of the cavern's entrance, but saw nothing. He heard the engine of another Jeep approaching and grinned fiercely.

"Too late, Benjamin," he spat. "You always were a little slow."

Keeping low, he moved to the cavern's entrance and ducked inside. There were no lights, and he heard no voices. He frowned. Those trapped below should be putting up a fuss by now, and he'd expected to see some trace of his people sealing things off. Instead he got silence and shadows. Empty darkness.

Black glanced into the cavern once, remembered Goodman, and stepped back out into the night. He was still alone, and he made his decision quickly. The last contact he'd had was with Goodman, and Goodman's station was off to the right of the entrance, toward the cliffs leading to the river below and beyond the mountain. He didn't know what was going on below, and he suddenly didn't care.

He thought of how close he'd come, how near he'd been to having Bessler's secret in his hands, and his vision swam. He saw red pinpoints of light and had to lean on the wall for support. It took a few moments to clear his thoughts, and in those moments the sound of the Jeep behind him grew louder. It was too much.

He lifted the radio to his lips, pressed the button to speak, and said nothing. He tossed the radio aside. Goodman had his orders, and if he didn't blow this freaking anthill off its roots, Black would do it himself when older business was finished.

He stepped away from the wall and turned back toward the sound of the approaching engines. He drew his standard issue US Navy .45 semi-automatic from the holster at his hip and checked the clip. It was full. Black smiled.

The approaching engine roared and Black stepped into clear sight. He raised the gun and took aim, waiting. There was only one clear path. Either the Jeep would stop where he'd left his own vehicle, or it would spin along the side of the cliff and come straight down the trail. Either way, he was ready.

Except that when the Jeep crashed into sight, it careened out of the trees to his left. Black spun, raised the pistol and fired, but he couldn't tell if he'd hit anything. He backed toward the wall, suddenly blinded by the single headlight of the approaching vehicle.

"Benjamin!" he screamed. He fired again, and again, backing up until his shoulder blades met the stone wall, but the Jeep kept coming. He had a last shot, and he held it, waiting. He shielded his eyes, trying to get a final glimpse, a last look into the eyes of the man he intended to kill.

Time slowed, and the figure behind the wheel of the Jeep came into clear focus. Black screamed, but it was far too late. He fired his final shot, and the bullet took Jonathan directly between the eyes. The Jeep never slowed. Within seconds of impact the fuel tank ruptured. The explosion shook the base of the mountain, and the flash lit the night like the sudden bolt of lightning.

Goodman felt the earth shake beneath his feet and his eyes opened wide. He broke into a run, diving toward the tunnels.

On the road the impact from the explosion nearly sent Benjamin's Jeep careening into a tree, but he held on, ground the wheel to the left, and plunged ahead toward the mountain. His mind filled with images of rushing water, drowning workers, and Black's sneering face. The others held on, grim faced, staring into the shadows ahead.

Silent and powerful, the river licked and lapped at the stone, rushing along over smooth stones and slick mud...hungry and waiting.

TWENTY-TWO

Benjamin fought the wheel of the Jeep, managed to keep it on the road, and roared down the final stretch of road toward the entrance to the caverns. The first thing he saw when he broke into the open was the wreckage of the jeep. Smoke billowed from the twisted, broken vehicle, but nothing moved.

It took a moment to park, another to be at the driver's side door of the fallen Jeep. There was no hope. Whoever had been behind the wheel was a charred, ruined husk. Benjamin staggered back, unable to look too closely. It was then that he saw the second body. Crushed between the jeep and the stone of the mountain, a crack in the stone running up from the center of the impact.

It was Black. There wasn't much left, but Benjamin recognized the clothing - and the dark hair, scorched by the flames and explosion, still held an eerie facsimile of its original style. Benjamin turned and retched. At that moment, the second Jeep skidded to a stop beside his own – Cynthia and Ellie leaped from their seats and hurried to his side. Benjamin held up a hand to keep them a few feet back, fought for control, and finally managed it.

"I'm sorry," he said softly. "Black..." He waved his hand at the wall, and the wrecked Jeep.

Cynthia glanced in the direction he indicated, but Elly ignored him, stepping close and steadying him.

"The workers are out," she said, "but we still have people inside. Are you sure it's over?"

The question brought Benjamin up short. Black might be out of the picture, but what orders had he managed to pass on?

Who was still in there – what did they believe, and how far would they go?

"I don't know," he said. "We have to get everyone out of there."

Cynthia had stepped away from them, and was inspecting the wreckage of Jonathan's Jeep. She turned, and trotted to where Black had left his own vehicle. Benjamin had all but missed the second Jeep in his shock.

Cynthia climbed in and rummaged about, looking for something. Elly turned and watched her, perplexed. It didn't take Benjamin as long to catch on, and he sprinted over to help, and moments later he came up out of the back seat with a triumphant yell.

In his hand he held a two-way radio, and without waiting to explain himself, he keyed the microphone and screamed.

"Abort. I repeat, abort! Black is down. The mission is scratched. Get out while you can."

He released the microphone, and they waited. At first there was nothing but static. The radio crackled once, and what might have been a very weak signal hissed from the speaker, then it died. Benjamin shook the radio, as if the action could bring a response and ease the tension, but there was nothing. He reached to key the microphone again, but before he could press it, a voice rattled out of the receiver, metallic, but clear.

"Black is down, copy."

"Abort," Benjamin barked into the microphone. "Pull out. Meet back at camp."

There was another slight hesitation, and then the voice returned.

"I'm afraid I can't do that," he said. "I'm not sure who this is - but it doesn't matter. If Black is really out, there's only one way he'd want this to end. Nothing for me back in your camp, or their camp, or anywhere else. See you on the other side."

The signal died, and Benjamin turned first to Cynthia in consternation, and then to Elly.

"We have to evacuate." He said. "Cynthia, see who you can raise. Tell them we don't know how much time there is."

He turned away, and Elly called after him.

"Where are you going?"

"I'm going to see if I can find that guy. There's only a couple of other ways in and out, and he has to be near one of them. Even if he's suicidal and crazy, he had to get in there somehow; if I can get there soon enough, maybe I can stop him."

"And get yourself blown up?"

"I'll be careful," he said, and he was gone.

Cynthia held the radio in her hand, indecision clearly mapped across her features.

"Do what he said," Elly snapped. "Get those people out of there."

Then, without another word, she turned and ran off after Benjamin. Her heart thundered in her chest from the unfamiliar exertion, and from the thrill of danger. She saw Benjamin ahead, not moving as quickly as she'd feared he would be. He wasn't aware of her following him yet, and that was also good. She didn't want him distracted by her presence, but if he was going to risk his life to save the work they had done in this mountain, the least she could do was watch his back.

She wished she'd had enough sense to grab a weapon of some sort, or at the very least one of the radios, but it was too late for that, and in any case she had no idea how to use the equipment if she had it. She cursed her own inadequacy, even as her frustration gave her strength. With a burst of speed she rounded the side of the mountain in time to see Benjamin slip around the next corner. She continued her hurried pace until she neared the spot where he'd slipped out of sight, then slowed and caught her breath, moving more quietly and carefully. If Benjamin thought there was danger ahead, it wouldn't be a good idea for her to rush into it headlong.

She stuck her head around the corner carefully. There was no one in sight, and ahead it looked as if the side of the mountain stretched all the way to the river. She stepped carefully into the open and moved along the stone wall slowly. There was no sound, and suddenly she felt very, very alone. If what Black had told them was no empty boast, this mountain could explode at any moment, taking her and Benjamin and anyone left inside with it.

Ahead there was a dark shadow on the stone face, and moments later she saw it was an opening. A path led away from it toward the trees. She scanned that trail carefully, but there was no sign of motion, and she still heard nothing. She moved closer to the opening and stopped, her back pressed to the stone. She still heard nothing, though the sound of rushing water was closer, and when she stuck her head around the corner and stared into the darkness, it grew to an echoing roar. She experienced a moment of vertigo, and wondered how those workers could stand it, being confined in this dark hole, the river rushing by them, threatening to crash through and wash them away forever.

There was no light. She tried closing her eyes to acclimate to the darkness, but it didn't help. She couldn't pierce the heavy shadows, and again she cursed herself for not being prepared. She didn't want to stumble into the tunnel blind, so instead she turned to the trail. It led away into the trees, and she guessed that it wound around to some short tributary off the road leading to the main cavern entrance. If they used this side entrance, they'd have to have access to it from the road, and that might mean that whoever was in there had left their vehicle where she could find it.

Elly had no idea what she might do even if there was such a vehicle, but she felt desperate to do something - anything - that might help, and there was just no way to know what she might find. If whoever was in that cavern got the best of Benjamin and came back out, maybe she could find a weapon that would force him back in before it was too late. It was a weak plan, but it was all she had, so she plunged ahead into the trees, moving at a trot, and moments later the mountain was obscured by the low-hanging foliage of the trees overhead.

Goodman moved carefully into the cavern. There were a lot of twists and turns, and since the original plan had called for remote detonation, he was going to have to be creative to make this happen. He knew he could set the explosions off with a single manual detonation, if he got the right one, and if he did it before they found him. He had no illusions of getting out of the cavern alive, nor any real desire to do it. His dreams, already cloudy veils over reality, were rising to full control of his mind. He felt the water rushing just beyond the wall like a pulse, and he longed to press himself into the stone and count the beats. He stopped for a moment and pressed the palms of his hands into the stone. They vibrated with power, and he closed his eyes.

In his dreams he stood, watching the rushing bubbling torrents of water rush through the tunnels. He shivered as the images returned. As he opened his eyes to continue, he heard a sound that didn't belong, discord in the flowing harmony of the river. He stood very still, and had almost convinced himself he was hearing things, when it came again. A clank, as if some bit of equipment had scraped on the walls. Someone was coming.

He thought back to the radio message he'd received to abort. He knew it hadn't been Black, and he didn't believe it was one of Black's men, either. There were codes and protocols in place, and none of them had been observed. He'd sort of half-expected that they'd evacuate and leave him to his business. It hadn't occurred to him anyone would have the courage, or the lack of good sense, to follow him into the caverns and try and stop him. Now he had to re-evaluate.

He was still about ten minutes away from the charge he intended as his target. If he moved quickly, he might outdistance his pursuit and still have time to accomplish what he'd set out to do. He didn't want to hurry it, though. He wanted to take his time and prepare for the moment - his last moment. They said your life flashed before your eyes at such times, and Goodman intended to get the entire show before he was flushed to oblivion.

That meant that he had to deal with whoever was back there, and the sooner the better. He glanced up and down the passage and saw that it turned up ahead about fifty feet. Without further thought he trotted to that corner and slipped around it into the shadows beyond. He pressed against the stone wall, wishing he could stand on the far side of the corridor where the water rushed just beyond reach. If he did that there was too much risk of discovery, though where he now stood he had to depend on his sense of hearing alone and the constant roar of the river masked all but the most glaring sounds.

He listened for the jangling clank he'd heard before, but heard only silence. Sweat soaked his collar, and for the first time since he'd gotten the word from Black that the mission was "on" he felt the nagging, biting touch of doubt. Who the hell was back there? Would it be someone he could easily overcome, or would it be some sort of South American commando? Were they armed? Would they be as quick to kill him as he would be to do the same to them? Had he left any signs behind him in the passage that could give him away?

He tried to remember if he'd been quiet as he proceeded through the tunnel, or if he'd been so caught up in the moment that it hadn't mattered. He had been expecting no pursuit, so there was no way to gauge how indiscreet his passage into the darkness had been. He didn't even know how close they were. The sounds he'd heard had echoed, and the tunnels tended to elongate and amplify sound. He cursed under his breath and spun toward the center of the mountain. It was possible, he thought, that the sound hadn't come from behind him at all. Were there others inside, still trying to make their way to the surface? Could some of the workers have been forgotten, or even remained behind?

He heard a soft scrape and pressed more tightly into the wall. The silence that followed grew, and grew, and suddenly he wasn't sure he'd heard the sound at all. He started to move back the way he'd come, but held himself in check by sheer will. If he committed back that direction, and the person he'd heard was actually ahead of him, they might get between him and his goal and prevent him from completing the mission. That was unacceptable.

His breath was harsh, and too loud, and he tried to bite it back and silence it. He had to make a decision and act. It was the only thing that would get him through this, and it was the only way to his goal. With a snarl of rage, he pressed off the wall, turned toward the mountain's heart, and launched himself down the dimly lit tunnel. The light pooled near strategically placed lanterns, and faded to black shadow between. Crossing those pools of light was like running through some sort of impossibly slow strobe light. He fought against the rising panic that threatened his concentration and scanned the corridor ahead, his hand on the hilt of his knife in case anyone blocked his way.

In the darkness behind, Benjamin heard Goodman's panic, and moments later, he followed, keeping as tight against the wall as possible. He kept as silent as he could manage without falling too far behind. He'd spent a lot of time in the tunnels, and he was familiar with their twists and turns. He also knew they provided plenty of places for an ambush if he didn't pay attention. He concentrated on the retreating footsteps and prayed that he could keep pace and, when the time came, maintain the element of surprise. Anyone crazy enough to bring a mountain down on his own head wasn't to be taken lightly, and Benjamin had plans for the rest of his life that didn't include being washed into a primeval river.

"Who are you?" he whispered.

There was no answer, and he followed the soft echo of his question into the shadows.

Elly found what she was looking for about two hundred feet down the trail and tucked in behind a small strand of trees. It was another Jeep like the one that Black had driven. She climbed up to the driver's seat and inspected the vehicle quickly. There were quite a few pieces of equipment she didn't recognize, and she left these alone. The key dangled from the ignition, left and forgotten, and she got a sudden chill. Would someone who intended to come back to the vehicle, even out here in the middle of the jungle, leave the keys where anyone who happened along could find them?

There was a shotgun on the floor in back, and tied in behind the back seat were tightly packed bundles she didn't want to consider. Warning labels were vaguely visible, and she assumed they were explosives. She didn't know what she expected to find, or what she would do when she saw it, but she felt a sense of urgency all the same.

There was a radio lying in the passenger's seat. It was silent, and there were no lights flashing, but she picked it up and turned it over until she found the power switch. At first there was just static, but then she heard a pop of static. She was on the verge of depressing the microphone button when a voice crackled out of the tinny speaker, startling her.

"We're pulling out," someone said hurriedly. "We've cleansed the camp. Air-twelve is waiting for loading."

"Copy," another voice chimed in. "But what about Goodman? We've heard from most of the others; Black is out, but Goodman was still live on the air until a while ago."

"Don't wait on that lunatic," the first voice replied. "He's probably decided to blow the mountain up and let it take him for a river-boat ride. I never trusted that guy - he has too many screws loose. If he doesn't get his ass back here, or make it to the airfield in time, we're leaving without him."

"Roger that," the second voice replied. "I hope he takes the Express Train to Hell, to be honest. If he takes out the mountain, at least it will distract the locals from our departure. "

The signal died, and Elly sat, stunned. Lunatic?

She turned and grabbed the shotgun out of the back seat, hoping it was loaded and ready to fire, and jumped back out of the Jeep. She pushed the microphone button on the radio and spoke rapidly, and as clearly as she could manage, hoping that Cynthia, or someone would be monitoring the signal and hear her.

"This is Elly Kassell. Benjamin has entered the caverns after a man named Good man. He is dangerous, and apparently intends to try and bring the entire mountain down on their heads. I'm going after them. Black's men are retreating to an air field and about to escape the island. If anyone is listening, let the authorities know - stop them."

Elly stared at the radio in her hand. She was unused to such equipment, and without an answering "Roger," she distrusted the green metal box's ability to carry her words to anyone that mattered. Then she shrugged and tossed the radio into the Jeep and headed back toward the cavern entrance, carefully keeping the barrel of the shotgun pointed forward.

"I'm coming, Benjamin," she whispered. "For what it's worth, I'm coming."

A few moments later she slipped into the shadowed entrance to the caverns and out of sight.

TWENTY-THREE

Goodman caromed off the wall with a grunt of pain as he rounded yet another turn. There were few side-tunnels; a fact he'd originally found comforting, since it made getting around beneath the mountain simpler. Now he wished for a maze. He wished for the tight, claustrophobic tunnels he'd crawled during his years of military service. Dark holes where you could get lost, or lose pursuit, and the biggest dangers ran on four feet, or slithered in silence.

He knew he should have plenty of time to finish the job, but he couldn't tell for sure how far behind his pursuit had fallen. His breath echoed loudly, and his feet pounded on the stone floor. It seemed his blood flooded his veins and joined with the rush of the river beyond the mountain wall, blocking his ability to hear. He knew he should just concentrate on the tunnel ahead, move forward and finish it, but the image of someone – anyone – creeping up behind him, shooting him, or stabbing him – anything that prevented that final rush, that flood of water and darkness that would wash it all away, maddened him.

Sweat matted his hair to his forehead and stung his eyes. He couldn't take a step without glancing over his shoulder; his progress slowed, and then, at last, stopped. He turned and dropped his bags to the floor. He pulled the knife from his belt and stood, facing the passageway behind him, scanning the shadows. He caught a flicker of motion, and then realized it was his own shadow. Something glittered, but it was light from the blade of his knife, and he cursed. He turned slowly, barely able to contain the urge to spin and slash at the darkness at his back.

Black and the others were forgotten. The mission – the plan
to blow the mountain wall and flood the tunnels, forcing an
evacuation – the carefully set charges - was banished to the
dark recesses in the far corners of his mind. He felt the tunnel
walls around him. Instinct kicked in, and his heartbeat slowed.
It was a big tunnel – he knew it was bigger than it should be.
He held the knife easily, dropping into a crouched stance.
Whatever was coming, whoever was trailing him, he was ready.

Benjamin stopped and held his breath. He'd heard the man
ahead of him stop, heard the clatter of equipment being
dropped, and the shuffle of feet, but now he heard nothing.
Had they reached the charge? If so, there were only seconds
remaining before the world – for the two of them – would end.
Benjamin wasn't ready to meet his maker, so he hesitated. Very,
very slowly he leaned out around the rounded tunnel corner.
He caught motion, and stopped. Someone stood near the center
of the passageway. He wasn't near the wall, and that was good,
because any charges that had been set would have to have been
carefully concealed, and that meant a crack in the wall, or even
a chiseled compartment.
    Benjamin tried to think. The man's behavior had been
erratic from the start. Any sane man would have taken off into
the jungle when Black fell, trying to catch up with the others in
his group and make an escape. Benjamin had been dealing with
Black for years, and had considered him the most dangerous,
and probably the least sane man he'd ever met. He had no basis
against which to judge the actions of someone this far over the
edge. He wasn't even sure why he'd followed, putting himself
at risk right alongside the crazy man.
    He felt like things had been going steadily downhill since
Elly's arrival in New York. From the initial abduction, to Black's
threats and attacks, and their wild ride to Pompano, and the
complex, the entire thing was a fiasco. He thought back to Lily
– to the things they'd done, and the things they all hoped to do
in the future, and in that second he knew. He could not let this
man ruin so many hours of work. He couldn't let this mountain,
this doorway they'd opened into the past, be slammed in their

faces by madness, all their work ruined and forgotten.

He needed a plan. He knew nothing of the man in the corridor, whether or not he was combat trained, or just a thug. Benjamin was trained, and he trusted himself in almost any situation, but there was no margin for error here. Not only his life, but the sweat and labor and dreams of many others depended on the next few moments. Not to mention Elly. If he failed her now and didn't return to guide her through the aftermath of this disaster, the entire project might fold. The secret might be released unprotected, or buried and forgotten for another hundred years.

He finally settled on a shot at surprise. It seemed like this man, Goodman, was walking a very tight edge. His actions were erratic and seemed to indicate he was ready to snap. Benjamin reached into a pocket and pulled out one of the tranquilizer shells he'd been carrying. He knew he wasn't going to get off a shot at such close range, and in any case he wasn't going to fire a weapon in the tunnel. There was no telling what it might hit if it ricocheted, and if they were actually close enough to the charge for Goodman to set it off, he might accidentally hit that and bring the mountain down himself.

He gripped the shell tightly, took a deep breath, and then whipped it around the corner, hoping it wouldn't strike Goodman or that the man wouldn't notice the quick flash of brass. There was a momentary silence, and then the shell struck stone. It banged and clattered down the passage, and Benjamin heard a quick, startled intake of breath. Then he heard Goodman move, turning away, and launched himself into the passage with a roar.

He saw that his ruse, for the most part, had worked, but Goodman was incredibly agile. Benjamin dove for the man's legs, saw the flash of the knife's blade, and barely managed to get an arm up in a sweeping block, diverting it from its intended path through his throat. He hooked Goodman's leg at the knee, and as he rolled past, he yanked hard. Goodman grunted as his legs flew out from under him, and Benjamin rolled up fast.

It was barely fast enough. Goodman hit the ground moving and swung again, intent on driving his blade into Benjamin's thigh.   Benjamin lashed out, kicking the blow aside and brought his boot back hard and fast into Goodman's chin.   It was enough to stun him, and Benjamin took the moment to kick a last time, driving his boot into Goodman's wrist.   The knife clattered off down the passageway, and Benjamin pressed his advantage, dropping down to crash his fist into the other man's chin. Goodman reeled and struggled to free himself, but Benjamin landed a second blow, and then a third.   He reached for Goodman's arm, driving it up behind the man's back, and held him pressed to the stone floor.

He was strong.   Benjamin felt the man's strength coiled beneath him and knew he could only hold him for so long.   He didn't know what to do.   He hadn't come prepared to walk out with a prisoner – he hadn't come in prepared at all.   Now he knew he had to figure it out, and fast.   If the man got loose he would either escape into the tunnels, or he would kill Benjamin, or both.   He had a heavy flashlight on his belt, and he knew if he could get it he could end this, but his position was too precarious.   If he reached for the flashlight he'd have to shift his weight and release his hold with one hand.   If he slipped, or if he didn't snag the light on the first grab, Goodman would be loose, and all bets would be off.

There was no choice.   He ground his knee up into Goodman's arm, pressed him hard and pushed off slightly, reaching for the light and holding on as tightly as possible with his right hand to Goodman's arm.

The ruse hadn't worked.   His shifting weight telegraphed the move, and ignoring the pain, Goodman brought his legs around, pressed a foot to the floor, and pressed back against Benjamin, sending him rolling off and reeling for balance, headed toward the stone wall at his back.

Goodman spun like a cat, and Benjamin saw him squat, draw something up from low on his leg, and cried out.   It was a gun, a small, wicked .22 that looked like a cannon at short range. Off balance, Benjamin couldn't dive for cover or react.   He cried out and raised his arm, and at that moment the otherwise silent passageway echoed with the sharp sound of a shotgun being pumped.

Things happened in a blur. Goodman heard the sound and spun, and Benjamin kicked wildly back, caught the wall with his boot, and propelled himself forward. In the passageway he saw Elly, a heavy shotgun in her hand, leveled at Goodman. Goodman was swinging his gun hand to try for a shot at her, and that was the moment Benjamin needed. He put all his weight and strength behind the blow, slamming the heavy flashlight into the back of Goodman's head. The man dropped like a stone, the gun flying from his hand. Elly cried out and backed away, and Benjamin winced, afraid she'd panic and pull the trigger. She didn't. Instead she stumbled back and toppled to the floor, sitting in a heap with the shotgun in her lap, an expression of shock painted so comically across her features that Benjamin nearly laughed.

Instead, he rooted through the bag that Goodman had dropped, found a length of cord, and bound the man's hands tightly behind him. He frisked the prone body for weapons, found nothing, and then turned to Elly, who still sat where she'd fallen, staring at him.

"Thank you," he said simply. "You saved my life."

She couldn't speak, but he was happy to see the blank stare leave her face, replaced with a wan smile.

"I pulled the trigger," she said. "Nothing happened."

He stared at her, then walked over and took the shotgun gently. He glanced down, and began to chuckle. The chuckle rose to a full laugh moments later and he had to lean on the wall for support.

"What?" she asked. He couldn't tell if she was angry, exasperated, or just frustrated, but the expression on her face only sent him off again. He couldn't breathe, and there was no way he could speak, so he stumbled closer, turned the shotgun, and pointed.

The safety, which was clearly marked, was set.

Elly stared at it dumbly, took the weapon from him, glanced up – and then they were both laughing. It was several moments before either could breathe, and several more before Benjamin though to turn on his radio.

"Benjamin here," he called out. "Cynthia, if you can hear

this, we are fine. Elly is with me, and we have Goodman. I repeat, we have a prisoner. We'll be at the west entrance, get someone over to pick him up."

Before anyone could answer, he turned the radio off and helped Elly to her feet. As she rose, she stumbled again, falling gently against his chest. Without thought, he wrapped her in his arms, and she didn't pull away. They didn't move until they heard Goodman groan. Then, with a last glance into the tunnels at their back, they dragged him to his feet and pressed him ahead of them, Benjamin now holding the shotgun, pressed it into the prisoner's back. They set off slowly, making their way back to sunlight, and safety.

Before they reached the entrance to the tunnel, Cynthia and two others met them. They took Goodman, who was fully awake again and crazy eyed with frustration. One of the men had handcuffs.

"What will you do with him?" Elly asked.

"All of the others have left," Cynthia told her. "We had people in place to head them off, but we were too slow. They may get caught when they land, depending on how well they planned, but they are no longer our problem. This one? I suspect we'll be handing him over to the local authorities. I believe they are going to be interested in the explosives that have been set. I doubt Mr. Goodman is going home anytime soon, though if he is cooperative, there might be some hope."

Elly nodded. She glanced around at the mountain, the cavern entrance, the armed men and finally at Benjamin.

"We need rest, food, and a bath. I want to know what's happened to Jennifer, and the others."

Benjamin nodded. "We can manage it from back at the complex, and check the pumps at the same time," he said.

Moments later, they were packed into several vehicles. One of the men had gone to where Elly directed him and retrieved Goodman's Jeep. They turned away from the mountain and the river beyond and rolled slowly back into the jungle, riding beneath a deep, heavy curtain of silence.

TWENTY-FOUR

They gathered around the conference table on the lower level of the complex, Elly, Benjamin, Edgar, Phoebe, and Jennifer, Marvin, Antoine, Cynthia and Anne. Each held a warm cup of coffee, or tea, and a nearly full bottle of cognac sat in the center of the table. The plant above ran smoothly, the twin generators pumping out power in unison, and the Bessler generators, decoupled, but powered up, leaving their signature tingle in the air.

The mood was somber, but the return of Jennifer and Edgar to the fold had lightened the mood some, and having the walls of the complex wrapped safely around them, and all the workers safe made a difference as well.

"It's hard to believe he's gone," Elly said at last.

"Black?" Cynthia asked.

Elly nodded. "It's funny, but he was the first person I encountered in this entire crazy operation, he and Jonathan, and now they're both...dead. I'm afraid I'm not used to people dying."

"None of us are," Benjamin replied. "I know that might be hard to believe after everything you've seen, but it's never been this crazy before. I'm afraid that your coming to America set off something in his mind – Black's, I mean. He's been content for years to chip away at us, sneaking around and spying, trying to infiltrate our operation. I never thought he would take it so far. Or, I guess I did think he might, but I pushed it to the back of my mind. Nobody likes to believe the worst of anyone."

They were silent a moment longer, then Cynthia spoke up again.

"What comes next? The complex is intact, though it will take some effort to smooth all of this over without alerting the locals. Teams are in the caverns now scouring them for the chargers Black had set, so that danger seems to be behind us."

Everyone turned to Elly, and she frowned.

"Well, as you are aware, I am not my grandmother. I can see how all of this came to pass. I'm not happy with it, and I'm pretty sure that if it had come to anything like this while she was alive, Grandmother Lily wouldn't have been any happier."

"A lot of good work is being done," Edgar cut in. "Most of us have dedicated our lives to that work."

Elly nodded. It was obvious that there was a very great deal at stake. If she just shut everything down, jobs would dry up, lives would be disrupted, and at the core of it all, her grandmother's life work would fail. That decision rested in her reluctant hands, and she wished, not for the first time, that she'd stayed in her tiny little flat in London, transcribing legal documents and typing deeds.

"I don't intend to let my grandmother's work, or that of any of the rest of you, go to waste," she said. "I also don't intend to allow this kind of intrigue to be part of our lives. If we are going to continue to bring Bessler's Wheel to the world, we are going to find a way to do that more openly. You've all made incredible progress, and from what I've seen here, and back in New York, you've got equipment at a level that we can begin to unveil it."

Benjamin started to speak, but Elly held up a hand. He fell silent, and she smiled and continued.

"I realize that I don't have all the answers or even all the questions yet. I'm not advocating an immediate release, or even that we unveil things next week, or year. I just want to know that we can safely bring this secret to the world before some other crazy man has a chance to steal it, or put people in danger as they have been here. This wasn't even just about us – we put the lives of a lot of people on the line, people who weren't even aware what they might have died for. I don't know about the rest of you, but I think anyone who believes that was an acceptable risk belongs on Black's side of the fence, and not on mine."

She scanned the group then, as if looking for someone who would disagree. No one moved, and all eyes were directed at the floor.

"Benjamin?" she said.

He glanced up, and she smiled at him.

"I would like to see a plan in the next couple of weeks for allowing those who are part of this operation to be slowly let in on what is going on. They don't need to know everything; certainly we don't want them to understand how the generators work. I want them to know, however, that the second set of generators is there, that we are researching something wonderful, and that they are part of it. The same is true of the local government, though I'd suggest we ask permission to 'begin' what we've been doing all along, and make a show of installing something beneath the diesels that they can believe is not currently in place. I doubt they'd take kindly to learning that their country had been used as a test-bed for new technology without their knowledge; I'm equally certain they'd be happy – eager, even – to be part of it if they were invited.

"If we take a more proactive and open approach throughout our operation, I believe we'll find that more interest from the sort of people we don't mind working with will ensue, and that the ability of men and women like Maxwell Black to disrupt things will be minimized. You can't steal a secret that isn't really secret. It may even be time to invite in some scientists or educators, on a very limited access basis, and begin to get other minds "spinning" – if you take my meaning."

Elly fell silent and Benjamin stood slowly. He looked around the table, barely able to conceal a smile, and then started chuckling.

"Of all the decisions that your grandmother made, Elly, I'm beginning to believe sending you to us was the best. You are right, of course. It is easy to get caught up in the adventure, and the intrigue, and to lose track of what is important. I'm afraid the events we've all just experienced have been a rude awakening. I hope you won't judge us on this short period. While there has always been an issue of security, this is the first time it's ever reached the point where I believed lives were at risk.

"I think your plan is wise and I for one am behind you a hundred percent, as I know Lily would have wanted me to be."

He scanned the others, who were nodding and whispering among themselves, and he smiled.

"I think you'll find we're all ready for some activities with a little less stress."

"Good," Elly said. She held up her tea cup, and the others followed suit with their coffee, cognac, or whatever was in front of them.

"I'd like to propose a toast," she said. "I'd like to toast a man who lived and died a very long time ago, but whose memory lives on through us. To Johann Bessler and his wheel."

"May it never stop turning," Cynthia added.

They drank, and Elly stood.

"I don't know about the rest of you, but I need some rest. Tomorrow, I want to get on the way back to New York. I have at least one thing I need to finish up there before I'll be ready to move on."

Everyone stood, and they shuffled out of the room toward their quarters. Benjamin stood watching until everyone had cleared the room, then he followed, turning off the light as he stepped into the hall.

In the huge chamber beyond the glass windows, the generators ran silently. He stood and stared at them for a long time, then turned toward his room and sleep.

Back in her room, Elly found that, despite her exhaustion, sleep was the furthest thing from her mind. She poured a glass of wine from the bottle someone had thoughtfully provided, and laid back on the bed, lost in thought. She found herself drifting from Pompano, and the complex, and Maxwell Black to her grandmother's journals. Bessler's story, so clear in her mind, was incomplete.

She was afraid that recent events had given her an insight into how things had ended for the inventor, but she wanted to know for certain. She reached for the journal and opened to where she'd left off dropping back into the story, but skimming. She knew she'd never be able to read the whole thing before sleep claimed her, but for some reason, she felt the urge to know how Bessler's story had come out. Sipping the wine slowly and balancing the journal on her knees, she returned to the 1700s, and to Bessler and his wheel.

The wheel must be powered by compressed air.

There is a mechanism that turns the wheel, bound to a handle beyond a wall and out of sight, manned day and night by Orffyreus's maid, his wife, and his servants.

There is a clockwork mechanism within the wheel, intricate and advanced, but needing to be wound eventually.

If the wheel could turn continuously for eight weeks, and still lift the same weight, it would be proof enough.

1727

"Bessler's maid, Anne Rosine Mauersbergerin, testified to authorities that Bessler's wheel had been turned manually from its beginnings in Gera. Bessler, his wife, his brother Gottfried, and she had taken turns to rotate the machine. Turning was carried out by a small crank in an adjoining room. She claimed that the posts had been hollowed out and contained a long thin piece of iron with a barb at the bottom which was attached to the shaft journal."

Professor Willem's Gravesande responded to the maid's allegations:

"...They say that a servant under oath, turned Orffyreus' machine, she being in an adjoining room. I know perfectly well that Orffyreus is mad, but I have no reason to think him an imposter... This I know, as certainly as anything in the world, that if the servant says the above, she tells a great falsehood... [During the examination,] I ordered the machine be dismounted from its supports, and we saw the bearings uncovered. I examined the bearings on which the journals rested and there did not appear any trace of communication with the adjoining room. I remember very distinctly the whole set of circumstances regarding that investigation..."

During official tests, hundreds of highly respected and

impartial people carefully examined the bearings and attested to the fact that no sign of fraud could be found, even when the wheel was moved from one set of supports to another. Regardless, the maid's testimony forever tarnished Bessler's reputation."

Courtesy of : http://www.besslerswheel.com

1745

Johann, who had given over the name of his birth and went solely by the name Orffyreus, came into the service of Karl II late in his life. His wheel, built, and rebuilt, broken and ignored, ridiculed, studied, denounced and coveted by so many that the records had grown muddled and dense.

Only one other man had ever shared his secret – Karl I, who had been his benefactor and supporter, had seen the inner workings of the wheel, though he'd never come up with the price of purchasing that secret. The pressure of standing up beside the truth and protecting it for so long, from so many, had taken its toll.

Barbara was gone. She'd never been strong, and their life on the road, under stress, attack, and often without funds, had taken its toll. Johann had underestimated the opposition, hatred, jealousy and spite his wheel would engender in men of science, faith, and positions of power. It was a wonderful invention, a great work of science, but – as it turned out – men of science were more interested in such wonders when it was their own genius behind them. No one wanted to admit what he'd done, at first, and after a time so much had been written, said, proclaimed and accused that they could no more back down than he could. Men of science were unwilling to be show nincorrect in their findings. Men of faith were unwilling to admit a miracle that didn't stem from their books, prophecies, or belief. Men of power listened to the latter two groups with much more attentiveness than was warranted, and the wheel fell dormant.

By the time Johann came to work in the halls of Karl

II, he was on to other endeavors. He still held his secret too precious to be passed on to anyone unwilling to pay his price – and was convinced that even if the price was met, he'd not find anyone worthy of sharing the knowledge. It was precious, and dangerous, and maybe the world wasn't ready for such a treasure. It was certainly willing to cast it aside – and Johann along with it.

There were other things he could do. He had continued his studies of medicine, and science, and his mind was as brilliant as ever. It was his heart that suffered. He missed Barbara terribly, and though he understood the pressures that had been brought to bear, others had betrayed him. The maid-servant, Barbara's confidante, had claimed the wheel to be moved by a series of levers, manned constantly by herself, or others of Johann's followers, in an elaborate hoax.

There was no way to know what she'd been offered, or what she'd been threatened with. The girl had never confided in Johann himself, and if she'd told Barbara before her death, it had never been revealed. In the end it didn't matter. It was more important to the world to denounce Johann's Wheel than it was to embrace his genius, and it was more important to his own sanity that he keep the secret. In the end, he knew, what mattered wasn't as much that the world share the secret, as that he possess it. He knew what he'd done. One of the smallest wheels still lay hidden, secreted away with his journals, in a place only he was aware of.

It had been one of his last great endeavors to conceal the work. He had designed and commissioned his own gravestone. It rested against the wall in the rear of his workshop, covered in a tarpaulin. He'd given explicit instructions to Karl II – who he trusted implicitly with everything but his greatest secret. The journals and the chest with the remnant of his wheel he entrusted to his patron. They were to be kept at Kassell, where Bessler had spent his happiest years, under the auspices of Karl I and now the son.

There were vague plans for other inventions that might have brought his secret to the world. Johann had drawn plans for a fountain that would shoot water continuously without need of any form of energy to run their pumps. He'd designed a giant organ that would play itself, running perpetually until its various pieces and gears wore out, or it was physically stopped. He even proposed a ship "Preservation Device" that could have helped prevent loss of life and goods at sea.

None of his inventions were taken more seriously than the original wheel. The testing, thorough, endless, and tedious, had proven nothing, it seemed. Despite meeting and exceeding every challenge, creating a wheel that spun either way, for instance, to prove that it didn't operate on a clock-like winding mechanism, and moving the wheel physically from one stand to another to prove there was no external motive force applied had only sharpened the wits of his opponents and brought on wilder and less-likely claims that were, despite their inherently ridiculous nature, accepted on the word of their proponents. The world, clearly, was not ready for the wheel, and in such a state, Johann was no longer inclined to provide it.

His current project was interesting, and held his attention well, giving him some peace from his past. He'd heard rumors out of Asia of windmills that operated with horizontally sailed "wings" and the idea had appealed to him. It was more efficient, less unsightly – and no one had yet accomplished the construction of such a device in Europe. When Karl II suggested that he set his mind to it, Johann accepted eagerly.

Now it was all but complete. The structure, built in Fürstenburg, stood four and a half stories in height. It was an engineering marvel, and Johann knew it. He knew just as surely that, no matter how miraculous it might prove, any reports of it to the world would be tainted by derision and reminders involving his wheel.

The day was lightly windy, and it was cool, but not yet cold. He entered the windmill on a lower level and climbed slowly and laboriously up the winding stairs. It was a Sunday, and work had halted for the Sabbath. Johann had come to be alone with his creation. The silent immensity of the windmill calmed him. He found that he could think more clearly when he was alone and surrounded by his work.

He thought back to the moment on his cot in that far away

room when it had call come together in his mind – when he knew he was neither deluded, nor insane. So many miles between there and where he stood. So many lives and loves; so many heartaches. He stepped onto the upper platform and strode to the center. You could look down into the gears and mechanisms of the place from the very top. When the windmill went into operation, you'd be able to witness that operation in full, allowing operators and engineers clear view of the workings in the case of a mishap.

Johann was not as spry as he'd once been. At sixty-five years, his back ached, and his joints had begun to stiffen when the air grew too cold. The climb to the upper story of the windmill had tired him. There was a railing to prevent one from toppling over into the heart of the huge, mechanical beast, and he leaned on it heavily. It had taken many men months of labor to construct this, working under Johann's close supervision. Engineers had been brought in who did not spend their days finding fault in his work, but instead marveled at it and became a part of it. It was a wonderful thing, and it would perform the work of a much larger traditional mill in conditions of lower wind.

He stared down into the depths of the machine, and his mind drifted. Deep down, he caught sight of a glimmer of light, a glow he couldn't place. There should have been no workers on the lower levels, and there were no lamps kept lit when the building was unmanned. He leaned a bit closer. The light had grown brighter, and as he watched grew brighter still. His long gray hair, which tumbled past his face as he bent over the railing, touched the edges of that glow, and he felt them pulled taut and held.

Johann cried out. He pressed against the railing, but his own efforts, combined with the steady pressure drawing him down, drew him up until he rested precariously on the wooden frame. He no longer had purchase to fight the imbalance. He could not make out the machinery below, but only the brilliant glow, drawing him forward and inward. In that moment he remembered the dream. He remembered the great organ and the way he'd been trapped within – and the miraculous secret that experience had imparted.

Below he saw a huge wheel, spinning endlessly. He tilted forward, slid into the light softly, and dropped. There was no thought, and no pain. He came to rest against the side of the wheel as it spun, and he spread out over it. The sides were malleable – he sunk within the stone and cried out. And was lost.

They found the man they knew as Orffyreus sprawled over the huge gears of the windmill. He had been broken by the fall, but physicians concluded that his heart had failed him. Despite the horrific manner of his demise, his features were peaceful, and he seemed to smile.

He was buried in an obscure graveyard and the stone, found in his workshop, was placed over the grave. The crate, and the wheel, were kept close to Karl II for many years, forgotten by all but a very few. The secret followed him to the grave, and beyond.

But he left a code.

EPILOGUE

Elly sat alone in her office. The window behind her was dark – there were stars beyond it, she knew, but with the illumination of the city below, they were blocked from view. So many things were like that – shining brightly, illuminating the mysterious, and lost to view.

She held a simple sliver of metal in her hand. If she was correct, it was the key. She'd put the wheel together so many times over the last few months that she was certain she had begun to live, and share, the frustration Johann Bessler must have faced when building it. So many times she'd set it in motion, only to see it spin, and spin, and eventually come to a halt.

At first she'd been convinced it was too old, that something over the years had shifted, crumbled, or changed, and that it had simply worn out before she had the opportunity to see it in operation. Then, each time, she'd gone back to the journals. She'd gone back to the notes her grandmother had left to her. She'd pulled it apart, bit by bit, studying each in its turn, and tried something new.

This time was different. Something in Bessler's own account had struck her – something about the workings of an organ. She had pulled out a different group of her grandmother's books this past month, and she now knew more than she'd ever expected, or cared to, about the workings of ancient antique organs. She knew something else, as well. She knew a secret, and she was moments away from proving it.

She slid the tiny bit of metal into place, and then very

carefully closed the central chamber of the small wheel, sealing it from sight. The small device sat on a metal base. The axle slid out on either side to rest easily on carefully machined braces. She'd used modern lubricants to remove all trace of friction, but otherwise the wheel and its components were just as Orffyreus had left them.

The door behind her opened, and Benjamin stepped quietly into the room. He stared at the wheel, and Elly smiled up at him.

"Is it?" he asked.

She nodded. There was no reason to discuss what she'd done, and she didn't feel inclined to philosophize. It was not a moment for words, but for magic. She reached out and pulled free the small dowel that held the wheel stationary. She gave it a tiny nudge with her index finger, and she sat back.

They watched as it began to spin smoothly, its motion steady and somehow eerie. They watched together in silence for over an hour, then Benjamin stepped p and laid his hands on her shoulders. She reached up and laid her fingers over his, then rose and stood beside him. A shaft of moonlight, or the beacon from some much taller building, shone in through window, somehow falling directly on the spinning, whirling wheel.

Without a word, they turned, and they left the room. Behind them, the wheel continued, spinning into a brave new world.

About the Author

DAVID NIALL WILSON has been writing and publishing horror, dark fantasy, and science fiction since the mid-eighties. An ordained minister, once President of the Horror Writers Association and multiple recipient of the Bram Stoker Award, his novels include *Maelstrom, The Mote in Andrea's Eye, Deep Blue, the Grails Covenant Trilogy, Star Trek Voyager: Chrysalis, Except You Go Through Shadow, This is My Blood, Ancient Eyes, On the Third Day, The Orffyreus Wheel*, The DeChance Chronicles, including *Heart of a Dragon, Vintage Soul, My Soul to Keep, Kali's Tale* and the tie-in novel *Nevermore - A novel of Love, Loss & Edgar Allen Poe, The Parting The Temple of Camazotz,* and *Crockatiel* for the original series O.C.L.T. and the memoir / cookbook *American Pies: Baking with Dave the Pie Guy.* There are more than thirty titles in all, including several short story collections. David can be found at http://www.davidniallwilson.com and can be reached by e-mail at david@macabreink.com.

David is CEO and founder of Crossroad Press, a cutting edge digital publishing company specializing in electronic novels, collections, and non-fiction, as well as unabridged audiobooks and print titles. Visit Crossroad Press at:

http://store.crossroadpress.com

Curious about other Crossroad Press books?
Stop by our site:
http://store.crossroadpress.com
We offer quality writing
in digital, audio, and print formats.

Enter the code FIRSTBOOK
to get 20% off your first order from our store!
Stop by today!